Four Nights
at Sea

Books by Demi Alex

The International Affairs Series

26 Hours in Paris

Four Nights at Sea

FOUR NIGHTS AT SEA

International Affairs

Demi Alex

LYRICAL PRESS
Kensington Publishing Corp.
www.kensingtonbooks.com

LYRICAL PRESS BOOKS are published by

Kensington Publishing Corp.
119 West 40th Street
New York, NY 10018

All Kensington titles, imprints, and distributed lines are available at special quantity discounts for bulk purchases for sales promotion, premiums, fund-raising, educational, or institutional use.

Special book excerpts or customized printings can also be created to fit specific needs. For details, write or phone the office of the Kensington Sales Manager: Kensington Publishing Corp., 119 West 40th Street, New York, NY 10018. Attn. Sales Department. Phone: 1-800-221-2647.

Lyrical Press and Lyrical Press logo Reg. U.S. Pat. & TM Off.

First Electronic Edition: December 2016
eISBN-13: 978-1-60183-601-4
eISBN-10: 1-60183-601-5

First Print Edition: December 2016
ISBN-13: 978-1-60183-602-1
ISBN-10: 1-60183-602-3

Printed in the United States of America

For my girls:
Beth, Elisa, Joyce, Mina, Penny, and Sheila
We can have it all.
Let loose.
Go for it! ♥

Chapter One

Charlie debated whether to kiss her boss or kick him in the balls. Paul was off his rocker with this one.

"That's right, ladies. This is your chance. We're going to feature the winning article in the Valentine's issue," Paul said, puffing out his mouth-watering chest and grinning haughtily. "The selected piece will join 'Aphrodisiac Foods from Around the World' and 'How to Say I Love You in Twenty Languages' in *City Wings*' Valentine's edition."

Holy shit! This was it. This was the chance Charlie had been waiting for. It was the break she needed.

"Our readers devour anything and everything having to do with international desires," he continued. "It's a way to escape the daily grind and dream of possibilities. Who would have thought New Yorkers were so romantic?"

Yes, Charlene—Charlie—Stanton wanted her writing to win. She wanted to publish a real feature, with her own byline, in one of the trendiest travel magazines for New Yorkers. No, she didn't want to compete against her friend and roommate, Kathryn Taylor, though. They'd worked together at *City Wings* for over two years, worked well together as copy writers and staff writers, and now Paul was pitting them against each other as feature writers. It was so messed up. A disastrous idea.

"Get out there. Do your research," Paul said, circling his hand above his head like he was a Texas rancher. "Lasso someone who makes your body hum, and write about the perfect place to find love, ladies."

"Seriously, Paul? Lasso someone who makes our bodies hum?" Kathryn rolled her eyes, then smacked her forehead with the back of her hand. "Wait. Hold on a minute. Wait . . . wait. I'm seeing a hand-some man, in a far off and romantic place like Paris, sweeping me off my feet."

Paris. Kat had to go and mention Paris. Like, why? Did it really matter if Paris was the most romantic place on Earth if neither of them wanted to fly over and find out?

Charlie didn't travel well and wasn't in the mood for a trip to the doctor in order to get a prescription so she could get on a flight. Kathryn had to stop speaking about the perfect place to find love on the other side of the Atlantic. How did one argue the romance of Paris?

Wondering why she'd ever picked up the vape stick when she'd never even smoked, Charlie reached for her pink, sixty-dollar vapor-izer, and twirled it in her fingers. She answered the silent question in her mind. The thing was a crutch. Something to keep her grounded when thoughts crowded her mind and she wanted to scream at the world. Screaming and throwing temper tantrums were not allowed in the grownup world. Puffing on vanilla-flavored vapor kept her mouth occupied. It kept her from engaging in unladylike behavior.

"I think we can take a small detour from the publication's travel angle on this," Charlie said. After all, living in New York did have its benefits when it came to an abundance of male prospects for the fea-ture. "Why can't a woman find love in her neighborhood, and *then* sail off into a foreign and exotic land with the love of her life?"

"If it's done properly, I can see it working. However, any featured lovers must take off in the end for a foreign destination." Paul nod-ded, tapping his fingers on the table as he considered her argument.

Maybe, just maybe, Charlie could convince the sexy tyrant to see things her way? Hope spread in her chest and she leaned forward in her seat.

"There is a pragmatic benefit, too," Paul added. "If we concen-trate on finding love locally, more of our readers will relate to the ac-cessibility of that goal and can dream of escaping to a romantic place with their loves."

"Exactly," Charlie said, breathing with relief.

Paul encouraged her to continue, so Charlie barreled on. "The dating scene has evolved so much over the past few years. There's always the chance of meeting someone at a bar or a club. Online sites host a bunch of events in this city. And let's not forget the old-fashioned way of being introduced by common friends."

"Great options." Kathryn looked doubtful. Charlie and Kathryn had exhausted all those options, but neither had found Prince Charming at a neighborhood hangout. Her friend was even more disillusioned than she was. Kat didn't believe that love could last. Yet she was blabbering about far-off and exotic locations. Maybe because Kat loved to travel, and Paul was willing to tag along?

Charlie was screwed. For some perturbed reason, Kat angled for Charlie to write about Paris. What was up with that? Wasn't she just arguing Paris was perfect for finding love? And, why couldn't they keep it in New York? Considering how many people lived and worked in Manhattan, if you couldn't find love in the Big Apple, you couldn't find it anywhere.

"How are those local options working for you?" Kat asked, snapping her fingers before Charlie's eyes.

Kat continued on her Paris Romance 101 introduction, but if Charlie was honest with herself, she had to admit she was just as disillusioned as her friend with the local love options. She couldn't truly get behind any romance for herself. Sometimes things weren't fair. Like maybe it wasn't about the location. Maybe it was about the fact that Charlie hadn't let any guy in since her divorce. She simply couldn't. It was too difficult to decipher their intentions. Did they like her for her? Or did they like her for her trust fund?

"Not fair," Charlie said. "Maybe it's been bad timing for me. I really haven't tried too hard. It's been difficult to trust anyone since my divorce, so maybe I'm the problem and the scene is just fine."

Paul cleared his throat and held up a hand. "You're not the problem, Charlie," he said, covering her hand with his own. "Your asshole ex is. So let's take jerks like him out of the equation for the benefit of this piece."

Whatever. She needed to relax. And just flirt. Like Kat and Paul were doing.

"This is a very incestuous organization," Charlie said, pointing from Paul to Kathryn to the door. "Between you two and the accounting department, a tree house should be the official headquarters of *City Wings*. You're all too tight."

The conference room filled with laughter. Paul and Kathryn had known each other forever, so they had no problem teasing or hitting below the belt. When it came to Charlie, they treated her with kid gloves. As if her divorce had been the end of her life. It hadn't. It had actually opened her eyes to what she really wanted. More than anything, she was so over the money-grubbing scumbags of the world.

Charlie was ready to move on from sitting-duck status. She was doubly ready for a real sex life—something she hadn't had with the ex—but she needed to learn how to compartmentalize physical and emotional.

Shit. Shit. Triple shit. She had to stop thinking so hard. Everything she wanted would come, after she had her byline. First, she had to prove herself as a competent and successful writer to her family. It was a matter of professional and personal honor.

"We're looking for love, not sexy interludes," Charlie said, an idea sparking in her mind. "Sexy interludes. But. Fine. Okay. Got it." She placed her palms flat on the table and stood. "If we're really looking for the perfect place to find love, why not a cruise ship? It's textbook romance. What about one designated for singles? Passengers board with an agenda. Just think how much fun we'll have writing about a cruise."

"Nope. There is no 'we.' You can sail away on a Love Boat, and Kathryn will fly off and take her chances in Paris," Paul announced. Kathryn tried to argue that he should reverse the assignments because she was nervous about running into a past fling, but thankfully he didn't budge. Paul insisted that Kathryn would benefit from a personal tour with Marko Renard, the man she'd placed above all others for years. He assigned her Paris. Charlie got the cruise. She sent up a silent prayer of gratitude. She didn't need the added stress of flying if she was going to concentrate on her feature.

"Good," Paul said. "Time for you ladies to bring out the claws and get down to work. You each have your assignment. Your expense accounts will be adjusted and ready to go by noon. See Justin for the details. Get me your stories by next Wednesday. I'll decide which one gets published in the Valentine's issue."

"On what criteria will the winner be chosen?" Kathryn asked.

"Whatever I want," he said with a devilish grin. "I'm the boss."

Two thousand dollars was more than enough money for round-trip bus or train fare and a reservation on Lovers Sail Tours. Just over a day on the bus, then she'd sail out from Miami on Thursday. Then off to romantic Cozumel; add the singles on board, and she was sure to get enough material for a winning feature.

Charlie reserved an inside cabin on the sixth deck and booked a port excursion. Lovers Sail recommended the "romantic" experience, and was even willing to pair them up if needed. Partners would be determined once on board.

After clearing her immediate departure from the office with Paul, Charlie went home to pack.

With her expandable carry-on-size suitcase and leather backpack ready by the door, Charlie grabbed her cell, opened the Seamless app, and repeated the last order of shrimp pad Thai, red curry beef, and two orders of the crab Rangoon appetizer. She finished verifying payment just as the front door crashed open.

"Charlie, I'm home," Kathryn called, her forehead wrinkling as she took in the packed bags.

"*Aowww.*" Charlie pretended to rush and hide the luggage in the closet. Relieving her friend of the large brown bag, she peaked inside and squealed. "Fuck-me boots! Way to go, babe."

"Got you something, too." Her friend dangled a smaller bag, stuffed with tissue paper, and dropped onto the couch. Kathryn patted the cushion at her side, but didn't offer her the gift. Instead, in a very animated and exuberant manner, she did the honors herself.

Charlie sat and clasped her hands between her knees. She watched her roommate pluck tissue paper from the bag and fling the sheets extravagantly over her shoulder. Amused with Kathryn's stripper imitation, Charlie covered her mouth with her hand and made her eyes extra big with excitement. "Should I blush before or after the big reveal?"

"I'm sure you blushed enough while you were packing," Kathryn said, pulling out a package of batteries and waving them in the air.

Charlie burst out laughing and grabbed the batteries. "Thank you. These are much appreciated and will be put to good use."

"I hope not," Kathryn said, lifting a red lace thong from the bag. "I think you could get more use out of these." Next came the black lace and lastly, the silk.

"You're too much," Charlie said. "You do know this is a work trip?"

"So what?" Kathryn replied, shaking her head. "A good reporter explores all avenues. *All*. Figured you could wear the granny panties the first night, but you'll need these for the next three."

Kathryn had assumed correctly. She had packed nothing but cotton underwear. Shaking her head, she stood and reached for the new lingerie. "For your information, I don't wear granny panties. They're cotton bikini panties. Practical. Pretty and sexy, too."

"Sure, if you're in high school." Kathryn scrunched her nose. "I take that back. Have you seen what those girls wear?"

"These are adorable," Charlie said. "Thank you." She walked the few steps to her suitcase and folded the new underwear into the outside pocket.

"Wait. One more thing," Kathryn said, dangling a skimpy, pink string bikini from her fingers as she walked toward the closet. "Pack this."

"No way," Charlie protested, sliding her palms over her hips. "Have you seen *these*?"

"I certainly have. You have a rockin' bod. You're not covering it with that stuffy one-piece you've had forever." She fit the bikini into the same pocket Charlie had placed the underwear in, then propped one hand on her hip and held out the other. "Give me that fugly suit."

"I like my fugly suit," Charlie replied, laughing and waving a dismissive hand through the air. The intercom buzzed. "Saved by food delivery. If you want dinner, you'd best be nice to me."

"I am nice," Kathryn insisted. "Didn't I just give you a sexy bikini and killer panties? Do I need to deliver a ripped man to your bed?"

"That would work," Charlie answered, plucking a five from her wallet for a tip and sashaying to the door.

Once they'd devoured the appetizers, finished half of each entrée, and switched dinners, Charlie confessed to packing mostly conservative outfits.

"My cruise-appropriate clothing is pre-divorce," she explained. "They're a little traditional, considering my mother had a hand in selecting every piece, but they're fine. I'm not cruising as a participant. I'm cruising as a professional observer."

"Seriously? You packed *those* clothes?" Kathryn placed the red curry beef on the coffee table and stood. She disappeared into the bedroom, clearly on a mission, leaving Charlie cringing on the couch from the noise of the massive storage bins being dragged out of the closet.

"I can't fit into your clothes," Charlie called, imagining her friend tossing short and skimpy dresses over her shoulder. "Don't bother. Even if I could get your miniskirts over my hips, they'd reach my knees."

"I'll admit we have different shapes. You're blessed with knock-out curves, I have more height, but we're almost the same size," Kathryn said, emerging with her arms full of casual, bright-colored clothes.

"They still have tags on them," Charlie said.

"I picked them off the clearance racks at the end of the season and haven't had a chance to wear them yet." Kathryn held up a neon-green tank top printed with a phrase about giving her coffee before speaking. "These will help with getting people to talk openly with you. They invite conversation." She held a pink one up to her chest. It read, *Ask Me*. "If being a non-intimidating professional is your goal, these will work in a casual setting. You could wear them by the pool bar."

"Yes," Charlie conceded, reaching for the tanks. "They're good, non-intimidating, and cute. If you don't mind me being the first to wear them, I'll take them."

"I don't mind," Kathryn replied, holding the bright-colored shirts high. "On the condition that you agree to take these dresses with you." She held up a barely-there little black number. The plunging halter matched the nonexistent back, which matched the tiny skirt.

"That's not enough material to cover my hips." Charlie held up a hand in protest. "Even if I'm five inches shorter than you, it's barely going to reach past my underwear."

"Don't wear any." Kat handed her the items in order. Colorful tanks. Miniskirts. Skimpy and fun sun dresses.

Sighing, Charlie stuffed them in her case and returned to the couch. "You need to look at it from my point of view, Kat. This assignment means something different to me than it does to you."

"What are you talking about?" Her friend gave her a sobering look and sat beside her. "It means a byline to me and to you. We've worked hard for our own features. Plus, it's an opportunity to break out of our loveless ruts."

"Kind of." Charlie reached for the electronic cigarette and took a long drag. "I'll admit that what you're saying is mostly on target. However, there's never been a doubt in your ability to make it as a writer. Your parents supported your career goals—maybe not financially so much, because they couldn't, but they always cheered you on. Paul hired you because he knew you were a capable writer. He had proof from your school days." She puffed on the pink stick and chased the vanilla-scented vapor with a waving hand.

"You're a great writer," Kathryn insisted.

"Thank you," Charlie said, folding her hands between her knees. "I like to believe that, but my family doesn't. According to them, the only reason for me to attend Columbia Journalism School was to find the right husband, which I recklessly overlooked during my undergraduate education. They think I was there for my M.R.S. degree."

"You are so much more than pretty wifey material," Kathryn said, her pitch a bit higher than typical. "You're such a talented writer, not to mention someone that I would always want at my side. Dependable, smart, hardworking, stable—"

"It doesn't matter." Where her family was concerned, her main objective had been to find the proper husband to grow her inheritance. Her shoulders dropped in defeat, but her determination rose in opposition.

"Okay. Let's talk about how this week will make a difference." Kathryn covered Charlie's hand and squeezed in support. "I'm here for you. Let's brainstorm the best avenues to prove that you're more than a pretty face."

Relief and gratitude flooded Charlie. She was so lucky to have a friend who believed in her. "I'm going back to the basics. Starting with the five *W*'s every investigative reporter asks: *Who*, *what*, *when*, *where*, *why* . . . I'm going forward with my intentions from the moment I embark. I'm going to interview all of my fellow passengers that are willing to share."

"Don't forget the *how*," Kathryn added, folding her feet under her bum. "I got it. Let's come up with all your key questions over a bottle of wine. That way, you're guaranteed not to miss anything you could use."

"Can't," Charlie said, checking the time on her phone. "I need to get to the Port Authority. My bus leaves in a little over an hour."

"Bus?" Kat shrieked. "Are you out of your mind? That's going to take forever."

"Twenty-six hours, to be exact. The same amount of time you'll have on the ground in Paris." Charlie winked and stood. She carried the dinner containers to the kitchen and set them on the counter. "If I take a flight, I'll arrive totally wrecked and the first two days of the cruise will be ruined. The load of meds I'd need to get my butt on a plane would take a huge toll on my body. I'll bus it."

Shaking her head, Kat gazed at the floor. "You're going to regret getting stuck—wait!" She looked up, excitement playing in her eyes.

Charlie looked at her friend, wondering what exactly the massive brainstorm was. "You know I'm on a tight schedule, right?"

"I got it," Kat said, holding an index finger in the air. "I have twenty-six hours in Paris. You have twenty-six hours on the bus. So you need twenty-six interview questions for the cruisers." She clasped her hands together and rolled her shoulders. "Trust me. It's our lucky number. Twenty-six! Everything twenty-six."

"Okay. If you insist." Charlie stretched up and wrapped her arms around Kat's shoulders. "I really have to go. I'll work on the questions while someone else drives. You never know who may be on that bus."

"You never know," Kat agreed.

Chapter Two

Almost thirty hours later, Charlie stripped off her clothes and co-cooned herself in the soft organic sheets for a few hours of un-interrupted sleep. Just before arriving in Miami, she'd made use of the travel app she referred to for research and had come across a great last-minute deal on South Beach. The hotel proved perfect. Oceanfront and balcony. Plush, king-size bed. Decadent and sweet.

She knew of the 1Hotels in New York, liked the environmentally friendly basis they were run on, and she was more than happy she'd decided to dust off her credit card and take a bit of time for herself before boarding the ship for work. Folding her hands beneath her pillow, she shut her eyes and thought of a late breakfast at Tom Colicchio's place.

Colicchio, her celebrity crush, was her absolute favorite *Top Chef* judge. Truth was, she'd been salivating over his meals for years. Maybe she wouldn't be eating his delicious short ribs for breakfast, but she'd definitely find something to enjoy.

Hugging a pillow to her chest, she let out a contented sigh and settled into the darkness. The next thing she knew, someone was knocking on the door, and bright sunshine snuck between a crack in the curtains.

"Room service," a slightly accented female voice announced.

She threw off the covers and reached for her bathrobe. "One second," she cried, fitting the slipper socks the hotel provided on her feet. She'd ordered coffee for nine o'clock, just in case she'd slept past her typical seven o'clock wakeup time. She had slept in. Life was so good.

"Good morning," Charlie said, opening the door and stepping back.

"Good morning, Miss Stanton." A smiling woman stepped into

the room and motioned toward the glass doors. "Would you like to take your coffee on the balcony?"

Morning coffee? Overlooking the ocean? A tropical breeze in her hair? Charlie's heart did a happy dance. "Yes. Thank you."

The attendant nodded and placed the tray down on a low table to pull back the curtains and open the doors. "It's a little chilly for a Miami morning, so you may want to stay bundled up in that robe or bring a sweater out here. I think it's in the low seventies at the moment."

Charlie considered the twenty-something degrees she'd left behind and laughed at the thought of seventies being *chilly*. "I will gladly suffer for such a beautiful view."

The other woman joined her in a quick laugh and arranged the coffee on the table for her. "Can I do anything else for you before I go, Miss Stanton? Perhaps request a full breakfast to be brought up?"

"No. I'm good. Thank you," Charlie said, reaching for her wallet to tip the woman. "I'm planning on breakfast at Beachcraft."

"Excellent idea. My sister is in the kitchen this morning. If you like huevos rancheros, I strongly suggest them. Gabriella is a real artist when it comes to frying eggs." The woman chuckled and pointed to her chest. "Tell the server to request them the way Mariellena eats them. Fried real soft so that all the goodness oozes and mixes just right with the other stuff."

"Wow. I'm suddenly starved," Charlie said, her mouth watering in anticipation. "I'll definitely ask for that."

"And sit outside on the patio area if it's available," Mariellena added. "The weather will warm up soon, and it'll be real pretty out there."

"I'm sure," Charlie said, walking the woman to the door. "FYI, this weather is a heat wave compared to what is happening in New York."

Smiling as she locked the door, Charlie turned and headed for the balcony to enjoy her morning coffee. She was on a second cup when her phone chimed an incoming call and had her racing inside to retrieve it off the nightstand.

Checking the caller ID, she quickly pressed the green answer icon. "It's so gorgeous here. I'm in South Beach. Surf, sand, and sun. Gorgeous, I say. Gorgeous!"

"Good-morning to you, too," Kathryn replied. "I was calling to confirm you've arrived in Miami and your bones are defrosting. But I guess I don't need to worry."

"Nope. No worries. I'm at 1Hotel on South Beach," Charlie said. "But the bus ride sucked. It was long and boring. Really, really boring."

"So no hottie on the bus?"

"Not one. The seat next to me was empty all the way down. It gave me time to work on questions and do some research on the cruise." Charlie stepped out onto the balcony and gazed out at the blue water, scraping her teeth over her lip. She wondered how her friend would feel that she'd hastily made a reservation on a sailing that was not simply a singles cruise, but was a Lovers Sail Singles & Kink Cruise. *Kink* being the part of the marketing she'd missed.

"So you're all set?" Kathryn asked.

"Yup. I'm grabbing a late breakfast at the hotel restaurant," she said, keeping the conversation safe.

Considering her sexual experience and non-adventures, she decided to omit the kink part of the sailing's description. She didn't bother to mention that not everyone was single either. Some were cruising for sex and kink, not romance.

Even though Charlie had been married, Kathryn knew the extent of her sex life. Really restricted. Really vanilla. Missionary on a schedule. She'd freak on her behalf and insist she not board the ship. Charlie focused on the good stuff. Focused on where she was. Focused on the byline.

"Hotel restaurant? Break out of the predictable and safe rut. Go somewhere special," Kat said.

"I am," Charlie said, twirling her hair and puffing on her vanilla-flavored Vapestick The kink part of the cruise was a definite break from the predictable. She didn't share that info, though. "It's Chef Colicchio's. I'm so psyched to try it."

"Then why are you still talking to me? Get going, girl."

Smiling and slathered in exquisite-smelling lotion, she dressed in proper cruise attire. She was a professional, would present herself as a professional, and use all the information she could gather for professional advancement.

Choosing to check out early so she could beat the lines on the ship, she left her suitcase with the bellhop and then strode through the lobby toward the restaurant, marveling at the nature inspired décor. She was looking up when she slammed—full-bodied—into a firm and warm obstacle. A strong arm wrapped around her back and a large hand settled on the curve of her hip.

"Steady there."

The deep masculine voice swathed her senses and stole her balance, causing her to sway and grasp at his shirt to remain upright. Milk chocolate–colored eyes looked down at her, heating her skin and sparking a sudden desire that flamed deep in her core.

"I'm sorry," he said. "I wasn't paying attention to where I was going. Are you okay?"

Was she really supposed to give him an honest answer? Or was she supposed to thank him for the way the contact made her body hum? Damn Paul for planting that thought in her mind.

She pasted a prim and proper smile on her lips, but didn't prevent her gaze from roaming down his muscled chest to the silver belt buckle above his nicely filled out black slacks. He had almost a foot on her in height, broad, strong-looking shoulders, and the chiseled features of a Ralph Lauren model. She couldn't see past him or over his shoulder, but neither did she mind the view she had.

"I'm fine," she finally managed. "My fault. I was distracted by the décor."

Ford didn't miss the flush crawling up the angel's neck or the darkening of her blue eyes. If he had his way, he'd continue standing outside the entrance of the restaurant until she offered him her name and number. Hell, he'd take anything she chose to offer.

This angel had a sexy edge to her that instantly placed his body on alert.

He let out a long breath, and with his free hand, swept a blond wisp off her pretty face. "I'm really sorry. Please allow me to make amends and buy you a drink."

Her pretty, pink tongue wet her lips and he saw the consideration in her eyes. Plus, her fingers may have released their death grip on his sleeve, but they were still curled around his forearm. *She feels the heat.*

"Please," he repeated, hoping to convince her he wasn't an ax murderer or the type of guy that picked up women in hotel lobbies. "I hear the mojitos are great when enjoyed on the patio. Very public."

"Mojitos for breakfast?" The twinkle in her eyes gave her away.

A definite devilish gleam, so he knew she wasn't as angelic as she first appeared.

"It is South Beach."

She laughed and glanced behind her at the bustling restaurant, and when she turned back to him, she slowly raised her shoulders and broadened her smile. "Well . . ."

"There you are, darling." His former stepmother's voice sounded from behind as a dainty hand swept over his back and a mental bell rang to mark the end of opportunity. "I told you I wouldn't be late today."

The beautiful woman dropped her hand from his arm and stared at his breakfast date. Why had Eugenia picked this day of all days to arrive on time? He felt the petite blonde fidget, but he refused to let her step away and tightened his fingers on the soft swell of her hip. Hell, she'd think he was a mental case if he didn't get it together.

"Miracles never cease, Eugenia. You've pleasantly proven me wrong," he said in a teasing voice, reluctantly breaking eye contact with the curious angel. He leaned over and kissed Eugenia's cheek. "We were just talking about how good the mojitos are here."

"They are *deliciously* refreshing," Eugenia agreed, enunciating each syllable with flare. Bypassing Ford and stepping up to the source of the uncomfortable swelling below his belt, his favorite ex-stepmother pulled the adorable, sexy woman into a hug. But being adorable and sexy hadn't prepared her for Eugenia's bulldozing. The angel's eyes grew big with shock. "I'm Eugenia. Let's get a table under one of the umbrellas, eh?"

"Eugenia," Ford tried to interrupt. "I'm—"

"Pleased to meet you, Eugenia. I'm Charlie. Thank you for the invite, but regretfully, I can't join you."

Was that to him or Eugenia? Ford studied Charlie's features, but quickly decided he didn't care who she addressed. He just wanted more time with her. His body hadn't reacted to a woman like that in forever. He adjusted his stance, hoping to disguise the eager interest tenting his pants.

"While I'd love to savor that mojito, this is a working breakfast for me." She tapped the laptop case on her hip. The startled angel had recovered and was as composed as a senator's campaign manager.

"Come on, sugar. A little break is good for productivity. Vitamin D will do wonders to keep you motivated and energetic." Eugenia was laying it on thick, but Ford didn't object. He needed an advocate in his corner. And he wanted to learn more about Charlie. "And it's been ages since I've met and gotten to know one of Ford's friends—well, at least a beautiful one."

The pink blush returned and marked Charlie's cheeks. Her perplexed gaze darted between them, but her smile held. Hell, she was good at awkward niceties.

"What do you do?" Ford asked.

"I'm a writer." Charlie paused as if trying to convince herself of the statement. "I'm working on a piece about cruising, and figured I'd add a pre-cruise angle. Have you heard of a publication out of New York named *City Wings*?"

"Yes," he replied, finally allowing her retreat and releasing his hold on her hip. "I used to follow *City Wings* when it was only a blog—before it became the go-to magazine for post-college New Yorkers and their travel dreams."

"I like that," Charlie said, a brightness in her blue eyes. "I'll be sure to tell my boss how you described us."

"Please do," Ford said, giving her his signature smile. The smile never failed him. Maybe now she'd stay with him? "Anyway, can we get you to reconsider that mojito if I promise to speak about *City Wings* ninety percent of the time?"

"I wish," Charlie replied, and from the way her eyes darkened with longing, he believed she did. "But I really need to review my notes. I haven't been with *City Wings* since the beginning, so I'm not an established writer there. I started as a copy writer, then worked on shorts as a staff writer, so this is my first chance to prove myself and earn a byline."

"Good luck, even though I doubt you'll need it. I think you're well on your way to writer stardom, sugar. When can we read this cruise exposé?" Eugenia asked.

"Hopefully in the Valentine's Day issue. But I'm not sure I'd call it an exposé," Charlie replied, shifting her weight from one foot to the other. "It's a feature about the best place to find love. I figured a cruise would be romantic and offer ample opportunity for *l'amour*."

"Now I understand." Eugenia looked from Charlie to Ford with a conspiratorial smile. "You should definitely pick Keaton's—"

"Ford," he corrected.

"Oh, darling, sorry about that. I don't care what you call yourself.

I love you anyway, *Ford*." His ex-stepmama laced her hand through his arm and stretched to place her red lips on his cheek in an exaggerated smooch. "Now, *Ford* can tell you a thing or two about cruising and love."

More than a thing or two, if she'd let him. He'd even be willing to show her.

"He's been working in the industry for over five years," Eugenia offered.

Charlie's gaze darted to the hostess station. "I'd better get going. I want to make it to the port with time to spare before boarding. Nice meeting you both. Enjoy those mojitos."

He watched her walk away, knowing she'd do everything in her power to deny their attraction. By the reaction of her body to his touch, it was clear such sensation was outside her comfort zone. But she wasn't going to be lost to him forever. He had no problem reaching out.

Thanks to Eugenia's bubbly manner, he had her name. Knew where she worked. And he'd be able to look her up when he returned to New York in two weeks. Two very long weeks, but worth every minute of waiting in order to savor the delectable woman for a few promising encounters.

"Let's go, darling," Eugenia said, tugging on his arm and starting for the patio. "We have less than an hour to catch up, and I have a list of things your father asked me to review with you."

"I'm not wasting our time together discussing a list of his demands." He'd much rather figure out how to connect with Charlie. "Besides, you're divorced. Why do you have to do his dirty work for him?"

"It's not dirty work. He wants to make amends with his son." Eugenia tapped long fingernails on the back of his hand as they waited for the hostess to return, smiling sweetly at him with the most patient look in her eyes. "He may be a bad husband, but he's a good daddy. Both to you and your little sister."

"How is my favorite girl?"

"Emily is well. Gorgeous as ever, and acing every one of her classes."

"That's my Em," he said, truly proud of his little sister. With an apologetic tilt of his head, he raised a finger and asked Eugenia to wait. "My baby girl is too important to rush over. I want to hear all the details. School. Swim team. Everything. Let's wait till we're seated so we can have a proper conversation."

The hostess walked up and he requested a table on the patio, noticing that the only available table on said patio happened to be directly behind Charlie. He pulled out Eugenia's chair and adjusted his seat so that he could enjoy the view. Long, blond waves rested on her slight shoulders, which were thankfully exposed—unlike the majority of what he believed to be her soft and pale skin.

His gaze trailed down her spine to a shapely backside, which graciously blessed that lucky seat. What a shame for such beautiful curves to be hidden beneath a matronly golf . . . what the fuck was that thing called . . . skort and such a roomy sleeveless polo. He concentrated on her arms and calves. They were certainly worth major appreciation. Ford settled back in his chair, folded his arms across his chest, and smiled.

The waiter poured sparkling water into their glasses, and they ordered their meals and drinks. He glanced at the great woman at his side, wondering how his father had managed to fuck up everything with her.

"Sugar, you're rather preoccupied," Eugenia said. She pointed at Charlie while scooting her chair toward his, close enough to whisper. "How about coming clean and telling your favorite stepmother how you two know each other?"

"There's nothing to come clean about. We literally bumped into each other just before you arrived. Your imagination has shifted into overdrive. Romance, romance, romance," he teased in a low voice. "But you are my favorite stepmother."

"And you're my favorite stepson."

"Your only stepson," he reminded. "Now tell my about the little princess."

"She's not so little, Keaton. Emily is turning thirteen next month, and she needs her big brother around. She misses you," Eugenia said, accepting a mojito and stirring it graciously. "Isn't your contract almost over?"

"It's technically over. The final sailings are a bonus. I need the financial padding to make the café happen and grow properly," he admitted. "If not, I may be delayed on the first store, and the second store expansion will be at least a year behind schedule." He knew what was coming next, so he braced himself.

"Just come home," Eugenia said.

"Em's birthday is in March," he pointed out. He covered Eugenia's perfectly manicured hand and looked her directly in the eyes. "I'll be in Louisiana for Emily's party, but I'm not coming *home,* as you put it. I'm disembarking in Miami, visiting with friends for a few days, then flying straight to New York. You're well aware of my plans. I need to wait for the returns from my bonus check to finalize the details before I can truly get anything off the ground. Just have my back with Em. I don't want her to feel neglected while I concentrate on my business plan."

"But you don't have to do all that. Your father has come around. He wants to finance your venture. You don't need to go back to your old boss and struggle on your own. Let your father help. He misses you, and he regrets the grad school incident. He's even willing to pay off your student loans and give you a clean slate for the future. Accept his apology and move past this all. You've made your point." Eugenia pulled her hand from beneath his and wrapped her fingers around his wrist, flashing him an earnest and dazzling smile. "Let your father help you build your java empire."

Ford shook his head. No matter how good a heart Eugenia had, she had a true weakness when it came to the stability she believed money afforded. Knowing the details of her tumultuous childhood, he understood. But it wasn't that way for him. Security didn't come from money. It came from his abilities and only his abilities. Money was a by-product.

"You know I love you, sweetheart." Ford switched their hands back to the original position. "You've been my best friend since high school. You've grown into the best mother a child could want. Hell, as a young bride, you were the best wife to my father. Actually, you still are."

"Ex-wife," she interjected. "Your father is a horrible husband, but he is a devoted, caring, and loving daddy. Possibly a good friend. Even if he's overbearing."

Choosing not to argue and upset her, he nodded. "You deserve honesty, so I'll be blunt. Not only do I not need the cover of the Keaton Fitzgerald Rutherford legal and financial umbrella, I don't want it. I'm not holding anything against Dad for not paying for my

MBA. I actually appreciate that. It taught me that I could rely on my-self and still get what I want."

"But the loans—"

"The loans are paid off, Eugenia," Ford explained. "They've been paid off." He decided to explain his choices and put her mind at ease. "Working on a cruise liner afforded me the opportunity to live very inexpensively. My rent, my food, almost all my living expenses were covered by the job. I was able to not only pay off the student loans, but to accumulate a nice savings."

"But that can't be enough, Keaton." This was the pragmatic part of Eugenia.

He met her gaze, and words were not necessary to communicate.

"You invested your earnings and have made a nice profit?" She guessed correctly, but was courteous enough to put it in the form of a question.

"You know I did," he replied. It was true that some of his invest-ments were riskier than others, but the payoffs had outweighed the risks. "I'm good to go, sweetheart. In just a few more weeks, I'll be okay. And if an investment pays off, as I believe it will, with my up-coming bonus I'll be able to act quickly and with less expense. That's why I'm staying on for the next two sailings. This bonus pay is separate from what I've already planned on and so is the profit it will yield."

"You have balls of steel, Keaton Fitzgerald Rutherford III," she cooed, laughter in her voice and admiration in her eyes. "You're still making it to Emily's birthday."

"You couldn't keep me away if you tried. I'll take any excuse to see my favorite girls," he said, leaning in and placing a kiss on the center of her forehead. "Now that you know I won't be asking you to clip buy-one-get-one-free peanut butter coupons for me, can you stop doing my father's bidding so we can enjoy our breakfast?"

Chapter Three

Ford scanned the bill, making sure Charlie's breakfast was included as he'd instructed, then slipped his credit card into the folder.

"So, when will I get an invitation to visit you in Manhattan?" Eugenia asked, after they'd caught up on Emily's accomplishments and schedule.

"Never," Ford replied, reaching into a pocket for the square envelope and sliding it across the table to Eugenia. "You never need an invitation. Just use your keys."

"You're giving me keys to your apartment?" Eugenia's hand covered her heart and moisture shined in her eyes. "I could never impose and walk in on you like that. What if I'm crashing on the couch and you bring a lady friend home?"

"Not happening." Ford laughed at the image of Eugenia ever "crashing" on the couch. "Don't worry about that. There's a second bedroom. The contractors are putting the finishing touches on Emily's bubblegum explosion as we speak. It will be ready for you to use any time after Monday."

"Wow, Keat—"

"Ford," he corrected.

"Ford," she relented, a tiny line of disapproval forming on her perfect forehead. "You must be paying a pretty penny in rent in order for your landlord to be so accommodating."

"It doesn't matter. Having you in my life makes any amount of money worth it. Come whenever you want," he said, brushing his thumb over her forehead to ease what she'd consider a horrifying potential wrinkle. "You never have to crash on the couch."

"You really have done well, Keat—Ford," she corrected herself.

"Not that I ever doubted what you could do, but it must be difficult starting up like this. I admire you."

He simply nodded, modestly appreciating her awe. "Thank you, Eugenia." He placed a loving kiss on her cheek. "I'm serious. You use these keys anytime you want. The alarm information is on the card. It's your city crash pad."

She pulled the card from the envelope and two keys dropped onto the table. Reading the information on the white cardstock, she hooted. "I have a city crash pad," she said, clutching the keys to her chest. "You make me feel like more than family. Thank—" She stopped mid-sentence and smiled up at an approaching Charlie. "Hi. How was your breakfast?"

"It was delicious. Thank you," Charlie replied graciously, before turning her attention and not-so-angelic gaze on Ford. "When I asked for my check, the waiter told me there was no check to bring me."

Ford grinned, but didn't speak. Why would she be annoyed?

"Perhaps it's included in the room rate," Eugenia offered.

"Perhaps," Charlie said, smiling at his stepmother but not at him. "But the waiter didn't ask for my room information. And he claimed it was taken care of anonymously."

"Busted. And with pleasure," Ford said. "It's the least I could do after I ran you over earlier." He raised his hands, palms up, to demonstrate she'd left him no choice. "Come on. Give a guy a chance to apologize."

"I ran into you."

He shook his head and shrugged. "Not how I remember it."

A dainty finger swirled through a blond tendril and a pensive look colored her face. If she could look any prettier than she had on first bump, she did just that as her shoulders relaxed and she smiled. "Apology accepted. Thank you."

"Good," Eugenia said, clasping her hands together. "Now you two go grab a taxi and get on to the port. Don't let him off the hook so easy, Charlie. He should at least deliver you to your ship."

Charlie blushed and shifted from foot to foot. *"Um."*

"Good idea, sweetheart." Ford squeezed Eugenia's shoulder and kissed her cheek. The woman was a genius. He owed her. He stood and looked down at her. "Are you okay getting back to the condo on your own?"

"Just fine," she assured, tapping the side of his thigh. "Get going."

"Love you," he said, walking toward Charlie, who stood silently, her lips parted, twirling a finger in her hair at a hundred miles a minute. "Ready?"

Charlie stared at the beautiful and confident woman who had just delivered the most attractive man she'd ever met into her hands. Unable to understand her reasoning, she simply nodded at Ford. Once he stepped up next to her and placed his hand in the small of her back, she once again searched Eugenia's face for permission.

"Go on, sugars. Enjoy your cruises."

"Thank you," Charlie replied dumbfounded. Either the other woman had an extraterrestrial amount of confidence or she considered Charlie totally repulsive and no competition. But the polite bombshell smiled too sweetly to be thinking of anything as nasty as that. It didn't make sense. Taking a deep breath, Charlie sucked in her stomach and let Ford lead her away, looking over her shoulder and waving to the other woman.

He kept his hand on her back as they walked, and the contact heated her skin, keeping her well aware of the effect his presence had on her. She had a few seconds of relief only when they'd reached the lobby and he stopped walking. She didn't slow, though, and moved ahead of him. His fingers closed on her wrist and pulled her back. "Do we need to collect your luggage, Charlie?"

"Oh," she breathed. She felt her cheeks heat once again. What the hell was it with all the blushing? Nervous laughter bubbled up in her chest and slipped past her lips. She shrugged, then corrected her reaction by straightening her back and glancing at the bellhop area. "Yes. That would help. Guess I'm excited to get on the ship."

Ford took her hand in his. "Excited about the cruise or the article?"

"Both," she replied, wondering how this guy was so sure she'd accept his touch and manhandling. Even more perplexing was the fact that she didn't just allow it; she liked the way his fingers tangled in hers. She settled her hand into his much larger one and enjoyed the way his thumb feathered over the back of her palm, coaxing her to complete her answer. "I think it's more about getting the byline. I need to establish myself as a journalist. My own feature will go a long way in proving I'm capable of a writing career."

"I get it," he replied, and she believed him.

Handing her claim ticket to the attendant, she collected her sensibility and looked up at the man with the strong dark features she was so inexplicably drawn to. "Sorry. I've just met you, and I'm imposing on your courtesy by professing career goals."

"Definitely don't apologize. I want to hear about your goals."

She decided not to reply and searched for the dollar bills she'd tucked in the outside pocket of her laptop case. But when the bellhop appeared with her bag, Ford immediately handed him a tip and reached for the handle.

"Let's go and get you one step closer to that goal." He led them out the front door and arranged for the taxi.

Seated in the back of the car, with her carry-on stowed in the trunk, she rested her laptop case against her thigh.

"You have an accent, but it's not real heavy, and I can't place it," she said.

"I was born and raised in New Orleans, but I spent a significant amount of time away from home when I was real young," he explained. "After I finished my bachelor's degree at Tulane, I moved to New York for grad school. So my Louisiana accent may be a bit diluted."

That explained his over-amorous personality. It was Southern hospitality, with a twist of old-world chivalry and a splash of arrogant male. Charlie needed to get control of her hormones and remember that this specific man belonged to another woman. Retrieving her iPhone from the pocket, she barricaded herself behind her Kate Spade case, then nodded and looked out the window.

"Makes sense," she said, continuing to concentrate on the steady stream of palm trees lining the street and pretending more interest in the gorgeous landscape than in the man at her side. "Did you choose a career with the cruise industry because you grew up near the Gulf?"

She could do this. She was a professional. Tapping the screen on her phone, she navigated to the notes section and her list of questions for the ship's staff. Asking him anything from the list was more like an interview than personal interest. She closed her eyes and took a deep breath. *Sure, keep telling yourself that.*

"I didn't choose a career in the cruise industry. It's a job, a means to an end." She felt his gaze on her back and the tingles dancing beneath it. "I have two more sailings and I'm done. Then, real life begins."

Unable to resist, she peeked over her shoulder. "What do you mean?"

"Coming out of grad school, I was loaded down with debt." He shrugged very matter of fact. "I needed experience in food service management to advance my career objectives. I started a job, not a career, on board in order to make enough money to climb out of debt and gain the necessary experience. I did. Now I'm ready to move on."

"To what?" She turned in her seat, meeting his gaze.

"Something of my own." His deep voice held a pensive note, but his posture was determined. "Sometimes you just need to break away and do what you want. Right?"

"I guess," she stammered, wondering who exactly he was talking about. Did he know her? Was she that easy to read? She needed to break away. She had. But she still hadn't gained what she wanted. "Does Eugenia support your decision?"

"I believe so."

"You don't know?" Stunned with her own reaction to his nonchalant attitude, she barely managed to hide the astonishment in her voice. Maybe his Southern chivalry wasn't chivalry after all. Maybe he was a narcissistic chauvinist who believed only a man's advancement mattered.

His masculine chuckle shook her from her reverie, and he stroked the back of his finger down her cheek, capturing her chin and guiding her to look at him. Meeting his amused gaze, the embarrassment of a wrong assumption bloomed in her gut.

"I think you may have the wrong impression of my relationship with Eugenia. She's special to me, but not as I think you believe. If I was romantically involved with anyone, or I was in an exclusive relationship, I wouldn't be wanting to touch you so much," Ford said, staring at her mouth as he spoke. "I wouldn't be obsessed with your lips, and I certainly wouldn't be wondering if they would yield and accept my kiss."

"Oh," she breathed, realizing she'd been holding her breath. She exhaled.

"Tell me what you thought," he insisted, still holding her chin and leaning forward to bring his mouth to within inches of hers. "I want the right to call on you when I arrive in New York. In order to have such a right, we need to clear the air. I want no pretense. No mistaken ideas."

Her heart hammered in her chest. He wanted the right to call on her.

"Unless, of course, you're in a committed relationship." His fingers traced over her left hand and skimmed the space where a ring would have been if she were off limits. "Unless you didn't feel what I did when I rudely, but thankfully, ran into you."

She shook her head.

"Tell me. Vocalize. I want inside that beautiful mind," he insisted.

"I assumed she was your wife or your girlfriend." Charlie's hold tightened on her phone, and she glanced down at her white fingertips.

"Neither," he replied, peeling the phone from her grasp. He tapped the dark screen and typed into it. "Eugenia is a friend and one of the stepmothers my father brought into our home. Actually, you can say I brought her home. Father married her. Eugenia and I have been friends since high school. And even though we are very close, we have never been anything but friends, and we will never be more than platonic family. But I understand your assumption. She and I are little more than a year apart in age, so she's more like a sister to me than a stepmother. More importantly, she's the mother of my baby sister. The only sibling I'm aware of and the princess of my heart."

"That's nice," Charlie said, relief coursing through her and managing a smile. "I mean it's nice that your little sister is the princess of your heart."

"She is," he repeated, and placed the phone back in her hands. "I've programmed my cell number and dialed out so your number has registered on my phone. Do you have any reservations about me calling you when we get to New York?"

His mouth was once again inches from hers, and his breath heated her lips as he spoke. His dark gaze held hers.

"No," she whispered, boldness and hope growing within her. He wasn't attached. He was interested. And he made her body *hum*. "Call." Leaning in toward him, she was surprised when he pulled back out of her reach.

"Two more things you need to know." His gaze returned to her mouth and her lips sizzled with anticipation. "First, I really want to kiss you. Second—and this is not because I'm presumptuous but because of the nature of your writing—I'm not a happily-ever-after kind of man. I'm definitely not a knight in shining armor or the romance-novel marrying kind, and I don't believe relationships last forever."

Pressure skidded across her forehead, but the sizzle on her lips flared to a burning desire. She didn't care. She wasn't looking for a husband. Charlie was going to practice what she preached and let loose. She'd give in to the physical attraction and enjoy the moment. "Kiss me, Ford."

His fingers traced over her neck and up her cheeks, cupping her face as he slanted his mouth over hers. Soft and gentle at first, his tongue slid over her lips and teased them apart, only to possess them with undeniable strength and passion that had her insides liquefied by the time he allowed her to breathe again.

"Beautiful," he said, groaning as his mouth lingered over hers. "You feel the need, too." He took her hand and pressed her palm over the strong beat of his heart. "This is so damn frustrating. I haven't had enough of you to hold me over for the next two weeks," he said, then kissed her again.

With the feel and taste of the man permanently branded in her mind, she took what he offered and pressed against him. She licked up his neck and nuzzled behind his ear. "We'll pick this up at a later time. You'll be in New York in a few days."

"Hell. Now that I've sampled that sweetness, ten days are forever away. I'll be there earlier." He let out a breath and tucked her head beneath his chin as he brought her to his side. "Until then, don't let me kiss you again. In the meantime, I'm going to have to keep myself occupied and resort to solving algebraic equations to stay sane. By the way, I hate math."

He kept his arm around her and his chin on her head, allowing her limited movement. His hand rested beneath her breast, and his fingers splayed over her ribs in the most possessive hold. She liked it. "Don't even look my way. It's taking a lot of control to simply sit here. And responsibility dictates that sit here is all we can do for now. Ten days."

"Ten days," she breathed, a longing sigh escaping her lips. And yes, her body was totally reacting to Ford in ways she'd never thought it was capable of responding to anyone, but she had to admit that she was more than a little turned on by his responsibility reference. She liked a man who claimed personal responsibility. That was damn sexy.

"*Chère*, I'd like to suggest we head back to Miami for that mojito we discussed earlier," Ford said, giving her a squeeze. "We can take an extra hour or so to get to know each other better. There's plenty of time before we need to board. We—"

"No. Not possible," she interrupted. No matter how much she'd like to spend the next hour with him, she wasn't going to be sidetracked. "This cruise is work for me. I need to stay focused on the feature. Interviews. Notes. Writing. There is going to be a lot to learn, and I'm going to need to interpret it without bias."

"I'll give you all the info you want about romance on the high seas. I've seen a lot of it." His arm had relaxed and draped comfortably around her. It felt good. Natural. "I've had more than five years to observe guests and their relationships. There are many options for romance. Some typical. Some really out there. I can even bet that this sailing will end up with some unexpected wedding ceremonies."

"Really?" She turned towards him, wanting to ask him so much more. "You see people get married every time?"

"No. Not every time, but we do see it. It's not like on TV with the captain performing ceremonies left and right. Doesn't work like that." With a determined finger on her chin, he encouraged her to face forward. "I warned you. Don't turn those gorgeous blue eyes on me, baby. I'm hanging on by a thread."

She laughed, but was truly flattered . . . no, empowered. Charlie didn't think she could ever have such an influence on a man.

"Excuse me," the driver called over his shoulder. "Which ship?"

"What?"

"Which pier should the taxi head to first?" Ford clarified, pointing to a billboard indicating they had almost reached their destination.

She rambled off the details to the driver and turned to find Ford looking at her with an amused smile.

"What?" she asked again.

"You're sailing on my ship," he replied, grinning like a cat that had just found a bowl of milk. "You're stuck with me, Charlie." Then, out of nowhere, a dark storminess shuttered his features. "You're on *this* sailing? You?"

"Yes," she said, wavering between being embarrassed about the title of the cruise and being excited that she was going to get more time with Ford.

"You realize it's a charter, don't you?"

Lovers Sail Singles & Kink Cruise. She nodded. "I know."

"Do you know the theme?" He was certainly looking at her now. The sexual energy had dissipated and was replaced by something she identified as having strong objection and control tendencies, perhaps judgment.

"Yes," she replied, pulling out of his embrace and sitting up straight. She wasn't about to justify her actions. No matter how attracted she was to him. She was a grown woman. A professional. "No biggie. It'll have to do. Especially since I discovered the nature of the cruise while I was on the bus ride to Miami."

"Bus ride?"

"Yes. A bus ride," she said, giving up all hope of remaining sexy in his eyes. She threw up her hands in defeat. It was over. Any chance she had at getting hot and bothered with the sexy Cajun was gone. "I don't like airplanes. And when I booked the cruise, I thought it was a singles cruise, not a singles-and-kink cruise. But I'm determined to learn everything there is to know about singles, romance, and kink. Happy?"

"No," he said, shaking his head. "You're not going."

"What?"

His dark gaze narrowed on her and his jaw set in hard angles. He paused a few moments, then blew out a long breath. "I know I have absolutely no right, but is there any chance that you could reconsider and not board this ship?"

"You aren't listening. I said I *need* this byline. I don't care what I have to do to get it. This is my chance to prove myself."

"At what cost?"

The driver pulled up to the passenger drop-off location. The taxi had stopped. She yanked on the door handle and pushed. Stepping out, she threw a fifty over the seat to the driver.

"Thank you, sir. Keep the change. And you," she turned back to

Ford, "thanks for ignoring my words. You have no right to tell me what to do. None. How do you get off thinking I care what you say? My plans matter. What I want matters. Forget this ride. Forget we met, forget—"

Without giving her a chance to finish, he shackled her wrist with his fingers and pulled her to him, while simultaneously springing from the cab. He towered over her.

"Stop," he said, placing a finger on her lips. "Stop speaking."

He kept her still and prevented her from moving away. But there was something more in his gaze than stubborn insistence. She just didn't know what it was.

Determined to remain in control, she pushed on his chest, and tried in vain to put space between them. He didn't budge. His grip grew tighter. It didn't hurt, but it wounded her pride. She really couldn't move.

"I'm sorry," he drawled. "I spoke instinctively and without thinking it through." His brown eyes gentled, and he looked truly apologetic. "The assignment is *that* important to you."

A frustrated tear slipped down her cheek. He lifted his finger from her lips and swept away the moisture.

"I apologize. I was thinking as a jackass of a man." His thumb traced her cheek, and he gave her a sincere smile. "I didn't mean to imply that your career goals aren't important. Not that it should matter what I think, but I truly believe you're willing to do what it takes to achieve success. I was being an overprotective chauvinist. Forgive me."

"Done. Behind us," Charlie said, taking a deep breath and dropping her forehead to his chest. She was accustomed to men being quick with their opinions and highhanded, and she was used to hearing them apologize for it. She couldn't meet his gaze and remain composed, so she just wanted to move on. She closed her eyes and inhaled his fresh scent as a consolation.

Some consolation. The distraction of his apology and concern was just as great as his sex appeal and annoyance. Charlie lifted her face to look at him. She had no choice. He'd already rattled her, and she couldn't deal with emotional upheaval.

"I have a job to do," she said. "I'm here as a professional, and being with you for only a few minutes sidetracked me. I can't afford distractions. I can't afford to fail."

"Okay. I get it." He shook his head and released her. He walked around to the open trunk and retrieved her carry-on. Setting it on the walkway, he extended the handle and closed her hand around the plastic. "They're serving a lunch buffet onboard. I'll meet you there at one. I'll be your biggest supporter and greatest resource. Promise."

He made a show of crossing his heart, then turned and strode through the crowd. She had no chance to object.

Chapter Four

Immigration had cleared the ship, so Ford was able to board immediately. He went directly to where his replacement was verifying the food delivery.

"How's everything going?" Ford asked, clasping the uniformed Jorge Ramos on the shoulder.

"Like clockwork," Ramos replied. "You checking on me, Rutherford?"

Ford shrugged. "You can't blame me for wanting to make sure there are no surprises. I'm still officially the manager on the sailing."

"Bullshit," Ramos said, signing an invoice and stepping back to allow the final crate of produce to be loaded. "We both know I've got this. Go up top and ogle those pretty women. They're all boarding with a great agenda."

"Which is?" Ford asked.

"To fuck and be fucked," Ramos replied with a smartass grin.

"Wipe that smirk off your face and keep your dick in your pants—at least where the passengers are concerned. Company policy is very clear." Ford glanced at the bustle of activity around them and wondered if any of his staff would lose his or her job by the end of the cruise.

"I know, Ford. This isn't my first time out, and I'm not about to risk my career for a hookup." Ramos looked up at the glass gangway and the many female passengers that were embarking, then he nodded toward Gabi, the sexy sous chef who had joined the crew the previous month. "Besides, I'm sure the female staff members will have the same frustrations as the men. There'll be many opportunities from within. Some delicious opportunities."

"You wish she'd give you the time of day," Ford quipped.

"I don't need all day. Just an hour here and there will do." Ramos was still watching the sous chef. Hell, he had it bad.

"You're whipped," Ford said, extending his hand. "I'll blend into the background. Let me know if I can be of any help."

"Will do, sir." Ramos accepted his hand and shook it. "Go get an eyeful and relax. You deserve it, Ford."

"Right."

Ramos was competent and perfectly ready for his own sailings. The man had handled the last two with no input from Ford, and he had done a damn good job. Taking the crew stairs, Ford made his way to his quarters and powered up his laptop. He had personal accounts to review and put in an order before they left port.

He knew he wasn't needed as food and beverage manager on the sailing. Captain Georgiou had requested he remain for the bonus trips to keep the less-seasoned crew focused during the charter. He was working incognito, interacting with the passengers as a supposed guest to make sure company policy was followed by both the crew and members of the group.

His current dilemma of the pretty little reporter bothered him more than it should. Even though they'd shared only a kiss, an irrational amount of possessiveness filled his gut. He didn't want her interacting with other passengers, especially not the sexually driven male guests. Not when he wanted her for himself. However, she was determined, and for reasons unknown to him, he couldn't let her investigate the happenings on the cruise without him at her side. Some of the Dominants would eat her alive, figuratively and possibly literally.

The hair on the back of his neck stood at attention, and he rolled his shoulders to get rid of the disturbing images. Fuck it. He had no choice. He dialed Guest Services.

"Alex, it's Rutherford," he said. "Book me the best cabin available." He could swing the financial burden of the ticket if it meant having a place to take her that wasn't officially off limits. Guests weren't allowed in crew quarters, and he wasn't allowed in a passenger's cabin, but if he purchased his own . . .

"Sorry, Ford. The ship is full. We have no available cabins." Alex chuckled. "You have a family member that wants to join the fun?"

"No." His idea to bend the rules went up in flames. Maybe he couldn't buy space, but he had a cabin and his passage was secure.

He just had to figure out how to attach himself to her and not get tossed overboard before they reached port.

He stripped off his clothes and stepped into the shower. Water always cleared his mind. He'd find a way.

Twenty minutes later, he strode onto the bridge and requested a private talk with Captain Georgiou. The captain agreed, finished instructing the other officer, then indicated Ford should follow as he led them out of the bridge. "What's up, Rutherford?"

"I'd like to touch base on something," Ford said, stuffing his hands into his pockets as they walked. By bringing Charlie's presence to the captain's attention, Ford could justify spending a lot of time with her. "There's a magazine reporter on board."

"I know," Georgiou said, surprising him. "Miss Stanton's publisher called to inform me this morning. Paul, her publisher and my friend's son, is concerned that Miss Stanton may be in over her head on this sailing. He asked that we keep a watchful, yet distant, eye on her. In case she requires our support."

"I met Miss Stanton in South Beach this morning. We shared a taxi to the port," Ford admitted, not feeling half as guilty as he should for what he was about to suggest. "I asked her to reconsider the assignment, but she's determined to do her job."

"And, like Paul, you have concerns?"

"More than you know, Captain."

"I see," Georgiou replied, rubbing his chin. "Ford, you are much more than staff to me. Over the past few years, I've watched you mature into a man who takes all his responsibilities to heart. I do not want you to ruin your hard work or tarnish your reputation by going against company policy, overstepping your duty, or engaging on a physical level with a guest."

"My assignment involves interacting with passengers during the group activities. If I happen to attend the same events she does, I'll be able to keep an eye on her," Ford blurted. "No conflict."

Georgiou shook his head and veered into one of the deserted bar areas. "Not smart, son." He leaned against a stool and motioned for Ford to sit. "I asked you to sign on specifically to keep the crew in check. We've also discussed how you need the extra money to meet your goals. You're jeopardizing what you've worked so hard for to be close to a woman."

"Thank you for the input," Ford allowed. "I appreciate that. However, I can handle the interaction. I don't want Miss Stanton placed in any compromising positions, unable to do anything about it."

"You're willing to risk your reputation for a woman you've just met?"

"No risk on my side." Realizing he was at the captain's mercy, for the first time in a long time, Ford humbled himself. "Please, sir. I give you my word. There won't be a reason to relieve me of my duties."

"You're more than taken by this young woman—to use polite language. Being with her in the sort of setting you know this sailing is all about will be temptation at its highest. She'll sleep in her bed, and you'll be sleeping alone—in your quarters. You can't step foot in her cabin, son."

"You have my word." He'd sleep in his cabin. She would sleep in hers. Period. He wouldn't allow her to sail alone, and knowing that he had no right to drag her off the ship before it left port, he'd keep his word and watch over her in the sexually charged atmosphere in a constant and unanswered state of arousal.

It seemed like an hour had passed before the captain nodded and held out his hand. Shaking Georgiou's hand, Ford contemplated the best way to break the news to Charlie. She wasn't going to be happy if she thought he was watching over her shoulder—which he definitely was.

As if reading his mind, the captain shook his head. "You know where to find her?"

"Yes I do." Ford checked his watch. "I'm supposed to meet Charlie at the buffet in half an hour."

"Charlie, eh?" Georgiou laughed and his perceptive gaze narrowed on Ford. "You sure you want to do this?"

"One hundred percent."

Charlie speared a mushroom and brought it to her mouth, then pushed chicken around on her plate. Her appetite had disappeared. She stared at her picked-over lunch, hoping they'd announce the cabins were ready and she'd get a reprieve from the onslaught of people. She was on activity overload watching the passengers file in and out of the restaurant.

"Hi, baby doll. Why you looking scared?"

She looked up to find a real hottie, who could have been his school's football star, wearing a pair of khaki shorts and a University of Miami T-shirt, grinning at her. "Who said I'm scared?"

"Your big blue eyes," he replied, friendly laughter joining his grin as he held out his hand. "Hi. I'm Quinn."

At ease with his friendly manner, she accepted his hand. "I'm Charlie."

Quinn waited for an invitation, which she freely gave by indicating the seat across the table, before he pulled out the chair opposite Charlie and made himself comfortable. She wondered why such an attractive and yummilicious jock needed a singles cruise to find love.

"I can read the question in your eyes," Quinn said, placing his muscled arms on the table and leaning forward. "I could ask you the same thing. Beneath that very reserved outfit, you're fucking gorgeous."

Swallowing her shame at being so transparent, but unmoved by the reserved outfit comment, Charlie cleared her throat. "I don't know what you're referring to."

"Sure you don't." His broad smile reached his eyes as he leaned even closer. "What's a nice girl like you doing in a place like this?"

Quinn wasn't being rude. He'd simply asked what they'd both been thinking. Charlie glanced at her notebook and then back at the handsome jock. *No time like the present to start,* she thought. "I'm working. Writing a Valentine's Day feature."

"Okay, I'll bite." Quinn leaned back in his seat, looking entertained with her explanation. He crossed his forearms over his broad chest and let his gaze travel over her conservative outfit. "What's the topic?"

"The perfect place to find love," she said.

"And you think Cupid carries a whip?"

"I'm not talking about whips," she objected, pushing the heel of her palm to her stomach to still the churning. "Some travelers may be here for the—*um*—leather goods, but I'm sure just as many are here to find love. I'm researching and writing about the perfect place to do that. I think a cruise fits the bill."

"Maybe," he said slowly.

"Why are you here, Quinn?" It was time to put on her reporter's hat and turn the questions on him. "You don't look like a guy who needs to be in an organized setting to find a date."

"I brought my date," he said with no hesitation. "And if you want me to be frank, I'm here for the sex . . . sex tips. No reason to get lazy just because I've landed the man of my dreams."

Her lips curled up in a smile. She'd been way off base. She'd missed it.

"It's not you. It's me. I seem to fly beneath most people's gaydar," Quinn teased. "It took me two weeks of ordering iced cappuccinos, double foam, and extra chocolate to get Luis to recognize my advances as more than friendly banter."

"Luis?"

"My man," Quinn explained. "Luis manages a café off campus where most graduate students hide from the noisy undergrads. I kept batting my eyelashes, but he never noticed. I tipped him so big, I practically spent a month's rent the first week there. Knocked up against him at every opportunity, and all he did was apologize for being distracted and bumping into me."

"Did you try speaking to him?" Typical man. Acted out, but didn't talk. Charlie shook her head in frustration. Men were so dense.

"Of course I did. At first, I tried starting a conversation about a car he was restoring, but he sidestepped that. He treated me like any other customer and totally ignored the sparks exploding between us. He claims not to have realized that I was interested in him at all. Wasn't even sure I was into men." Quinn shook his head in disgust. "So you're not alone in missing those vibes—because, baby doll, he missed them, and I was sending them out loud and clear, whereas with you, they may have been mixed in with other signals."

"How'd you get him to notice you?" Charlie asked, drawn into the love story. Nervousness melted away, and she found herself leaning towards the extremely good-looking man in order to hear every word.

"It was a Friday night. I was the last one there, and I pretended to be absorbed in my studying rather than in Luis."

"That's so cute," Charlie said, feeling the warm fuzzies spread through her.

"Not really. I sat there, sporting a very painful boner, watching the man I wanted sway to music as he mopped." Quinn placed one fist over the other and pretended to mop to a sensual rhythm. "I finally got the nerve up to approach him, wrapped my arms around his hunky torso, and grinded up against his tight tush."

"Wow!" Tush. So cute. She brought her hands to her chest and sighed.

"Yeah, wow. He decked me. Luis turned around and landed a right hook on my face. He thought I was a mugger or something."

"Holy cow," Charlie said, unable to stifle her laughter. "That must have really sucked. You're seeing stars for all the wrong reasons."

"It gets better," Quinn said, holding up his hand. "The cut beneath my eye bled like crazy."

"Did you tell him to call 911?"

"Fuck no." He laughed and waved a big hand in front of his face. "I told him to kiss it and make it better."

Charlie placed her elbows on the table, interlaced her fingers, and rested her chin in them. "Go on."

"He started muttering some stuff in Spanish and stomped off to the back of the shop. I mean, I knew what I knew. He was definitely into men and all, so I knew I hadn't misjudged the sparks."

"How'd you know he was gay? If he didn't know about you, it makes sense that he wasn't all that in tune with things."

"Nah, I knew." Quinn puffed out his chest. "Maybe I was the surprise Midwestern jock, but Luis had a bad boy reputation. He was into sex. Men. Women. It didn't matter."

"So he's bi?"

"He refuses to put a label on it. It makes sense. I've been with women. Loved being with them. But I prefer my man. However, there are a few women I wouldn't turn away from," Quinn explained. "It's just that I want him. Love plays a major part in the physical relationship for me."

"That's refreshing," she admitted. "So tell me what happened with Luis."

"Like I was saying," he drawled, winking and rolling his hand for emphasis. "After he'd come out about his sexuality and his father had disowned him, he turned into one of the biggest studs in Miami. Men, women, both . . . made no difference where he parked his dick. His nightly conquests fueled the gossip vine. Not only does he have the highest-grade equipment, he knows how to use it well."

She grinned in challenge.

"Don't doubt. I know what I'm talking about," Quinn said. "You'll agree when he shows up. Luis is hot."

"Fine. So he ran off into the kitchen. What'd you do?" The writer in her needed to reach the ending.

"I sat up, with a lot of effort I may add." Quinn reached for the hem of his shirt and she swiped at his forearm. "Shy, eh?"

"No," she replied. "I just don't think you should strip in public."

Quinn chuckled. "You're in for many surprises this weekend, Charlie."

"Whatever," she said, dismissing the mischievous smile on his face. "Go on."

"I managed to pull my T-shirt over my head and used it to apply pressure to the cut. Mr. Rico Suave returned with a baggie of ice, but when he saw the blood soaking through my shirt he reached into his back pocket for his phone and insisted on paramedics. I was done waiting for him to notice me. I called on my high school grappling moves." He demonstrated, stretching his legs under the table, and wrapping his feet around her ankles. "Within seconds, the man was writhing beneath me on the floor."

"I get it," Charlie blurted, covering her face with her hands.

"You're blushing."

"Am not."

"Are so," Quinn said, pulling at her wrists and settling her hands on the table between them. "Don't worry. I won't give you the details on how he finally got the message that I wanted him, but he did."

"I figured that much." Heat flooded her body and she squirmed in her seat. "So you're here to make sure there's enough spice in your sex life."

"Oh, there's enough spice," Quinn bragged. "I want to add more and keep it that way. Luis is more experienced than I am. I want to explore and learn."

Charlie sighed. She'd envisioned a great love between Quinn and Luis, and now Quinn wanted to explore. "You want other partners?"

"Not what I said," Quinn insisted. "We're open to sharing together. But that isn't what this is about. We're committed to each other and we're planning to get married next year. I want to keep him so damn hard and ready to erupt at my touch or glance."

She fanned her hand in front of her face and lifted her hair off her neck.

"You're beet red. It won't do," he said, shaking his head. "On this cruise, you're not only going to have to dress the part, which means heading to your cabin and getting out of that uptight outfit, but you're going to have to loosen up if you want to get that info for your writing." He wrapped his hand around her fingers, holding them still. "If you keep reacting like that, some Daddy Dom is going to throw you over his shoulder and lock you in his cabin for the whole cruise. Unless that's what you—"

"No." Charlie shook her head. "I'm not getting carried off to some cabin. I'm not getting involved with anyone. I'm here in a professional capacity. That's it."

"Sure, baby girl. That's a lot of protest for one tiny question."

"It's the truth," she said, using her free hand to pluck a grape from the bowl and pop it in her mouth. She was a professional.

"What's his name? He hot?" Quinn pushed.

"Miss Charlene?"

Charlie looked over her shoulder. Ford was there with a distinguished looking uniformed man at his side. "I'm Charlene Sta—"

"I know," the older man interrupted. "May I please have a word with you, Charlene?"

Ford stood silent, hands behind his back, glaring at Quinn.

"Hello, Captain." Quinn stood and leaned near her ear. "No last names in public spaces. Now, if you want, squeeze my hand and I'll go."

She squeezed.

"We're in 6411. Leave me a message and I'll come find you," Quinn whispered. He gave her a quick peck on the cheek and said good-bye.

A momentary flutter of comfort. Quinn and Luis were only a few doors down from her cabin. She was in 6418.

As the captain sat in the seat Quinn had vacated, Ford slid next to her on the bench. He made himself comfortable, resting his thigh against hers.

Chapter Five

"I'd like to personally welcome you onboard, Charlene." The captain wasted no time getting to the point. "I'm Captain Georgiou, and I believe you've met Keaton."

"I have." Charlie nodded and glanced at Ford without turning towards him. He wished she would, because then she'd show she felt some personal comfort with him. But she didn't. She held her own, keeping a respectable distance. "Thank you, sir. It's nice to meet you."

"Your publisher, Paul Lallas, is the son of a friend of mine. When he realized it was my ship one of his writers was sailing on, he extended the courtesy of informing me about the purpose of your trip."

Charlie straightened her back and immediately appeared inches taller. One fist balled on her thigh, the other hand snuck beneath the hair at her nape. "I assure you that I have no preconceived notions and do not intend to depict the cruise line in any specific light—especially not negatively."

"I'm not worried about censorship, Charlene. Nor am I concerned about the performance of my crew or the beauty and efficiency of my ship. You can write what you observe and truly believe."

She relaxed and stretched her fingers.

"Paul explained you are researching a feature on the perfect place to find love." It was a statement, but the captain paused and studied her face.

"Yes, sir."

"I'm honored that we made that list," the captain added.

"There is another reporter investigating the same subject in Paris," Charlie offered. "It's hard to top the city known for romance, but I figure a cruise is a good option for readers."

"Very true," Georgiou agreed. "Paris is perfect for love, but so is the sea. When passengers come onboard, they leave worries and responsibilities behind. Mundane daily tasks are temporarily suspended. Every need is taken care of, and our guests can choose to rest, explore, or be pampered. Keaton and I have witnessed many romantic connections and reconnections." He glanced at Ford for confirmation.

"We certainly have. A cruise vacation is conducive to love and romance," Ford agreed. "However, this sailing has unique qualities."

"I realize that," Charlie said, finally turning to Ford, even as her gaze narrowed in warning. "I didn't when I first booked my ticket."

Her fingers twirled around a lock of hair. Ford shook his head and grinned. She toyed so adorably with that silky blond mane when she got nervous.

"Either way," she said, her attention back on the captain, "I believe the information I gather will lend itself to the feature by its mere nature. I'm sure there will be romance and love."

"I'm in complete agreement," the captain confirmed. "But I—we—have a few concerns. Being that this charter is of a more carnal nature, it produces situations that other sailings do not."

"I can handle it," Charlie insisted.

"It's not about you handling the Lovers' group. And if any such thought originally came to mind, please know that Paul insisted you are more than capable of taking care of anything thrown your way." Georgiou gave Ford a cautionary look, urging him not to interrupt.

"Thank you," she breathed.

Her soft breath sounded. The tense stance of her shoulders released and her hands turned palm up on her thighs. Disregarding how much like a lust-struck puppy it made him appear, Ford looked directly at her. He shifted to his left and enjoyed the brightness emanating from the woman. She was glowing. Her blue eyes sparkled. And a big, bold smile graced her gorgeous face.

"My concern is with how you'll be received by the other guests." Georgiou raised an eyebrow, and his gaze turned laser sharp. "Kinksters are typically willing to share the intricacies and experiences of their love lives with people interested in learning about their lifestyle. However, Paul said you intend to keep this trip on a professional level."

"That's true. Complete professionalism is my goal."

"I understand," the captain said. "This means you do not plan to seek the same fulfillment other guests are looking for from the programs, and you do not intend to develop a personal relationship while on board."

"No," she huffed. "My only intention is to write my feature." Clearly annoyed with Georgiou's line of questioning, those pretty shoulders tensed again and she crossed her arms over her chest.

"Perfect. This is very good. Your presence and intent works for both of us," Georgiou said, nodding and smiling as if he'd totally missed her displeasure. "Miss Charlene, Keaton thinks he's found a way for the two of you to make your work much easier. He suggested working together on some level."

"I'll escort you to the events you choose to attend," Ford added.

"What?" Her mouth dropped open and her pupils dilated. "Why?"

"I've worked this particular group's events for the past four years. I'm familiar with the programming, as well as romantic developments from other sailings." Ford didn't mention that he'd seen her first, and if anyone was going to touch her, it would be him.

"I believe he will be a great source of information for you," Georgiou concluded. "An insider, with knowledge of cruise ship romances, enriching your research material."

The man was a genius. Conniving and manipulating, but a genius. Ford leaned back in his seat. How could she refuse to spend time with him after the captain had pointed out he'd be the perfect resource for her feature?

"Thank you for the offer, but I don't need a chaperone."

The captain shook his head and held up his hand. "By allowing Keaton to accompany you, you will help him do his job. He needs to monitor the events, blend in with the guests, and report to me so we ensure the company guidelines are followed."

"We can achieve our objectives independently," Charlie argued. "I don't want, and won't stand for, a chaperone."

"Definitely not a chaperone, my dear. Consider him an assistant of sorts."

Ford didn't appreciate the assistant title, but if it got her to agree, he'd take it.

Charlie quieted and seemed to consider the benefits the captain outlined, but her eyes had shuttered all emotion. It was impossible to read her, and Ford couldn't determine which way she would decide.

He had two options: Sit back and leave it to Georgiou to sway the stubborn woman and make her see the benefits of having a man at her side. Or he could ignore the captain's suggestion and convince her on his own. While appreciating the captain's effort and respecting his authority, Ford wasn't about to chance leaving Charlie in the lion's den alone. This woman being physically available to the group's participants wasn't an option.

"I could really use your help," Ford said, covering her shaking knee with his palm, his fingers aching from the contact. "Having a female partner would make my job much easier and validate my presence in the workshops."

"Why?" Charlie asked.

Ford couldn't lay it on thick or Charlie would see right through his plan. The woman wasn't gullible. Worse, the captain was eyeing him with concern. If Ford overstepped, he'd be out of a job and off the ship in no time.

"There is a certain level of audience participation expected, and the other guests may be suspicious of non-participating newcomers," he explained, removing his hand from her knee and alternating a pointed finger between them. And that was the absolute truth, so he went for broke. "As an undercover employee of the cruise line, I'm still bound by the rules of my employment, so my interactions are restricted. It will only take a few close calls for others to question the authenticity and sincerity of my presence."

Thankfully, her hackles receded, and he saw the reporter surface as she analyzed his words. Her intense blue gaze met his, searching his eyes before dropping to his mouth. A blush crept up her throat and settled in her cheeks. Fuck, she was a tasty shade of pink. What the hell was he thinking, putting himself in such close proximity without being able to have her? He would never survive the weekend.

"Staff and crew are not permitted in passenger cabins," the captain elaborated. "If Keaton is expected to *interact*"—the man used air quotes for emphasis—"with other guests, but continuously doesn't follow through, he will look suspicious. Possibly be outed by his actions or non-actions."

"Oh," she whispered, her gaze still caressing Ford's mouth.

Ford needed to appeal to her good sense and make her choose him. "We'll make a good team, Charlie. And we'll both accomplish our goals while not compromising our principles."

"I'm not sure. It could backfire." Her finger twirled, creating a perfect curl.

"Working together will allow you to remain undercover if you're comfortable doing so," Ford pointed out. "It also keeps your research honest." Score. Ford liked that one. Honest research seemed to be her game.

Surprising him, she shrugged. "It doesn't make a difference to me. Besides, Quinn already knows I'm a writer on assignment."

"Quinn?" The name left a sour taste on Ford's tongue.

Georgiou held up a hand to keep Ford from continuing his questioning. "I'm curious to hear what Mr. Quinn said upon learning you are writing a story."

Her nose scrunched in the cutest manner and the pink returned to her cheeks. "Something about not blushing so much, dressing the part, and letting loose to get the material. Otherwise . . ."

Ford leaned closer to hear, but she didn't continue. Rather she clapped her hands.

"Okay. I'll do it," she said. "I think we could help each other." She turned and looked into his eyes. "I'll be your cover." With a dainty yet firm grasp, she moved his hand off her thigh to the pleather cushion. "You'll be a great source of information. Not only about this specific voyage, but I can pick your brain about romance and cruises in general."

"Perfect. I'll leave you to figure out the details." The captain pushed back his chair and stood. He smiled and took Charlie's hand in his. "If I can be of any help, please let me know. And don't forget to take advantage of all the amenities our beautiful ship offers, Charlene. She'll certainly make you smile." He turned to Ford and shook his hand. "Good luck, Keaton."

"Thank you," Ford said, wondering if his captain truly knew how much strength he'd need not to be thrown off at the next port. He had to finish the cruise. Just sitting in the casual eatery with the woman had his groin protesting the imposed distance. He could only imagine how he'd react if she decided to participate in any scenes for the sake of research.

"Why did you introduce yourself as Ford, when it seems like everyone who knows you calls you Keaton?" Charlie's gaze darkened as she questioned the difference in names.

"I prefer Ford. Keaton is my legal name, but it carries a lot of family baggage and bullshit I'd rather not deal with." He cleared his throat. "What cabin are you in?"

"I thought you aren't allowed in passenger cabins."

"I'm not," he replied. "I want to join your section for the muster drill. Perhaps pick you up so we could review the group's itinerary and decide which workshops we'd like to attend?"

"I'm meeting with Quinn for the lifeboat drill," she lied, standing and giving him her back. She looked over her shoulder. "Chat after we set sail—starboard, by the pool?"

She had no idea what she'd asked for, but he couldn't hold back a grin. "Sure. Whatever you want." Ford stepped closer to her and placed a hand on her shoulder, keeping her attention on him. "Be sure to check the itinerary. Later." He brushed his lips over her hair and left.

Chapter Six

Charlie presented as a prim lady, but she wasn't a stupid one. She had her own agenda, and she didn't appreciate being saddled with a babysitter. What the men didn't know was that she'd actually chosen to accept the handsome babysitter. Better to suffer the arrogant sex-on-legs than to be thrown over a Daddy Dom's shoulder and be carried away. Presenting herself as part of a couple would make her job easier.

That was her story and she was sticking to it. It didn't matter that her chest squeezed so tight each time she was around the man it kept oxygen from reaching her brain. Nor did it matter that the ache between her legs pulsed like crazy when he looked at her with those intense eyes.

Sighing, she closed her hand around the handle, lifted her carry-on, and started down the staircase. She knew one thing for sure. He, Ford, Keaton, or whatever he called himself, wasn't going to get her hopes up. He'd warned as much. He wasn't the relationship kind of man. And the intensity between them wasn't a casual fling kind of energy. She'd end up heartbroken if she got involved. She'd steer clear.

The flutter in her abdomen disagreed, but she knew better. She'd spend time with him to make her job easier and more efficient, but she wasn't going to admit how much she ached to lie beneath him and have him take her completely. She fanned her face with her free hand and pulled at the golf shirt sticking to her heaving chest. Shit. He'd be the sexual experience of a lifetime.

Whatever. She didn't have time for fantasy. She had a job to do, and she was going to freaking enjoy doing it.

Charlie stopped at Quinn's door and knocked, disappointed when there was no answer. She'd reviewed the afternoon's schedule, and she needed a cohort like Quinn to accompany her. Quinn equaled comfortable and free.

Shuffling a few feet farther into the passageway, she found her cabin and slipped her keycard into the slot. Before she had the chance to make it inside, laughter sounded from down the hall. She looked up and saw the handsome couple wave.

"Look at you, Miss Fancy," Quinn called, walking right up to her and planting a kiss on her cheek. "Guess we're meant to be. We're even on the same deck."

"Practically neighbors," she replied, giving him a big smile and waving a hand diagonally from her door to 6411.

"Charlie, meet Luis. Luis, this is the pretty lady I told you about." Quinn made the introductions, and Luis took her hand and brushed his lips over her knuckles.

"It's a pleasure to meet you, Charlie. I can see why you made quite an impression on Quinn. You're stunning."

Not only was Luis as hot as Quinn had described, but charm oozed from his pores. A bit older than Quinn, but sexy as shit, Luis sent her insides into a frenzy.

His pewter-colored short-sleeve shirt stretched over his sculpted chest and showcased the colorful tattoos on his impressive biceps. Black jeans casually hugged his trim hips, the jeans worn in all the right spots. When his dark gaze met hers, bad boy vibes wrapped around her awareness, until the corners of his full lips lifted into a dazzling smile and put her at ease.

She could definitely see why Quinn was taken with him. The man exuded sex appeal. With his confident saunter and exotic Latino looks, Luis could pass for Enrique Iglesias from afar. And if his personality came close to matching his looks, it was no wonder Quinn was so in love.

Once Quinn pointed out that her accommodations were more deluxe than theirs, she pushed on her door and the threesome moved into Charlie's cabin to discuss a few of the events.

"Told you it was fancy," Quinn repeated, rounding the seating area and strolling past the large bed to the balcony. "We went for an inside cabin."

"So did I," Charlie said. "I don't get it."

"Maybe they upgraded you? After all, you're a big-shot reporter," Quinn replied.

"Ha ha," Charlie said. "I wish." She placed her small suitcase in the closet and indicated the men should make themselves comfortable. "Actually, I need to ask you a favor related to my big-shot reporting."

While Quinn sat on the edge of the bed and leaned forward, his elbows on his knees, Luis remained standing and crossed his arms over his chest. He looked down at her, raising a dark brow in question.

"After reviewing the cruise specifics, I've decided that it may be more beneficial to keep the feature on the down low. I want to get a true perspective on my subject matter, and approaching guests with a list of questions may not be the best way."

"True," Quinn agreed, standing and taking a few steps to the lighted desk area. He studied the welcome basket and lifted a ribbon of condoms. "While all lifestyles are represented on this cruise, some people may shut down if they feel like you're observing them in a petri dish environment. You should mingle."

"Agreed." Charlie clasped her hands between her knees. "I can use some friendly faces to navigate the waters."

"Anything to do with that dark hunk of man who glowered at me on deck? I thought he was going to throw you over his shoulder and stomp out of the restaurant," Quinn said.

"No. Stop with me being thrown over shoulders," Charlie said, pushing welcome thoughts of being thrown over Ford's shoulder out of her mind. "I'll be working with that dark hunk of a man at some of the events. He needs a partner as cover for his work." She explained about Ford's position and what the captain expected of him.

"Right." Quinn returned to her side and folded the condoms into her hand, closing his fingers over hers. "If you need us, we're here for you. We're willing accomplices and friendly faces."

"Thanks," Charlie said, feeling the heat crawl up her neck. "I don't want to be a buzzkill. I don't want to get in the way—"

"You won't be in the way," Quinn insisted.

"You could be part of the way," Luis said, his gaze smoothing over her. "If you want to be, *pequeña.*"

"Um," she breathed, shifting in her seat, her hand still enclosed in Quinn's. She looked between the men and understanding dawned. They were inviting her to join in their sexual explorations. Shit. Shit. Triple shit. She'd messed up. "I didn't mean to imply that I should be your third wheel."

"We know," Quinn assured, pulling her hand into his lap. "We're in the friend zone. Got it. Luis is offering an additional option, should you want to venture that way. I've already told you that we enjoy variety in our bed. You, as a friend with benefits, would be awesome. But, if that's not what you want, we're cool. Friendly faces and accomplices."

Quinn was sincere. No hidden plan in his words.

"Thanks," she whispered, releasing her breath. "I thought we could attend some of the workshops together."

"We will," Luis said. "No worries, *querida*."

"*Querida?*" Charlie asked, looking at Quinn for clarification.

"Sweet thing. Darling. Honey," Quinn explained. "You've made a definite impression and sure connection with Luis. He doesn't take to most people. But sweetheart, you're hard to resist."

Luis wasn't as easy to speak to as to look at. He watched Charlie and Quinn, but didn't talk much. His dark eyes seemed to process more than she admitted. He seemed almost amused. An edge of anticipation scraped over her consciousness as the corners of his mouth formed a promising smile.

"Luis and I have marked the workshops we're interested in attending." Quinn pulled the program from his back pocket and handed it to her. "You're more than welcome to join us, Charlie. Being together should make it a little easier for you to dabble in what you'd like to explore."

Reviewing the schedule, she was pleasantly surprised to find that he'd marked a few of the events she'd already decided on. She nodded. "Thanks. I really appreciate it."

"Pick Your Mate." "The Dating Game." "PDAs." Those were a few of the titles Quinn had starred. She'd also starred them.

"Want to start with tonight's Sail Away party?" Quinn asked, pointing to "Erogenous Zone Happy Hour."

"Perfect," she said, glad he'd invited her. "I know singles make up the majority of guests, but I appreciate the opportunity to walk into an event together. Thank you."

"One condition," Luis said, raising a thick finger in the air. His dark gaze met hers, looking directly past her professional façade. "You need to agree to be honest and accept your nature. Regardless of your preconceived notions."

She wrinkled her forehead, unsure of what he was implying.

"True nature, *querida*. Be honest. That's all. Agree," he cautioned.

A peculiar heaviness filled her stomach. There was obviously a purpose for Luis's bold request, but whatever his reason, it unsettled her. "I'm honest."

"You need to accept that honesty," he pressed.

Nodding, she reached for her vapor stick and took a needed drag. She exhaled and waved a hand through the scented cloud, considering what it would entail to accept her *honest* nature. Nothing too difficult. She knew what she wanted. Sort of. "I agree."

"Good girl." Luis smiled, leaned over, and stroked his thumb down her cheek. He extended his other hand to Quinn, who accepted it and stood. "Change into something a little more comfortable. We'll pick you up when they call for the muster drill."

Relieved that he'd answered her unasked question on the dress code, she sighed and followed them to the door. "Thank you."

Once she was alone, she face-planted onto a pillow, punching her fists into the other pillow. "Shit! Shit! Triple shit!"

This cruise was everything she'd ever dreamed of and then some. It was a chance to take her career to a higher level with her very own byline. It was also a chance to have the sex she'd always wanted. Plenty of opportunities.

"Why can't you indulge in what Quinn and Luis offered?" Charlie cried to the empty room, flipped over, and sat up to look into the mirror. "Why can't you just do casual?"

Because she was a romantic fool and wanted tingles dancing on her skin when she was with her lover. No matter how good-looking Quinn and Luis were, they were, as Quinn had pointed out, in the friend zone. She wanted them as friends.

"They're not like Ford," she cautioned her reflection. "He'll break your heart." She dropped her arms in an exasperated gesture and shook her head. "Just stick with the research, Charlie. Have fun, and if you can't find the right guy for a casual affair, you'll make do." Done speaking to her reflection, she glanced at the goodie basket and the rubber penis that was displayed in the center. "Whatever."

She turned away and walked to the closet.

The horn sounded as Ford made his way to the lifeboat drill. He hadn't needed to ask her for her cabin number to know which muster station to attend. He already knew. But there was something about the woman that had him wanting to keep her to himself. Did he want her to need him? Or did he want to claim every inch of her as soon as possible? This infatuation made no sense. He needed to figure out more specifically what he wanted.

Passengers crowded the assigned spots, forming tight should-have-been rows of boisterous and rowdy people in the afternoon sun. Between the bodies moving to a salsa beat and umbrella topped drinks and beer bottles lined up along the railing, the guests in his particular station looked to have started their vacation well ahead of setting sail.

Ford scanned the group and spotted his petite blonde. She wasn't alone and she wasn't distressed. That Quinn guy had his hand on her hip and was shaking his jock ass to the music as they swayed to the beat. The jock held an oversized piña colada to her lips and urged her to drink. And with his arm wrapped so intimately around her, his forearm rested on the skin above her breasts.

"No way," Ford muttered. If anyone's forearm was going to brush her tits, it would be his. He'd seen her first. They had an agreement. He moved forward, pushing through the party, but stopped in his tracks when a second guy grinned at her and touched a finger to her chin. The second guy winked at Charlie and licked his fingertip.

What the fuck? Ford thought, unable to look away. *She's sandwiched between All-American and Latin Lover.* He groaned, holding his fists against his thighs. Charlie didn't need his protection. She didn't need his help. She had it all under control, and she blended in just fine.

Charlie caught him watching and raised her hand. Her fingers fluttered a hello.

As he restarted toward her, Ford knew he was screwed. Maybe

she didn't need him, but he wanted her. He'd never been the kind of man to turn his back on a challenge. And Charlene Stanton was definitely a challenge. He was going to spend the whole cruise in purgatory: looking, craving, tasting, but not having.

Admittedly more than a little drawn to Charlie, he wasn't about to ignore the ache in his groin completely. For some fucked-up reason, he couldn't, wouldn't, leave her alone. Once he'd had his fill of that delectable softness, he would then move on to business as usual. It was Lust 101—homework required.

Quinn finished the drink and stepped away, placing the empty glass by the railing. Ford moved to the spot he'd vacated.

"Hello," he said, lowering his face and brushing his lips over her mouth before the Latin Lover. "Started the party without me?"

That was an asshole move. He'd never needed to mark his territory with any other woman.

"Nah," she said. "You arrived on time. We're just getting started." Her bare shoulders rose and her sweet butt moved in an inviting wiggle. She held out her arm to the Latin Lover. "This is my friend Luis."

Ford moved behind her and pressed his body against hers, snaked an arm across her middle, then extended a hand to the other man. *Her friend.* Who cared? As long as it was his arm brushing her skin. He'd make sure it would be his arm every time from this point on.

"Nice to meet you," he said. "I'm Ford."

Quinn returned as the two men clasped hands and shook. Ford didn't miss the way he winked at Charlie.

"You met his boyfriend, Quinn, earlier," Charlie said, leaning back against Ford's chest to give him easier access to Quinn's extended hand.

Ford nodded and quickly shook the All-American's hand. "Good to see you, Quinn. I'm Ford."

Boyfriends or not, Luis and Quinn had room on their roster for an addition. If he had anything to say about it, Charlie would not be drafted. Ford was keeping her exclusively on his team.

He draped his arm down her body and settled his hand on the curve of her hip. She fit perfectly against him, and he nuzzled his way just below her ear. "You still up for chatting starboard after we sail?"

"Absolutely," she replied. "We're also planning on the happy hour party." She glanced at the jock, who was wearing an amused grin. "What's it called?"

"The Erogenous Zone party," Quinn said.

"Right," Charlie said, nodding and turning back to Ford. "Care to join us?"

"Absolutely," he said, throwing her enthusiasm back at her. "I go where you go."

The drill leader blew his whistle. Ford settled his chin atop her head, inhaling the coconut scent of her hair deep into his chest.

Purgatory.

Chapter Seven

"You're meeting *him* starboard?" Quinn asked when it was just the three of them walking back to their cabins. As Charlie fit her keycard into the slot, he touched her arm and made her turn to look at him. He fixed her with an inquisitive stare.

"Yup. We set it up earlier," Charlie explained, stepping back from the doorway and letting him into her cabin. Luis waited for her to enter and followed. "Why?"

"Have you read the material provided by the group?" Quinn insisted, reaching for one of the pamphlets on the counter and offering it to her.

"I've read most of it," she replied, taking the paper and returning it to the pile. "I have a job to do. I can't spend all my time learning about kinky sex and all it offers. I have to concentrate and write about the perfect place to find love. I need to look at the big picture, not the details."

"*Mi querida*, that Ford guy has his mind set on a very specific detail," Luis said. "There's no big picture with him. He all but pissed a circle around you, marking you as off limits to everyone else onboard. I'm surprised he let you walk back to your cabin with us."

"He has some work thing to see to," Charlie said. They weren't obligated to be together all the time. "We're looking out for each other, while meeting professional needs. It's a professional arrangement. We're not even considering this a friendship."

"It's not a friendship," Quinn agreed. "Read the damn material. This is a cruise centered on sexual exploration and expression, not on finding love. Love and friendship are byproducts and possible results of the sex. They're not the purpose. Plus, there are certain parts of the ship that are clothing optional—no clothing needed or expected."

"The starboard side of the lido is such a place," Luis said.

"Shit. Shit. I missed that. Triple shit." She dropped onto the edge of the bed and hid her face in her hands. Her stomach did continuous somersaults, so she appreciated her lack of appetite at lunch. "I'm not a nudist. I wouldn't be caught dead naked in front of a bunch of strangers. I can't sit on deck in the buff."

Luis laughed. He hooked a finger beneath her chin and angled her face upwards. "If you're with him, that won't be an option," he said, dropping a reassuring kiss on her forehead. "We won't be an option."

"What?" Her eyes burned and alarm pulsed in her mind. "Nobody, and I mean nobody, dictates who my friends are. Never."

Luis's laughter continued. "Oh, *querida*. You are such a refreshing pleasure. I'm glad we're friends."

Quinn nodded in agreement. He leaned over and kissed her cheek. "Very happy we're friends."

"Me, too," she admitted, feeling a twinge of regret in her core. What would it be like to be involved with two men like Quinn and Luis? They were handsome, charming, considerate, and totally sexy. Her shoulders dropped in disappointment. No matter what they were or how easy it was to be with them, they hadn't ignited a fire low in her belly the way Ford had. It burned hotter each time he touched her. But she wasn't relinquishing control to him or anyone. She was working.

"I say who I associate with," Charlie said. "No one else does. I won't be around anyone who tries."

"Don't sell the man short," Luis warned. "Ford may be possessive, but he's not an idiot. I doubt he'd ever try to name your friends or restrict your nature. And as far as we're concerned, I'll admit to holding onto hope that you'd change your mind until I saw you respond to him. Every inch of your skin turned the prettiest pink. Your nipples went so hard and your pupils dilated. No question. He's not meant for your friend zone. We are, and we'll be in your corner every step of the way."

Talk about being a straight shooter. Luis didn't bother with extra words for the sake of niceties. He placed it all on the table, making it absolutely certain she was on board with his understanding of the situation.

"However, *pequeña*, that doesn't mean that I'm negating our previous agreement," he continued. "And if you're honest, which is what you agreed to, you'll admit to wanting to meet him on any terms."

"Almost any terms," she said, pointing a finger in the air. "I'm not going naked."

"Trust us, sweetheart. He won't allow you to expose that body," Quinn said, grinning and waving a hand in the air. "If you strutted in naked, he'd tackle you to the floor and cover you up himself. He's not about sharing."

"Whatever. I'm done daydreaming," she said, groaning and pushing against Quinn's massive back. "Just go. I'll deal with Ford. You guys have it wrong. Our relationship is a business relationship. He has no right to say what I do or don't do."

"If you say so, baby girl." Quinn stood, pulling her up and into a tight embrace. He brought his mouth to hers and gave her what felt like a good-bye kiss. "Just have fun."

"May I?" Luis asked, stepping up and gazing into her eyes.

Charlie licked her lips and nodded. She wanted this. Wanted to know what it was like to be given the control and feel treasured.

With one hand tight at her nape and the other cupping her cheek, Luis turned her to face him. He pressed his thumb to her chin and her lips parted. He slid his lips over hers, swept over her tongue, and feasted on her curious desire. Pressed against his hard body, she felt the length of his arousal against her belly. Another good-bye kiss. "Be honest, *querida*."

"I will," she breathed, reaching for the back of the chair and her balance.

"If not, we're getting back in the game," Quinn warned, walking ahead of Luis and out the door.

"That's a promise," Luis added, latching the door behind him.

They'd accepted her decision, agreed to play by her rules, and shown her they wouldn't abandon her and let her go at it alone.

She lowered to the chair and let out a long breath. And friends or not—not that it was typical to kiss her friends like that—those men were master kissers. She should be clawing at their backs and begging them to stay. Luis and Quinn offered her every decadent fantasy she'd never had the courage to dream of, but no matter how dizzying their kisses, they didn't burn through her like Ford's.

She was doomed. He wasn't allowed in guest cabins, and so he wasn't allowed to give her what her body craved. Officially, they worked together and therefore were allowed to interact because they provided cover for each other. That included being a couple for the other guests' eyes, but never really being together. It would be four nights of torture.

Or, if she was smart, she could keep things easy with Ford, forget about the supposed date they'd set for ten days down the road, and enjoy the carnal company of two sexy-as-fuck men. They looked good, tasted delicious, and smelled like heaven. There was no doubt in her mind that Quinn and Luis could more than physically satisfy her and teach her things that books were written about.

She shook her head. Nothing was going to happen with Quinn and Luis. She wasn't wired like that. Her mind didn't rule her body. Her heart did. At the moment, her body was preparing for heartbreak.

Grabbing the pink bikini bottoms, she walked into the small bathroom and prepped for self-imposed celibacy . . . again.

Ford checked the bedside clock and reached for the phone. He dialed Charlie's cabin, and laughed at the bothered manner with which she answered the phone.

"Hello. What has you so breathless?"

"I didn't expect the phone to ring," she replied. "I was getting dressed."

"In that case, may I suggest we change our meeting spot?"

"No. I'm good with it," she insisted.

He could picture her lips in a pretty pout and her proud chin jutting high. She must have read about the starboard side, but was too stubborn to admit it would be too much for her. He wondered how she'd really handle the scenes.

"Do I need to bring extra sunscreen?" Ford asked.

"Depends how easy you burn."

"Cute. I'm not the blonde in our pair. Unless . . ." He didn't bother to hide his laughter. It was easy to envision her blush at his implication and he liked that.

"Funny, Keaton."

"Ford. And I'll meet you by the elevators in five." He wanted to add that *clothing optional* meant she should be dressed and not on display, but he held back. She'd go naked just to annoy him. He went for casual. "We'll ride up together."

"Fine. I'll see you in five."

She disconnected, and he felt the loss.

He hurried out of his cabin and up the staircase to their meeting spot. He stared at the entrance, praying she'd walk through in more than a sarong. She did.

Charlie wore the same strapless blue dress she'd been wearing during the drill. Her full breasts were perfectly outlined by the elastic that hugged them, and the tips still beckoned for his lips to close around them, but there was enough material flowing around her body to keep it covered.

"Hi," he said, crooking his arm and offering it to her. "Ready?"

"As I'll ever be," she replied, fitting her hand through his arm and resting her dainty fingers on his forearm. "Luis and Quinn said that starboard was clothing optional."

He nodded, pressing the call button for the elevator, then covering her hand with his. "And privacy optional."

"What does that mean?"

She looked up at him, adorable and way too cute, and he considered hiding her in his cabin for the duration of the trip. She was sweet and innocent, at least on the surface, and he didn't want her exposed to the eyes of others. Fucking unreasonable, he knew.

"Privacy optional means you may see more than you're prepared to see," Ford said. "Are you sure you still want to talk there?"

"I'm sure," she said, squaring her shoulders. "I'm a professional observer. I'm with you. No one will bother me."

"They better not," he said, feeling good that she'd thought of the fact that she was with him. He pressed the button for the top deck.

Chapter Eight

Ford led her to a high top near the railing overlooking the pool. "I figure we can review tonight's program with a little peace from here. If you like, we'll make our way down when we're done."

So, he hadn't exactly complied with her request to chat *on* the lido. He'd taken it on himself to give her a bird's-eye view first. He didn't want her in the center of the action. And no fucking way would he risk another man's hands reaching for her tempting little body. He'd probably find himself in a fistfight, and the captain wouldn't hesitate to yank her away from him and have him thrown overboard. Well maybe not literally overboard, but he'd be relieved of his position and off the ship, shattering not only his opportunity to have Charlie, but also his ability to secure the remaining money for his café.

He kept quiet while she looked around, then climbed up on the stool without any objection. She glanced down at the party and scanned the crowd with intense curiosity. Her gaze stopped at a group gathered on two lounge chairs that had been pushed together.

Two women, a brunette and a redhead, were sprawled naked on the blue and white striped towels. The redhead was on her back, her legs spread wide, and on display for the guests. The brunette was on her side, massaging the redhead's breasts and rolling dark nipples between her fingers.

When a man dropped his head and suckled an offered tit, the brunette moved her hand between the redhead's thighs. A second man stepped up behind the brunette and kneaded the pale globes of her ass. He whispered something in the brunette's ear, and the woman slid her fingers into the redhead with a great show of zeal, as the redhead lifted her hips to the brunette's pumping.

"Are they part of the group's entertainment?" Charlie asked, leaning over the railing as if searching for a director. "A show?"

"No," Ford said, closing his fingers around her wrist. "You can say it's a show of sorts, but not organized. Some couples, oftentimes more than a few as you can see, have fun in public. The only rules are that their actions be consensual and not harmful."

"They're guests?" Her big eyes matched her surprised tone.

"Yes," he replied, standing and moving behind her. He snaked an arm around her middle and held her close as she pushed up the footrest. He shifted to hold her securely and her breasts rested on his forearm, causing his libido to go into overdrive. He intentionally moved his hold lower so as to not torture himself. "Does it turn you on to watch while the brunette fingers the redhead? Does the idea of a woman's touch make you horny?"

"Not usually," she replied, her tone more scientific than sensual. "But this is sexy as shit. I'm amazed at how free and comfortable they are with their bodies. All of them."

The man who had whispered to the brunette motioned for someone to approach. An employee of Lovers Sail appeared, outfitted in only a stainless-steel cock cage, and held out a tray of condoms. The man chose one, tore off the packaging, and rolled it on. He then selected a tube and squeezed the lube into his palm, dismissing the server with a toss of his head. He settled on the chaise behind the brunette and lifted her right leg.

Ford pressed his arm across Charlie's abdomen as he tightened his fingers on the soft swell of her hip. He didn't bother watching the scene below them; rather, he studied the expressions rolling over Charlie's face. She didn't look away from the thrusting bodies, and the writhing limbs didn't bother her. She was intrigued and, if he wasn't mistaken, she was extremely turned on. "You like that?"

"It's interesting," she breathed. "I like the freedom to do what feels right." She turned in his arms, her breasts brushing across his ribs. "Is that an orgy?"

"Considering he's fucking her ass, while she's fingering the other woman and sucking another guy's dick, who happens to be playing with the redhead's tits, I'd say it's an orgy," he said, chuckling as she burrowed against him but turned back to look.

"There is another guy sucking one of the redhead's boobs," Charlie added. "And a fourth guy lubing up behind him."

"Officially an orgy," Ford confirmed, intrigued that she was so into it. "There is also an ordinary and boring couple going at it by the bar." He pointed to the man bending a woman over a stool and pumping into her for all he was worth.

"Ew." She jumped away from her stool and onto his toes, practically crawling up his body and wrapping her arms around his neck.

She was so into the group activities, that her reaction to the single, heterosexual couple shocked him, and he hardly had time to secure her curvy little bottom in his hands. He leaned back and looked at her face. "What's wrong?"

"You think someone did it on this one?" She pointed to her seat.

Laughing, he cupped her ass and lifted her against his body. "I doubt it. Wrap your legs around my waist, and I'll keep you off any potential fuck surfaces."

"Okay," she said, surprising him again. "It's kind of nasty to think of their jizz all over the place. I'm not about exchanging bodily fluids with strangers."

"Duly noted. No bodily fluid play with others." Ford laughed louder, and the movement of his chest had her sweet ass filling his hands.

Charlie didn't want her flabby butt jiggling against him. "You're laughing at me." She smacked his shoulder. "Stop it. You know it's gross."

"You know the table and stools are clean," he replied. His large palm cupped a fleshy ass cheek as he grinned at her. "Our staff has received extensive training on properly cleaning the ship for the sailing's specific activities, and the event organizers have their own crew of sanitizing engineers. The surfaces are clean. Plus, sex acts are restricted to certain venues. This isn't one of them."

"Really?" Charlie asked, searching the tabletop and stools for stains.

He leaned just far enough back for her to moan in protest at the absence of his solid chest against her rapidly beating heart. Ford smiled and caressed her cheek, and she couldn't help but relax against his hand as he guided her face to look at him. Her whole body relaxed. Charlie stopped tensing her thighs, stopped attempting to lift her butt from his palm, and accepted his strength.

"Trust me," he breathed, dropping a kiss to her forehead. He took a few steps toward one of the many piles of clean towels provided exclusively for this journey, then placed it around her neck. "Besides, we just set sail. I highly doubt anyone has discovered our special spot."

She smacked his shoulder again.

"Now, you stop it," he said. "I wouldn't expose you to anyone else's fluids." He pushed the hair from her face.

"Thanks," she said, resting her cheek on his shoulder. "Can I just stay up here until we walk to a clothing-not-optional part of the ship?"

"Of course." Ford tucked her notes beneath his arm and walked across the deck. He slipped past the automatic doors to the elevator, and then pressed the button for deck five. "We'll head to the wine bar. It's usually quiet at this point of the cruise. You can update me on all your plans there."

As Ford stepped off the elevator, Charlie slid down his body and made quick work of lowering her bunched skirt past her hips. "Thanks for the ride."

"Any time," he replied. "Besides, carrying you around makes us look like a real couple. It's all good."

Damn. She'd forgotten. She was only pretending to be so aware of his body and the way it made her skin feel hot. With a flick of her wrist, she flipped her hair over her shoulder and took her notes from his hold.

"Yeah. Looking like a real couple helps." And just to prove to herself that it wasn't a big deal, she snaked her arm around his waist and hooked her thumb into a denim belt loop. "So how's *your* work going so far, honey?"

"It's getting better with every mile we put between us and the shore." He draped his arm over her shoulder, and his hand dangled dangerously close to her breast. "How about your work?"

Glancing down at his hand, she licked her parched lips. She had to rein in her body's reaction. It wouldn't do to feel his almost-touch to her core. It was innocent. Casual. It didn't mean anything. This—he—they were working.

"Other than wishing I could puff away my nerves with vanilla, peachy keen."

His fingers squeezed her bare shoulders and stilled her walking.

He turned her toward him and slowly slid his palms up the sides of her neck, lifting her chin with his finger. "You're doing great."

She was not. All she was doing was feeling the buzz traveling through her body with his every touch and craving a drag of vanilla to compensate. No surprise after all the sex they'd witnessed. Who wouldn't want a smoke after a mind-blowing orgasm—or to distract from the pulsing between her legs?

"Congratulations on quitting." His fingers feathered up and down her skin, keeping her immobilized and staring into his dark eyes. "The cruise should help with that since smoking isn't permitted in most public spaces. You shouldn't feel as tempted. I'll help, too. I promise."

"I didn't quit," she admitted, shaking her head. "I never smoked cigarettes, but I got hooked on those flavored vapes after my divorce. Like a crutch. I'm trying to stop. Regardless, it's a bad habit, and the truth is that when things get tough, I ache for the darn thing."

"I'm still helping," he said, trailing those tantalizing fingers down her arms and entangling his left ones in her right. Tugging gently, he fit their joined hands against his side and rubbed her fingers. He continued down the mirrored corridor. "Every time you get a craving, instead of reaching for the electronic thing, squeeze my hand. I promise not to let things get bad."

"You're kidding, right?" She lifted her free hand to just over her right ear, where she typically stuck the pink stick, but came up empty. She'd left it in her cabin. No vape. No quick inhale to calm her. She twirled her finger into her hair. "Why do you want me to squeeze your hand?"

"Just to let me know. Then, it's out of your hands and my responsibility to keep you occupied." His broad shoulders lifted in the most casual gesture, but the man was as serious as he was crazy. "You squeeze, and I'll take it from there."

"If you say so," she said.

"I say so."

As if touching the very thing that caused the craving would ease her pain. Ford had no clue, so there was no use in arguing with a delusional person. You couldn't win because they didn't employ logic. On the other hand, he was offering help with no strings attached. That was rare in her life. People had always wanted something from her.

Ford guided them into the wine bar and pointed to a table near a large round window, looking out just above the water level. "What's your pleasure?"

You are, the little voice in her head said, and heat raced over her skin at the thought of sharing all sorts of carnal pleasures with him. Pulling her hand from his, she slipped into the tightest section of the booth. "That's rather direct, Ford."

"While I'd like a truthful answer from those lips about what you're insinuating, I was referring to what you'd like to drink." He flashed a panty-melting grin and slid in beside her. "We're going to get to know each other real well. There's no reason to feel uncomfortable."

"Who said I'm uncomfortable?"

Still grinning, he stilled her finger and lowered her hand from her hair. "You did."

Once again, he intertwined their fingers and kept her from inching away. The feel of his solid thigh against hers was too good. The assurance of his company unsettled her. She'd always fought for self-empowerment, and she didn't want to need a man, but she liked being with him. Charlie glanced at their joined hands in his lap and shrugged. He didn't need to know every little detail. They'd just met. It made no sense to expose herself and bare her soul, no matter if she wanted to confide in him.

"I'll take a Coke," she blurted, her gaze skirting over the ornately decorated lounge. Gold accents on the cream-and-white fixtures gave the sense of an ancient Greek gathering spot. There were even some naked statues in the corners. "I'll hold off on more alcohol for now. Tempting as it may be, I need to keep my faculties intact."

"I'll look out for you, Miss Charlene." He tilted his head to the side, and he regarded her with steamy questions in his dark eyes. She couldn't look away, so she focused on breathing through the sizzle. "Nothing you don't want will happen."

"How do you know what I want?" Her heart pounded in her chest. She wanted so much more than she'd say. So much more than she could handle. She managed to look away and shifted in her seat. She needed space.

"The one thing I won't stand for is you hiding from me, Charlie." He pulled her back against him. "Ten minutes ago, your moist heat was steaming up my belt buckle."

She glanced from the denim-clad package to his waist. "I don't see a belt."

"Okay," he said, chuckling and leaning over and pressing his mouth just below her ear. "No belt. The button on my jeans." His lips lingered and he drew a sensitive earlobe into his mouth, groaning as he suckled the tender flesh with slow enjoyment.

Charlie wanted to object. Wanted to pull away. Instead, she dropped her shoulder and bent in closer. The man had talent, and as his tongue swirled, she wondered what else it would warm and entice.

"Ford," she whispered. "You're killing me. I know you shouldn't kiss me like that in public. But I like it. I don't want to stop."

"That's it, baby. Don't hide from me," he said, trailing his tongue down her neck and closing his mouth on her collarbone. "In Miami, a fuse lit between us. You can't deny it. I can't stop thinking about you. Can't stop wanting you. I've been hard from the moment you ran into me this morning."

"I didn't run into you," she objected, a devilish smile on her lips.

"You have no idea what you're doing to me." Still showering her neck with wet kisses, he responded by pressing her hand over his erection. "*This* is because of you. The way you look at me. The way your sweet scent fills my nose, and I can't inhale enough of it into my lungs to breathe easy. The way your hand fits in mine and makes me want to hold it every minute it's within reach."

"It's not me. It's this ship and the theme of the cruise," she said, shrugging away from lips that scrambled the logical part of her brain.

"How can you be so smart and beautiful, yet have no idea of the effect you have on those you open up to? Even when you only offer a tiny glimpse of yourself." He tilted her chin up and met her gaze. He touched his mouth to hers and his breath tantalized her lips, but he didn't kiss her. "You dropped your shield for a few minutes because you thought I was a nonfactor. Now you're stuck with me. I saw you. You're so damn intoxicating, Charlie. Warm heat and heaven."

An ache pulsed in her center, and her lips burned for his kiss.

"You want more than you let on, *chère*. Wanton desire burns in your core, and it's my intention to stoke that fire until you're begging me to release what you keep tucked away. Have no doubts. I want you. And I will have you."

Oh, excuse her! How did he know what she'd only just learned?

"Charlie, don't think when you're with me. Experience. There's no right or wrong in what you feel. Not when it's you and me." His thumb pressed on her lower lip as he slipped it over her tongue. "This mouth, these sweet lips, are mine, baby. And when you're ready, I'm going to do everything to them that I've been imagining all day."

Moisture dampened her bikini bottoms, and she squirmed in her seat to relieve the pressure between her legs.

"So stop hiding, Charlie. You hide behind a curtain of respectability and decorum, denying the very thing you want to set you free," he continued, using his thumb to spread moisture from her mouth onto her lips. "The shield also dropped when you thought no one was looking and no one would notice. Your nipples peaked and your eyes grew so fucking dark as you watched that orgy unfold on the lido. I thought I would come in my jeans watching you get so turned on. It's not the ship or the theme of the cruise. You fucking do this to me. And because you do that to me, you don't get to hide behind a wall of propriety."

He groaned and his groin lifted against her hand. She gasped in surprise when her mind cleared and she realized what she was doing. Her fingers curved around his width and the heel of her palm stroked over his long outline. She was touching him in public.

"Don't think about stopping," he warned, his mouth replacing his thumb for a soft kiss. The ragged exhalation of his breath sent shivers down her spine.

"We're in public," she rasped. "The bartender is in here."

"Patrick," he called to the bartender, "we'll have two Cokes, please." Ford didn't move away. Didn't give her mouth reprieve from his lingering touch as the words vibrated against her lips. The steady pressure and burning desire fueled a want deep inside her. "I'm going to kiss you now. Let me in, Charlie."

Her lips obliged and her tongue instinctively relented to the demand of his mouth as she welcomed his exploration and arched her back to press her chest against his. His taste swept aside any inhibition she had and stoked her desire for more of the sexy man. She sucked his tongue and lost herself in the heady flavor of his kiss. She wanted his mouth on her, everywhere, and she wanted to feel more of the way he made her skin tingle and her core ache.

Her teeth skimmed his bottom lip as her tongue smoothed over the firm softness. "Lord, Ford. You can kiss."

"There's a lot more than that. Promise," he said, leaning back and motioning the server to approach and place their Cokes on the neighboring table. Once the bartender had done exactly that, Ford cleared his throat. "Patrick, check on the stock set to be delivered for the evening. I'll keep an eye on the bar for you."

"Yes, sir," Patrick stammered. He tipped an invisible hat and walked out of the lounge. Charlie and Ford were completely alone.

Chapter Nine

The sweet little thing at his side was an enigma. According to his findings, Miss Charlene Stanton was born and bred for the stuffy country-club life. She'd married a rising finance star. He'd screwed her and her family over. She'd gotten divorced and had disappeared from appropriate social events.

A humbled Charlie had surfaced in the workforce. She'd taken a job far below her qualifications and family's influence. Lived in a small apartment with a roommate. And was currently determined to make her own way as a journalist. Ford had no doubt she had her reasons.

"Since this is likely one of the only times we'll have real privacy, I'd like an honest face-to-face conversation. Sit up here," he said, taking the towel from her shoulders and spreading it on the table in front of him.

She hesitated, was about to object.

"Please," he added. "No one is here. It's just us. Plus, you'll have a killer view of the sunset while we chat." He needed to lead her slow and easy, offering her what she wanted with no conditions. Tapping into her basal needs for adventure, while she worked at securing career advancement, was key.

"Okay."

She shifted and he secured her hips, lifting and placing her before him, arranging her dress beneath her so she sat on it as well as the towel. Positioning her feet on either side of his hips, he tapped the outside of her left thigh and prevented her from scooting away.

"Don't argue," he warned. "Let me speak."

Twirling a long strand of hair, she nodded. "This is new to me.

I'm not used to discussing intimate details with men. Typically, I stick to work."

"I know how important your assignment is to you," he said. "It's obvious you want it bad, and it's obvious you're going to do anything to get that byline."

"How is it obvious?" Charlie asked, her sweet, pink tongue wetting her lips.

"*Chère*, you rode a bus from New York City to Miami to board a kink cruise."

"I told you," she interrupted. "I thought it was a singles cruise. I'm writing about the perfect place to find love."

"I heard you," he said, unable to keep from relieving the itch in his palm by stroking his hand over her thigh. "But you discovered it was a kink cruise, and you still boarded. It may not be what you originally thought, but kink intrigues you."

"There's a lot to see. It's interesting." Her chest and neck turned pink with her admission. The sexy way she blushed was so distracting. He'd need to keep her in dim lighting if he wanted any control over raging hard-ons.

He had to give her everything up front to keep her at his side. There was no way in hell he'd allow room for anyone else. With the Latin Lover and the All-American already chomping at the bit to get to her, he knew other men would queue for her attention at the first opportunity.

"Yes, it is. There's also a lot of material for your feature," he said. "Some of the research may be unconventional, but sprinkling that spice in your writing will only make for a better read."

The conversation shifting to work seemed to ease her stress. The anxious stance of her muscles had relaxed, and she grew receptive to their conversation.

"So, you're going to write a bang-up feature—no pun intended—and I'm going to share information from past observations on a cruise ship. We'll be together, sharing our time and collecting material, while we cover each other's job-related tasks. We need to work well together. Have understanding. Fair enough?"

"Yes," she replied in a soft voice. "Perfectly fair."

"But, Charlie, you can't deny what's here." He gestured one hand between their chests, while smoothing his other hand over the back of her knee. "We have strong chemistry. Heat."

Once again, her blue eyes turned as dark as the sea. She inhaled sharply, and the skin on her thigh prickled against his fingers. Her body's response urged him on. Charlie felt the heat. She wanted the connection. But she needed a push.

"You're going to drop those walls you've built around yourself, *chère*. You're going to let me see to your needs. All of them. And I will see to them." He leaned in between her thighs and fit them about his upper body. "You want to explore the kinky things on this ship. There's a little nymph inside you who likes things in an adventurous way that you've denied, but you need a safety net to set her free. I'm that safety net. You only need to trust me."

He could see the struggle in her mind. Charlie wanted to let go, but she wasn't sure how. It pained him that some fucker had stolen her carefree ability. "Let go, baby. It's just between us. You and me. You have my word that I'll catch you."

"What if you don't approve?" Charlie asked, scraping her teeth over her bottom lip. "What if it's not appropriate and you don't like it?"

There it was. There was the issue that plagued this gorgeous woman. It wasn't even about her trusting him. She hadn't raised any concern about him catching her. This was about Charlie and how the outside world perceived her. Damn. She didn't get it. She defined appropriate. She needed to like it. And absolutely no one else had a right to approve or disapprove.

"Who squashed your spirit, baby?" Ford smoothed his palms up the sides of her thighs. "I'd like to know and pound them to the ground."

"I don't think you could take on almost everyone involved in my entire upbringing." Charlie laughed softly and shook her head. "Besides, they meant well. They didn't know how to deal with my curiosity and opposition, so I was told exactly what they expected from me."

"And did you give them what they expected?" He traced a finger along the elastic of her pink bikini and let his other fingers enjoy the feel of her beautiful thighs. Smooth as silk and creamy soft.

"I tried." She shook her head again. "I couldn't do it."

"Good. You're pretty amazing the way you are, Charlie." He

curved his hands around her waist and pulled her closer to the edge of the table, closer to him. "There's only one thing I wouldn't like."

Disappointment filled her eyes and a line creased the center of her forehead. She looked down, pressing her lips together as she exhaled. "There always is."

"I wouldn't like it if you were committed to another man," he added quickly. "Anything else you want, I welcome."

"Anything?"

Fuck. What was he getting himself into? Why did he feel the need to agree and wipe the expectation of disappointment from her face at any cost? She could want the Latin Lover and the All-American.

Her eyes didn't say that, though. She wanted acceptance. She wanted freedom, much like the freedom she'd lusted after while watching the orgy.

"Anything," he breathed. "I'll be your net. You jump."

"And what do you get out of this arrangement?"

He got his time with her. Simple. She did something to him he couldn't explain, and he'd do whatever it took to make her smile. He didn't want her to smile like a senator's wife on the campaign trail, but in that free and heartfelt manner he'd glimpsed.

"Blue balls," he admitted. "Like the captain said, I can't join you in your cabin. Trust me, I can't lose this job. I tried to buy a ticket so that I could secure a passenger cabin and get around the rule of guests not being allowed in crew quarters and crew not being allowed in a passenger's cabin, but the sailing was full. Company policy is very strict. If we're found together outside of the public areas, or we engage in anything sexual outside Lovers Sail's activities, I'll be fired and put out at the next port. I don't want to be left behind and waiting, Charlie. I want to be with you."

He trailed his palms up the side of her body, tracing her curves, until his thumbs played at the full undersides of her breasts. Her nipples hardened. She didn't squirm or hide her approval.

"I know. The personal consequences for you are big," she said, nodding in agreement. "That's why I don't understand why you want to be my safety net."

"Because I get you. Any part of you that you want to give me."

She studied him for a long minute, then covered his left hand with her own and brought it to her breast. "I want to give to you. And I want to take."

"Yes," he groaned. "Thank you." His right hand curled around her nape, and he lowered his head and demanded her mouth in an immediate and hungry kiss.

He took what she gave. Claimed it as his, and knew that regardless of what he'd agreed to, he wouldn't share her sweetness with any other man. She was his and his alone. He would see to her every need and desire as long as she was willing to put up with a man who wasn't made for long-term relationships. He'd keep it all in the present.

Ford swept his tongue past her lips and lost himself in her heavenly taste, wishing he wasn't the kind of man he knew he was. Wishing he was capable of holding onto Charlie for a long, long time, but knowing he wasn't made that way.

When they came up for air, she tangled her fingers in his hair and angled her face to meet his gaze. She smiled and licked her swollen lips.

"Good thing for you and your balls this is a kink cruise," she whispered, glancing down at his fingers playing with her breast through the dress. "I'm guessing it's allowed for you to maul me in public?"

"You're guessing right." His thumb skimmed over a puckered nipple. She moaned, and he licked his lips at her response. "It may not be the most traditional way to get to know you, or the most suitable form of attention to give you, but it does allow us to be together. It isn't optimal, but I don't care. What may be inappropriate in other settings is encouraged here. I don't mind if you don't."

"I'm learning that I really like inappropriate attention."

"Then let's be inappropriate together," he said. Ford traced the blue elastic of her dress and slowly worked down the material until he'd exposed a full breast. "More beautiful than I'd imagined," he said, licking over the pale skin. "Delicious, too." She arched her back and offered him more, tangling her fingers in his hair. "You're so amazing." Groaning, he sealed his lips to the hard pink tip.

Charlie gasped as Ford suckled her deep into his mouth, and her body simmered with yearning. She dropped her head back and closed her eyes, feeling the tug of desire all the way to the moist heat between her thighs. The warmth of his mouth, coupled with the scrape of his teeth over the sensitive flesh, sent shivers dancing on her chest.

"Tell me what you want," he rasped, his lips still on her.

She moaned in protest, aching for his mouth to return. Her body ached for his attention. "Please."

"Please what, baby?"

She raised her head and met his gaze. With uncertain hands, she freed her other breast. "Please take me in your mouth. Let me feel the zing of excitement. The warmth. The heat."

He lowered his lips to her new offering, placed soft kisses on the sensitive skin and around the rosy tip, before he sucked it deep and nibbled on the hard peak. As his mouth worshipped her breast, he guided her hand beneath her skirt and settled it inside her bikini bottoms. His fingers skimmed over her hip, and the tie released. Cool air swept over her damp center.

"Charlie, show me what you like," he said, biting gently on her nipple, while joining her right hand with his and sliding their joined fingers between her wet excitement. "Show me, *chère*."

"Here?"

"Right here. Right now," he said. "Charlie, you want this. Take it. I want your taste on my fingers and the scent of your excitement in my mind when I leave you. Let me hear what you like. Show me what you do when you're alone. Let me see you lose control. Come for me."

Slipping her finger between his, she slid her thumb up to her clit and circled the pulsing nub. "I don't . . . I can't."

"Fingers, baby." Ford coaxed, moving his hand back to her breast and rolling her nipple between his thumb and index finger.

She slid two fingers into her heat and thrust, while her thumb stroked her clit.

"You look so hot getting yourself off, Charlie. If it wasn't for the damn surveillance camera, I'd be laying you out on the table and—"

"Camera?" Her hand stilled.

"Keep playing with yourself. Add a third finger," Ford demanded, pinching her nipple until it stung. "The camera is at your back. Only I can see you, so pink and shiny, so pretty and wet."

He leaned back against the cushion, nodding his approval when she slipped a third finger deep inside her and pumped her hand faster.

"You're so beautiful, baby. I can't wait to put my mouth on you and get you nice and ready for everything we'll be doing together." Sliding his thumb through her slick folds, he swept over her clit and sent sizzling electricity through her body. "That's it. Hurry. Get yourself off before Patrick returns and hears your hand slapping your gorgeous wetness and the throaty moans that are driving me insane."

Shit. The bartender could return. He would see what she was doing.

"That's right. Patrick will know how naughty you are if he catches you. He'll know you like the thrill of sex in public places. The thrill of getting caught." Ford brought his thumb to his mouth and spread her cream on his lips. "And you're not going to stop working yourself until you come for me."

Excitement mixed with trepidation, and Charlie's heart raced. She brought her left hand to her mouth and licked up and down two fingers, coating them with her saliva before she lowered her hand and fit them on either side of her sweet spot. Determined to come quicker, she squeezed, rubbed, and pumped until it was difficult to breathe.

Keeping her gaze locked with his, she felt her legs tremble as he rolled a nipple between his fingers, and her orgasm made its appearance, building quickly and simmering through her body. She bit her lower lip and moaned real loud.

"So fucking hot," Ford said, sweeping his thumb over the sensitive bundle of nerves. "Now, baby, now. I've got you."

She shattered into the marvelous prism of release and collapsed into the strong embrace of the man who truly had her. No judgment. No expectations. She could just feel. Strong hands smoothed down her back as he held her hips and pulled her onto his lap. She dropped her head onto his shoulder and buried her face into his neck, breathing hard to resurface, as she straddled his lap.

"That was the sexiest thing I've ever seen," Ford said against her hair, dropping a kiss on the top of her head and adjusting her dress to cover her breasts. "I can't wait until we disembark in Mexico. I'm going to take you so hard you won't be able to walk straight for hours."

She couldn't speak, but she sighed her agreement. No one had ever looked at her with such longing, spoken to her with heated desire, or made her feel so wanted. Even the use of his very, very descriptive words made her feel excited . . . more like wonderful.

"Hey, boss. Need a refill?"

"Not yet, Patrick," Ford replied, still holding her, still caressing her back. "Thank you."

If she could have, she would have moved. Instead she giggled against his neck and remained cradled against him. "Good thing he didn't catch an earlier elevator."

"Hm. Good thing," Ford repeated, sliding his fingers through her hair. "It was very close, though. We'll need to work on improving your time."

She laughed and finally managed to push up and look at him. "You're something else, Ford. Are you expecting me to be the Energizer Bunny or something?"

"Or something," he said, earning a playful punch on his shoulder.

"How about you discreetly tie my bikini bottoms in place?" Charlie asked, adding a sweet smile when he didn't display any intention of doing so. "Pretty please."

"I don't think so." He tugged on the side that was still tied and released it. "How about we agree that you wear dresses, and only dresses, for stolen moments on the ship?"

"Unless you're going to be stingy with those stolen moments, I don't have enough dresses," she countered. "Not possible."

"Do you have a dress that you could wear to dinner?" Ford asked, his dark eyes sparkling with mischief as his palm caressed her naked ass.

"Yes, but it's short. Real short. My big butt will be—"

"Nothing is too short for this cruise. We'll get more dresses for later. And I love your just-right butt. It's lush and curvy and fits perfectly in my hands." He pulled the bikini bottom from between their bodies and tucked it in his pocket. "Skirts will do as well. Did you pack any skirts?"

She nodded.

"No panties tonight. Wear the short dress and leave this one on the bed."

"Ford, that's irrational. I'm soaked. I smell like sex. Everyone will know."

"Not that I mind, but do you really think anyone on this ship will notice? What's more important is that I'll know and you'll know." He brushed his lips over hers. "I don't care what anyone else thinks, and neither should you. I'm going to make sure you get what you want, over and over, all day long. It's bad enough I can't take you to bed, but I'll be dammed if I can't have easy access to that beautiful sweetness."

Her body heated and tingles danced on her skin. "You're serious, aren't you?"

"Very," he replied. Lowering his hand between their bodies and beneath the skirt of her dress, he slid a finger through her swollen folds and turned his wrist to rub her clit with the heel of his hand. "I love how wet you are."

"Boss?" Patrick called from across the lounge. Ford held still and looked at him. "There are a lot of passengers milling around, and I think we're going to be busy earlier than usual. I tried to reach Juan to come in early, but there's no answer. Christina said something about catching a nap, so her phone is off the hook. Would you stick around so I could run down to her cabin and let her know? I'll be back in ten minutes."

"Of course," Ford replied, pushing two fingers inside Charlie's tight heat. "Can you improve your time and come for me before he returns?"

She nodded and dropped her face to his neck, aching to feel her body soar again, and believing he was her safety net to jump.

"Good answer," he said, placing a kiss at her temple. "I want you all over the hand I'm going to use to take care of my personal problem once I'm in my cabin."

A fling with Ford promised more ecstasy than she ever thought existed. She'd take it. She'd take him. Even if it was temporary.

Chapter Ten

Charlie snuggled against his neck and inhaled his masculine scent as she tried to regain control. She drew deep breaths, her chest heaved, and her heart pounded against his. Her pleased body writhed as he stroked the lingering euphoria of her orgasm and soothed her moans with a kiss.

"That was very, very beautiful, Charlie," he whispered against her ear, encouraging her with kisses. "You did so good. You have no idea how you make me feel. How hard I am because you're in my arms, available to me. Can you imagine how much I want to bury myself inside you and lose myself in your snug little body?"

Damn! She tightened around his fingers and the urge to move against his hand overwhelmed her. She'd completely lost it. With all decorum tossed aside, she remained in a state of physical ecstasy, exposed and vulnerable in a public space, feeling no regret for her blatantly wanton behavior.

"I can," she said. She couldn't compose full sentences and she didn't care. She licked a path up his neck and gently sucked his earlobe into her mouth. "I want. Can't move."

The vibrations of his chuckle passed through her chest and traveled to her pulsing clit. She closed her eyes and simply felt. She couldn't think. It was crazy. She was crazy. How could she let her body take control of her sensibility?

She didn't know how much time had passed, but eventually she came down, her breathing settled, and the spasms receded. Charlie lifted her head and glanced between her legs. The blue material of the dress rested on his tanned hand, which disappeared beneath it. His thumb circled her nub, in slow and soothing caresses.

"Look at how pretty your cream shines on my hand. You're so

wonderfully responsive and give so well. It's taking all my control not to bury my face against you and lick every drop of your sweetness." Groaning, he removed his hand and adjusted the skirt of her dress. He then brought a finger to his lips and sucked it into his mouth.

Her breath caught and her stomach did a somersault.

"Do you realize how utterly delicious it will be when I taste this directly from the source?" He continued the verbal and manual assault, not giving her a chance to process it all in her mind. Her body simply reacted.

"I can't believe we're talking like this. Actually, I can't believe I'm doing this," she whispered.

"We are. You are. You did. Twice. And I'm so grateful you did. What a treat," he said, stoking her desire and eliciting a heated response. "I'm looking forward to more. So much more."

The idea of more made her dizzy. Yet she wanted more. So much more.

"What about you?" She lifted her head, the inequality of their situation suddenly dawning on her. The sexual gratification had been one-sided. "I came twice. You didn't."

"I'm not keeping count, sugar. I wasn't exaggerating when I said that watching was the hottest thing ever. Those little hands moving inside that pretty treasure is so sexy. Your gorgeous breasts bouncing free and teasing me like cherry-covered desserts are so sexy. Everything about you is sexy."

"But you?"

He shook his head. "The camera was pointed at your back, which means it was pointing to my front." He tucked her hair behind her ear, tracing the curve with his fingertip. "Plus, you're covered by the skirt of your dress. They can't see a thing—other than the bulge in my pants when I stand up."

"Think about math problems," she suggested, remembering their conversation in the taxi and giving him sass. "That should offer some relief."

"Nothing but you will give me relief, *chère*. I'm too far gone." Ford cupped her face and caressed her jaw with his thumb. "I can't stop touching you. You better write that article fast, because when this cruise is done, you won't have any time to use the laptop. The only kind of lap you'll be seeing is my lap."

"Rather cocky, Mr. Ford." The sharp inhale of air and the color punctuating her cheeks proclaimed her willingness, still she didn't hide her smile. Even after two climaxes, his words made her clench in anticipation. "This is crazy, but I like it. I've never been so focused on pleasure and so on edge in my whole life."

"Glad to hear," he said. "Know, and have no doubt, that I want your beautiful body draped over mine, your lips on every inch of me, but Patrick will be returning at any moment. Two orgasms will have to hold you for now."

I've never had two orgasms in a day, let alone back to back, but this can't go on. We won't be able to work together. We can't, she thought, slanting her burning lips over his mouth in direct opposition to her words. "One last kiss."

It was a quick kiss, because Patrick returned the moment their lips met.

"I'm keeping you pasted to my side for the next four days. If for no other reason than your body responds to my touch and your mind wants what I know about *cruise romances*, you can let loose. Enjoy. Stay in the moment."

"You can't keep touching me. I lose focus, Ford. I need to focus."

"Come on, *chère*. Let me walk you to your cabin, the one that's off limits to me, so you can get ready for the Erogenous Zone event. You'll enjoy tonight's activities. After happy hour, there's dinner, and then the 'Always Kiss Me Good-Night' workshop." He turned his body and helped her to her feet, adjusting her dress once she stood. Then he took her hand in his and intertwined their fingers, bidding the bartender farewell as he led her to the door.

Walking to the staircase, she squeezed his hand, signaling the craving for a puff. He stopped on the first step and turned to face her on the landing. He grasped her hips and pulled her body against his hardness, claiming her mouth in a rewarding kiss.

"I want your taste on my tongue as much as you need the distraction." Seemingly willing to give her what she wanted, he feasted on her mouth and nibbled on her lips until a tiny moan escaped her. "But I can't say I blame you this time, sugar. We'll find some other way to satisfy that oral fixation." Ford trailed a finger over her swollen lips in a more than suggestive manner, and her tongue darted out to taste it. "For now, I think I'll kiss you again."

Charlie's mind filled with erotic images as she melted into Ford. Thoughts she knew she should push out of her brain. The man was surreal. Knowing her secret desires and giving without strings—literally no strings, when it came to her string bikini—he fueled her fantasies and answered them with ease.

She could do this. She could enjoy sex and not put her heart on the line. After all, a fling plus Ford equaled perfection. He didn't ask her to give up anything. He actually offered support in reference to her writing. It could work. No expectations. Just the here and now.

"Fine. But you're getting the short end of the stick," she said, looking into his dark eyes and hoping he wouldn't tire of her too quickly. He was clearly far more experienced than her and much more adventurous than she'd ever believed she could be. Ford had already proved those points.

"No, sweetheart. It's you that will be getting the stick; the whole, thick, long, and stiff stick. It's me who will be delivering the pleasure," he said, smacking the underside of her bare ass and laughing at his own corny joke.

She squeezed his hand again, angling her face up for another kiss.

"Baby?" He brushed his mouth over hers and licked along her lips. "Why are you suddenly wavering?"

She let out a long breath. "I was weighing it all out. Don't misunderstand, but I have research to do. An article to write. And instead of methodically interviewing guests and drawing conclusion, all I can think about is . . ." She let her thoughts trail off. All she could think of was how badly she ached for more of his touch. She wanted *his* hands on every inch of *her*. His mouth following. She wanted to drop to her knees, discover what made his knees weak, and explore his body with her mouth.

"You need to stop, Charlie. You can't look at me like that on the stairwell and expect me to stay under control."

"Sorry," she whispered. "I think I'm turning into a nympho or something."

"Or something." He chuckled and traced his finger down her nose. "But don't stop. Embrace it, baby. I'll take care of the ache. You write the article, trust me, and this will be an unforgettable weekend." He twirled a strand of her hair as he curled strong fingers around her nape. "It already is for me."

"Me, too," she admitted.

"Let me get you safely inside that damn off-limits cabin before I get thrown off the ship." The too-good-to-be-true dreamboat dropped a kiss to her forehead, and then swatted her backside. "Let's go. I won't let you lose focus."

She managed a smile and placed her hands on his shoulders as they descended the two flights of stairs. He walked her to the door, kissed her to within an inch of her passing out at the threshold, then swiped her keycard in the lock.

"Give me ten minutes, and connect your cell to the ship's Wi-Fi. I'll activate the account. We can iMessage if needed." He gently tucked a strand of hair behind her ear and trailed a finger down her cheek. "I'll be by the elevator at six o'clock. Then we're off to the Erogenous Zone."

Charlie nodded and stepped into the cabin. She watched him pull the door closed. Letting out a long breath, she pressed her back to the cool surface and slid to the floor, holding her skirt tight against her naked thighs for cover. Shit. He set her body on fire. As far as she was concerned, *he* was the Erogenous Zone. She was totally screwed— while not getting literally fucked. He offered a chance to experience the sex of her lifetime, but they had to remain in public areas.

Her sex pulsed with the mere idea that she could have been caught and seen as she was getting off. It had been a real turn-on knowing that the bartender could have strolled back into the room. A turn-on knowing that the camera was catching her back arch and tense as his magical fingers filled her and brought her exquisite pleasure.

What the heck was she supposed to do about the need to have him inside her? She wanted him like she'd never wanted anyone. And if she was honest, it had absolutely nothing to do with the theme of the cruise. It was him. Not just the physical allure of a good-looking man, but the way he got her.

In spite of not knowing her before the morning, Ford understood her determination and supported it. Identified with it. On that basis alone, she'd be drawn to him, even if she knew she shouldn't be. Confusion and frustration mixed with a peculiar sense of hopefulness.

What the hell had she gotten herself into? Why didn't she have the spine to rule out interaction with a man who meant sure heartbreak?

She rose to her feet and pushed the suddenly restrictive sundress down her body. Stepping out of the pooled material on the floor, she walked to the center of the room and stood before the mirror. Heat stained her skin and a dark love bite branded the pale flesh on her left breast.

Tracing her fingers over his mark, she felt her breasts grow heavy. The ache returned between her legs and warm moisture gathered at her center.

She needed a cold shower.

Ford tucked his hands in his pockets, and his fingers found the damp material he'd confiscated from Charlie's wonderful hips. Once she leaned over that railing to observe the activities on deck, the emotion displayed on her face had all but handed him a map to the treasures she'd kept hidden away. No amount of Internet searches would have revealed so much. She'd unknowingly dropped her shield and charted his way.

He stepped into his cabin and immediately shrugged off his shirt. Unbuttoning his jeans, he pulled her pink bottoms from his pocket and curled his fingers over the tiny bikini.

"Oh, baby. Did you really think I'd let you go nude just because we met on the starboard side of the pool?" He shook his head, thinking of her peeling off her dress and jumping into the hot tub . . . not if there were other eyes present.

He couldn't imagine the competent-yet-shy professional flaunting that perfect body for all to enjoy. But then again, he'd never imagined sex would be the way to break past the barriers Charlie had erected to keep herself safe.

The reserved woman was curious. She wanted adventure. And he was more than willing to oblige her if it meant she'd let him in.

"What is it about her?" Ford asked aloud.

It wasn't his style to act impulsively. But when it came to Charlie, he had. He'd invaded her privacy. Rejoiced in her sexual curiosity. And grabbed at the first straw she'd offered him. He wanted her. He was going to have her. All that remained was to figure out the terms.

By releasing her inhibitions and making her embrace her desires, he'd managed to chip a bit of that protective wall with each orgasm. Fuck, he'd keep her in a continuous state of arousal, making her come nonstop, if it meant she'd open up and be with him for the next few days. He needed time to sate his own desire for the woman and work her out of his system if he was going to get his mind straight and succeed in his own endeavors.

From the first moment he'd looked into the deep blue of her eyes, and heard her sweet voice, he'd wanted her. No logic. No reason. He just did.

The one thing he'd learned after the fiasco with his father was that he not only had the desire to go after what he wanted, but he had the determination and ability to achieve what made him honestly happy.

As for Charlene Stanton, she too had a specific plan to get what she wanted. The reasons evaded him, but he guessed she'd repressed her needs for so long that she had focused intently on one thing—her career—to make it through. She'd denied her sensuality and hidden behind golf skorts and a laptop to assure her professional success.

Well, he wasn't about to let her retreat inside her shell. Not when she had him beside her. Not when her body reacted the way it had.

Knowing the time in the wine lounge would likely be the only time he'd touch her properly all day, frustration was just something he'd deal with. "If it were up to you, you'd drag her off the ship and keep her to yourself," he muttered, placing the pink bikini in his bedside drawer. But she wanted to stay on the boat and write her feature, which meant he had an added reason to keep his job and remain on the ship.

No mistakes. He stood and shucked his pants. No minimizing her goals. He took off his boxers and his cock saluted at attention. "You're going to do everything in your power to help her."

He walked into the bathroom, turned on the water, and stepped into the shower.

"You're going to give to and get from that beautiful woman until you're both satisfied and ready to move on."

Ford squeezed liquid soap into his hand, leaned his forehead on the shower wall, and fisted his erection.

Chapter Eleven

Tugging on the hem of her dress, Charlie held Ford's hand as they entered the grand lounge. Quinn waved to them from a high bar table in the corner, and she whispered for Ford to lead them over to her new friends.

"Hello," Luis said, offering his hand to Ford for a quick shake before turning his attention to Charlie and placing a not-so-chaste kiss on each of her cheeks. "*Querida*."

Releasing Ford's hand, she gave Luis a tight squeeze and a quick kiss on his jaw. "Hello, sir," she said in a low voice. "Am I embracing my honest self enough?"

"Making a good start," Luis replied, sliding his index finger down the curve of her nose. "Keep it up."

"*Gracias*." She turned to Quinn and stepped into his outstretched arms. "Hello, my friend."

"My pretty baby doll." He groaned and wrapped her in a big bear hug. "Do you need to keep reminding me about the friend status?"

She laughed and managed to reach far enough to place a kiss on the side of his neck. He groaned again, earning him a quick slap on his chest. "Cut it out, Quinn. Friends don't groan."

"Some do," Quinn said with a grin, and leaned close to her ear. "Others growl."

Ford wasn't exactly growling, but she could feel his stare burning into her back. She stepped out of Quinn's embrace and reached for Ford's hand. "So how is this happy hour going?"

"Good. Seems like it's a nice crowd to party with. Lots of beautiful people," Quinn said. "The mistress of ceremonies was announced right before you arrived." He pointed to a tall woman with a perfectly smooth caramel-colored complexion and straight black hair hanging down to her ass, who was wearing a leather dress that fit her body like a glove. "Mistress Gwyn will review the cruise guidelines in a few minutes. In the meantime, what can I get you guys to drink?"

"What are you drinking?" Charlie asked Luis, glancing at the tall glass with the refreshing-looking orange concoction.

"This?" Luis swirled the stirrer. "Not mine. It's Quinn's Sloe Comfortable Screw," he continued, holding up the glass in a toast and meeting Quinn's gaze. "His second of the afternoon."

"What can I say?" Quinn shrugged and leaned his head toward Luis. "This man's turned me into a slut for his slow and comfortable—"

"Enough." Charlie held up her hand, palm out. "I don't want to know details about your sluttiness, Quinn."

"Too much about this sexiness to cover in a simple conversation," Quinn said in a comical tone, moving his palms down his chest and showcasing his muscled body. The other men laughed. "I was just going to order Luis an All Night Long. He likes sweet things in his mouth."

"Since we're keeping with personal identifiers, I think the lady would enjoy a Grey Goose Screaming Orgasm," Ford added.

"And for you, my friend?" Quinn asked. "A hair-raising Leg Spreader perhaps?"

"Would love that, but once again, in keeping with the truthfulness of our situation, I'll stick with the Jack and Coke," Ford replied.

More laughter erupted as Quinn signaled for the server. He added a round of Blow Jobs. "For good measure."

Charlie relaxed as they all chatted and got to know each other. There was easy banter among the men, Ford and Luis finding common ground on the café front, and there was no tension to be felt. The butterflies in her stomach relaxed and gentle warmth filled her chest. Things were good in Charlie's world. Good indeed.

When the server returned with their drinks, he placed whipped cream–topped shots in the center of the table and reminded them of the proper way to drink them. *No hands.*

"I'm always up for a good Blow Job," Luis said, sliding a shot glass before Quinn. "Come on, *tipo guapo*. Show me what you do so well."

"I love it when he calls me handsome." Licking his lips, Quinn smiled a private message to Luis, then linked his hands behind his back.

He bent his tall frame over the table and closed his lips over the rim of the glass. Swallowing as he straightened, he kept his gaze pinned on Luis as he downed the creamy concoction and returned the empty glass to the table. "Want a taste?"

Luis nodded and kissed his partner, tapping his joined hands and releasing them. "Perfect, love. Just perfect."

"My turn," Quinn said, offering Luis a shot. "Take it deep. Don't let a drop slip."

Placing his hands flat on the table on either side of the glass, Luis opened his mouth wide and closed his lips around the glass. He tossed his head back, and Charlie watched his throat work as he swallowed the drink. A clearly mesmerized Quinn watched, too. The handsome athlete actually groaned his approval.

"Not fucking fair," Ford interjected. "I'm stuck with Jack over here."

Luis lowered the empty glass to the table and released it. "That's too sad, my friend. You have the prettiest woman at your side and you're choosing Jack."

"Not choosing," Ford said, trailing his fingers up Charlie's side and heating the bare skin just beneath the halter of her dress. "I choose Charlie any day."

Quinn handed Ford a Blow Job in approval. *"Salut!"*

"Cheers," Ford replied, making a show of sucking the whipped cream into his mouth and then turning up the glass.

"You used your hands," Charlie pointed out. "I thought we said no hands."

"I thought you like my hands?" Ford asked, touching the tip of his nose to hers.

Heat filled her cheeks and she looked away. She did like his hands. Liked them very much.

"It's your turn, baby doll." Quinn placed the shot before her and offered to lift her up so she could reach, but she shook her head and stretched her arms out.

"I've got this. Doesn't have anything to do with height," she said, licking her lips. "It's all about the technique." She sidled up as close to the table as she could and slowly licked at the sweet cream until it was gone. Then she opened her mouth and caught the glass with her teeth, inching closer to the edge.

"You're killing us," Quinn said.

"Agreed," Luis said. "Not very *querida*-like now."

"Shhh . . ." Ford interrupted, holding her hair back from her face. "I'd like to see her finish."

And she did. She lifted the drink and slowly tipped it back, noisily sucking the sweet cream between her lips. Once she'd lowered the empty glass on the table, she used her finger and wiped at the sticky goodness clinging to the corner of her lips and offered it to Ford.

"Well done," he said, closing his lips around her finger.

The gentle caress of his tongue around the tip tickled her deep inside the center of her being. A sense of accomplishment bloomed within her chest, and she released a breath of contentment. Peculiar how his approval made her want him more. Made her want to please him more.

"Welcome to the Tenth Annual Lovers Sail Singles and Kink Cruise," a very attractive man announced. Dressed in a white button-down shirt and a casual pair of khaki pants, he didn't broadcast kink. Rather, his tousled blond hair and deep tan suggested he was a fun, beach-bum kind of man who had cleaned up for the event.

"I'm Bodhi." Yup. Definite surfer dude. "Second in command to Mistress Gwyn. We are pleased to announce that our Lovers Sail event is completely sold out."

Applause and cheers filled the lounge as participants linked arms, exchanged kisses, and some even looked shyly around the room.

"We have a record number of event virgins joining us this year, so we strongly encourage you to keep appropriate play in the appropriate places. While many of us have embarked on this voyage with the intention of living our carnal pleasures, some have joined us because they'd like to simply explore and learn, while even more desire to find their soul mates and true loves. We also have many guests that have boarded as couples or groups. Nice mix. Everyone is welcome. With mutual respect and consideration, we'll all get what we want and need. This trip will rock!"

Bodhi's easy manner and words of encouragement made Charlie smile. For once, she'd have all she wanted and needed. Writing material on finding love. Carnal pleasures she'd only dreamed of. Four days of everything.

"I'm available to *all* of our guests," Bodhi continued. "Virgins, curious, dabblers, and masters, don't hesitate to reach out throughout the entire cruise if I could help make your experiences more pleasurable. Just pick up any of the ship's courtesy phones and Guest Services will contact me. Trust me, my sexies, I'll find you."

"I've met him," Ford whispered against her ear. "Bodhi is a real stand-up guy. Much more intense than he appears, and certainly worthy of the trust people place in him. He'd be a good person to interview—informally and with consideration for his anonymity, of course. I believe he works in the broadcasting industry."

It wouldn't have mattered if Ford had been reciting the Declaration of Independence, she just liked the manner in which he leaned into her and shared. He worked on keeping her focused. Every nerve ending in her body rejoiced when his breath swept across her ear. "Thanks."

"It is with great honor that I present to this most gorgeous group Mistress Gwyn," Bodhi said, strolling to the edge of the stage to offer his hand to the mistress of ceremonies. He escorted her to the microphone, and once he'd adjusted the stand to the proper height, he bowed and backed away.

"Thank you, Bodhi. As always, it's a pleasure to have you at my side." The woman turned and indicated her assistant, waiting for the group to quiet before positioning her ruby-red lips near the microphone again. "Welcome, my friends." More applause. "We *will* make this event the most pleasurable one yet. That is a promise, and I always keep my promises." Whistles joined the exuberant cheering. "However, before we officially embark on our adventures, I must insist on reviewing a few housekeeping rules and guidelines to make this good for everyone." Mistress Gwyn's tone changed from welcoming cheerleader to strict disciplinarian.

"On that note, thank you. You please me very much," Ford whispered.

Puzzled, Charlie glanced at him. "What are you talking about?"

"You follow directions well." He cupped her bottom and smoothed his thumb over the place where her panty line would have been below her waist. "Not only are you beautiful, smart, and talented, you're wonderfully obedient and willing."

Obedient? No one had ever called her obedient. She was the notorious black sheep of the family. Always bucking convention. She'd been branded as stubborn and headstrong. Never obedient.

"Soon enough, you'll discover how pleasing others gives you

more control than any strong-armed insistence does." His lips brushed over the sensitive skin behind her ear, sending shivers through her body. "You have my undivided attention, *chère*."

As Charlie tried to process his words, the servers handed out postcards. They had small print on both sides: one with rules, the other with abbreviations.

"Let's start with a review of guidelines," Gwyn said. "Please flip the cards to the white side with blue lettering. We have very few rules, but they are for your protection. There is zero tolerance for anyone who refuses to abide by them, so let's educate everyone on these policies. Feel free to pick up extra postcards and share with anyone who is not here. They are also listed in the daily bulletin the cruise company provided in your cabin."

The crowd stilled and the noise level dropped to silent.

"First, we only address each other with first names while on board. If you wish, you may choose to exchange personal details once the cruise is over. However, you may *not* ask someone to share his or her details if they are not offered."

Charlie felt like Gwyn was speaking directly to her. She glanced at her friends and shrugged. She'd broken that rule before she'd even been aware of it. The captain had been correct when he suggested she work under cover.

"No worries," Quinn said, leaning down in discretion. "We want to exchange information and keep in touch after this is over. We're good."

Even without hearing what Quinn had said, Luis nodded stoically. Ford simply caressed one hip and bumped the other gently. "All good," he said. "We boarded knowing each other. Just like an established couple. We get to explore more now."

"Consent is first and foremost the greatest necessity in all of our activities," Gwyn continued, holding two long fingers in the air. "If anyone is found insisting on non-consensual acts, that person will be placed in isolation and removed from the general population. Once we make port, he or she will be escorted off the ship, and depending on the situation will either be handed to the police or will need to make arrangements to return to Miami on his or her own. Consensual play only, folks!"

"Though consent may include rough, sometimes painful, play," Luis warned. "Be careful where you wander, *niña*."

"That's my concern," Ford quickly announced. "She'll be with me in every public area. I've got her."

"I'm sure you do. It's good to know," Luis countered. "Just don't be mulish, Charlie. Heed Ford's directives."

Did they think she couldn't handle herself? That she needed a big, bad man to make it through the events?

"Rule number three," Gwyn announced. "No blood play or acts that may require medical attention, consensual or not."

Aw, shit. Shit. Triple shit. Fear—actually dread—crept up her spine. Charlie inched closer to Ford. He wrapped a protective arm around her body and brought her against his tall frame.

"Due to our location and the limitations of onboard medical facilities, we cannot condone participants enjoying such play. It is too risky and your safety is too important." Gwyn held up four fingers.

"Rule four is common sense: condoms." She paused and looked around the room. "Condoms must be used for every act in public places. Staff is continuously on hand all over the ship. All you need to do is indicate the need for a prophylactic and protection will be instantly furnished."

"Any act?" a man called from the floor.

"Anal or vaginal," Gwyn explained. "Ladies, we also offer female condoms, however they are a bit trickier when you're in a passionate hurry to fuck. Familiarize yourself with the forms of protection before you need them."

Hurry to fuck? The elegant woman had said fuck. She'd clearly validated the appropriateness of fucking, and no one seemed appalled by the terminology. Rather, more couples had come together and were exchanging sensual caresses and loving looks.

"And while public displays of affection are always allowed," Gwyn said, extending a graceful arm toward the couples, "we do ask that you respect personal preferences of the participants in events intended for beginners. Our events are a success because of the courtesy and respect you all extend to each other. Respect is to be given and expected. At all times."

A man standing approximately ten feet to Charlie's right, dropped to his knees and raised his hand for Gwyn's attention. When she acknowledged him, he hooked his fingers into a second man's waistband, making it obvious that he wished to expose his partner to everyone's view. "May I show my desire for my man, Mistress?"

Mistress Gwyn looked around the room. "This is a B, beginner's, event. All must be comfortable. Are there any objections from our guests for a physical display?"

"No."

"Go for it."

"Show us what you got, dude."

"You may proceed," Mistress Gwyn said with a smile.

The man lowered his partner's shorts. He lovingly stroked his hand over a long and thin erection, then asked, rather loudly, for the other man to fuck his mouth.

Groaning in appreciation, the man receiving the blow job opened his eyes and met the mistress's gaze. "I was planning to propose this weekend," he said, holding the other man's head steady and pumping into his mouth. "Andrew beat me to it."

Andrew released the other man's thigh and flashed a gold wedding band, receiving a loud round of applause from the onlookers. He continued to suck, rolling his husband's balls in his hand like a set of dice.

"We were married on Fort Lauderdale Beach this morning," the receiving newlywed continued, closing his eyes and sinking deeper into Andrew's mouth. "Sharing the good news with all our new friends," he said, grunting the last two words and impaling Andrew's mouth as he buried himself deep and stilled his thrusts.

Andrew moaned in pleasure and slowly released his husband. Acknowledging the group's congratulations, he beamed with happiness and smiled. "Thank you, everyone. We'll be consummating this marriage all weekend long. Mostly in private."

Andrew's husband helped him up from his knees and claimed his mouth in a passionate kiss.

"Congratulations to our honeymooners. Many years of love, happiness, and passion," Gwyn said, allowing time for the newlyweds to enjoy their spotlight.

When the crowd had settled and Andrew was wrapped in his husband's embrace, Mistress Gwyn tapped the microphone. "That is how it's done, my friends. We share our joys, encourage our sexual needs, and always with the utmost respect to each other. Please remember that there is no video or photography allowed. We only share with each other. Thank you for requesting permission, Andrew." He nodded. "And thank you everyone for celebrating our newlyweds."

"Trumpets" played and the lounge filled with Jason Derulo's proclamation. Charlie felt the rhythm deep inside her as the song suggested, and her body hummed. Some sang along, while others raised their glasses in a toast.

"That's number nineteen," Charlie whispered to Ford. "So far, I have answers to seven of my twenty-six questions."

"I don't get it." Two lines marked the center of his brow.

"I'll explain later. When we're alone," Charlie said, slipping out of his embrace. "I'm going to congratulate them personally. Be right back."

Chapter Twelve

Ford watched as Charlie offered her hand to the couple, but instead was pulled into a group hug. He smiled to himself like a crazy man, shaking his head at the fog of oblivion that hovered around her awareness. She had no idea of her effect on others.

Comfortable, sweet, and open with strangers, yet a bit mysterious and protective of something he hadn't managed to figure out, Charlie attracted people into her sphere. He couldn't imagine anyone not wanting to hold her close. He knew he did. Something about the woman warmed his chest in an unfamiliar sensation, and he couldn't stop wanting more of what she made him feel.

Concentrating to block out the background noise, he could faintly hear their conversation. He smiled at her heartfelt congratulations. Wasn't surprised with their jubilant responses. And then she was making arrangements to meet with them and discuss their beach wedding. Perhaps in the late morning on Friday, after they'd had some time to celebrate privately. *There's the competent reporter*, he thought, an inexplicable sense of pride filling him. As if he had anything to do with her professional success. He shook his head and watched her make her way between the group and back to his side.

Extending his arm, he welcomed her. "Seems like you make a nice impression on everyone you meet, *chère*. They don't mind the interview?"

"I'm undercover," she reminded, lifting a pretty brow in emphasis. "It's not an interview. I'm just curious. We're going to chat about the romance of beach weddings."

He nodded and fit her against his chest, resting his chin atop her head. "Of course you are. It's all about the romance."

"The most romantic place to find love," Charlie elaborated. "Looks like Andrew and John have done just that."

The music faded and the mistress stepped up to the microphone.

"Let's take care of the remainder of our housekeeping items so we can get on with the main events," Mistress Gwyn announced. "Please flip your cards over to the blue side with the white lettering. Here you will find a quick reference guide to the level of explicit sexual content intended for each event. There are six categories."

Ford looked down at the card Charlie studied. Her dainty finger skimmed over the categories, not hesitating on any of them.

"B is for *beginners*," Gwyn announced. "We have a large number of virgins—and no, my dears, I'm not speaking about people who have never had sex. Perhaps taking your time at one of the B events would be a nice introduction to our special itinerary. As you saw earlier, even if various displays are not planned, with consent things may develop and evolve above the intended levels of sexual intensity. Please communicate your preferences or limits to the group leaders should you feel uncomfortable. We promise to honor and respect your wishes."

More than a few breathed in relief.

"V is for *vanilla*. In V activities there will be no escalation of the preset expectations. These workshops and activities will help enhance a monogamous couple's private bedroom activities with instruction and discussions, rather than demonstrations."

Yet another round of relief sounded from the group. Ford was surprised at the number of first timers. In past years, kink ruled the decks and it was difficult to navigate through the sexual activities without being swayed to join in and participate. Maybe his staff, especially the ones assigned to the chaste and fun discussions, had a chance of making it through the sailing intact. He'd speak with Ramos about varying their assignments to assure they all had a break from the in-your-face sexual stimulation and constant state of arousal most events guaranteed.

An oldie but goodie sounded on the speakers and Usher's voice floated through the air. The mistress moved away from the microphone as couples filled the dance floor, following the song's advice of "Nice and Slow."

Charlie's hips rolled and his groin rejoiced in the luxury of each brush. He curled his fingers around those wonderful curves, careful to keep her skirt smoothed and her upper thighs covered. She dropped her head back on his shoulder. Ford inhaled the coconut scent, curved his body over her petite frame, and rested his cheek against her hair. "I can get used to this, *chère.*"

She didn't say anything, but her hand moved under his sleeve, and her fingers closed around his bicep in acceptance. He would have hooted in victory if it wouldn't make him look like a fool, so instead he brushed his lips over her hair and watched as Quinn urged Luis onto the floor. Ford held her in his arms and watched the others dance, enjoying the sense of togetherness with a peculiar sense of calm.

The volume was lowered and Gwyn spoke above the soft music.

"VbC stands for *vanilla but curious*," Gwyn said, glancing at the dancers and nodding at a few in particular. "These events are structured to expose you to possibilities, while keeping you well within established parameters for your comfort. I encourage newcomers to venture into at least one of these programs. You never know what you may learn about unexplored desires."

At the rhythmic intrusion of three staff entertainers strutting onto the dance floor, a new song mixed through the audio system, bodies parted then joined in the finger snapping. Two women in black lace lingerie and one man in black leather pants took center stage, dancing suggestively to the sultry jazz of Peggy Lee's "Fever." Their lithe bodies gyrated with sexual invitation until the men in the audience tugged on their collars and the women fanned themselves.

The man collapsed over both women, cocooning them in an embrace, and the music ended.

"Ménage?" Charlie asked.

"Perhaps," Ford answered. "Or maybe just plain physical indulgence."

"MC stands for *more than curious*," Mistress Gwyn said. "At this level of participation there will not be any preset boundaries. You will need to establish your own. Expect much more physical interaction and participation."

Catcalls and whistling from the audience encouraged their leader to continue.

"K is for *kink*. Complete exploration and exhibition. You need to be committed to these activities before entering the venues. If you lack experience, familiarize yourself with the terminology and guidelines in one of the MC sessions first. Just as we pride ourselves on offering virgins and newbies a safe space to learn, we also pride ourselves on offering a space for our kinksters to gain the utmost satisfaction."

Charlie squeezed his hand and turned. Her blue eyes had gone as dark as the deep waters of the sea beneath a full moon, but no worry marked her pretty face. "That makes sense. After all, it is a kink cruise. Respect goes both ways."

"That it does." With a finger on her chin, he tipped her face closer and lowered his mouth to claim a slow and tender kiss. Her lips parted and he savored the delicious flavor of Charlie as her soft moan escaped their joined lips. He stroked down her throat, over her shoulder, settling his palm over her quick beating of her heart. Not for a moment did he break the passionate kiss nor their locked gazes, simultaneously answering her request for relief from her craving and testing if she'd raise her defenses between them. She didn't.

She accepted his attention, welcomed his touch, and didn't shy away from the public display.

"I'd like for us to attend Always Kiss Me Good-Night," he said, more than satisfied with her acceptance.

"Okay," Charlie said, her warm breath feathering over his lips.

"Perfect," Ford replied. "There's one more category."

"M is for *masters*," the mistress said as if on cue. "Not only Masters or Sirs and submissives, but individuals who have mastered the lifestyle in any way. These activities are recommended only to experienced members of our group. The play will be intense. The scenes are determined by the participants and not by the staff. Please respect this space. It is a passionate and fortifying time for many of our guests."

At that point, the evening's schedule of events was displayed on a screen behind her. Each activity was clearly marked with a suggested level.

"This brings us back to the rules of respect and consent. These are prerequisites—across the board—in any category," the mistress insisted. "Enjoy. Find pleasure. Find love. Our staff is available to help you achieve any of these goals throughout the duration of the cruise."

"Thank you, Mistress." Bodhi returned and bowed at the waist. He reached for her hand and brought his lips to her knuckles.

The audience showed its gratitude and understanding with applause.

Mistress Gwyn remained stoic, yet her eyes shined with compassion. "Thank you, my friends. Thank you for entrusting Lovers Sail with your needs. And with a kiss, I declare the official start of the Tenth Annual Lovers Sail Singles and Kink Cruise. *Passion sur la mer.*"

Gwyn touched an elegant hand to her lips and threw the group a kiss.

"Passion on the sea," Ford translated, but quickly realized there was no need as Charlie shrugged her agreement. His Charlie had understood. "You speak French?"

"*Un peu*," she replied. "Four years in high school. Four years in college."

"*Venez ici.*" He called her to him, realizing she'd just shared a tiny piece of the past she'd tucked away as she shimmied like the cutest pixie up against him. Wondering how he'd been so lucky to bump into such female perfection, he spread his hands above the soft swell of her ass, aching to raise her skirt and feel the full smoothness in his palms. Instead, he whispered a thank you and kissed her.

Quinn cleared his throat, stepped up practically between them, and ended the kiss. "Get a room. This is a B event."

"You playing with my pain? You know we can't get a room," Ford said. "What are you? Some kind of sadist?"

"Hardly," Quinn said, sporting a handsome grin. "More of a masochist if I enjoy being here with you, watching you two get it on."

"Good one," Charlie said, looking up at Quinn through lowered eyelashes and walking seductive fingers over his defined abs. "Who says you should watch?"

"I do," Ford quipped.

Quinn laughed and raised a hand in the air. "Ford, you don't have to say a word. I know my place." He looked over his right shoulder. "So I figured I'd do my friends a favor and let them know the captain is heading straight for us. How believable does he want you to be?"

Fuck. Not as believable as he felt. He stepped back from Charlie and spoke at Quinn. "Be a friend and pretend to be seducing my woman."

"My pleasure," Quinn said, saluting him. "Come, baby doll."

"That's what he said," she teased, allowing the jock to wrap his arms around her. "Just before he planted that hot kiss on my lips."

space. "I'd like to get back to my cabin and write for a little. Can you please let Ford know I'll see him at dinner?"

Quinn and Luis exchanged puzzled glances, but nodded.

"I'll walk you to the cabin," Quinn offered, crooking his arm for her. Covering her fingers with his hand, he spoke to Luis. "Be back in a few."

Chapter Thirteen

"Why would you let her go off like that? Have you seen what's happening on deck? She's not used to all the explicit scenes or the people who would want to involve her in them." Ford walked into the almost empty dining room and scanned the tables.

"She's not on deck. She went to her cabin in order to work. Quinn walked her to the cabin, made sure she was locked in, and is now picking her up and escorting her through the torrid halls," Luis said, his tone dripping with sarcasm and strained as if his patience was being worn thin.

Ford wasn't taking the bait. He pushed his hands into his pockets and walked to the table. At Charlie's request, he'd arranged for them to be seated with her friends.

"You're being totally unreasonable. Are you seriously that dense that you'd keep her from working?" Luis asked.

"No," Ford quipped. "I know better than that." He pulled out a chair and sat, facing the maître d's podium. "She's hell-bent on getting this piece to press, and I'd never stand in her way. What I don't get is why it's so important to her. Has she mentioned anything to you?"

Luis exhaled loudly. He shook his head. "No. She just keeps insisting that she's a professional and has a job to do. Reminds me of when my father refused to accept that I liked sex with men . . . I was hell-bent on fucking any man who stood still long enough, just to prove to my dad that I wasn't going to marry a good girl, settle down, have kids, and please him. I rebelled so much that I quickly lost sight of what pleased me. It took meeting Quinn to realize what I had been doing. I'm lucky he was so patient and insistent with me, or I never would be here today. The man is as stubborn as a mule. And I'm thankful for that. My father still won't accept us, but that's his problem. Not mine."

Ford nodded his agreement. He knew the stress of parental pressure. "I get that. I do. Fathers can be massive dicks. Mine is."

He could feel Luis studying him, but he refused to look back at the other man. No need to bond with Luis when all he wanted was answers on what drove Charlie. He pretended to read the menu instead.

"Tonight we eat off the International Aphrodisiacs menu." Ford dropped the folder to the table. "If you do oysters, I suggest the oysters with champagne-vinegar mignonette to start."

"What the hell is mignonette?"

Much to his surprise, Ford found himself identifying with the man he'd originally considered competition. He grinned, remembering his own reaction to the peculiar serving of a Louisianan staple. "Think of it like a dressing. The oysters are broiled, topped with creamy butter, sweet grapes, and then dressed with herbs and the tart vinegar. They're great."

Luis nodded, easily accepting the suggestion. "You really do know your food."

"More or less," Ford admitted, intent on keeping the conversation easy. "Comes with the job. Plus, I like to eat." Spotting Charlie and Quinn walking through the door, he stood, pulled out the chair next to his, and waited for them to approach. Once she rounded the table and came to his side, he rubbed his palm over her back and bent to kiss her cheek. "I missed you. Glad you're finally here, *chère*."

"Me, too. But I wasn't gone that long. I just went back to make some notes I didn't want to forget," she replied, touching his cheek and gracing him with a beautiful smile. "Are we sitting here?"

"Yes, ma'am." The remainder of the guests faded into the background as she squeezed his hand in a private message. He tipped her face up to his and looked into her eyes. "Yes, ma'am," he repeated, touching his mouth to hers and giving in to his very own addiction.

Her soft lips yielded and welcomed him with a soft sigh. The intoxicating taste fueled his desire for more, the painful evidence swelling in his pants, but he kept the kiss tender and short. Guiding her to sit, he inhaled her scent and fought the urge to pull her back into his lap. Fuck the ship. Fuck the cruise. Fuck her article. He wanted what he wanted.

"I got a lot of work done. The happy hour party was full of surprises, and I had to get it all into a file. I think this kink cruise has more romance than I anticipated. The people on board are an assortment of personalities and I really think they're going to make great inspiration for a piece that will appeal to many of the readers. The feature is going to rock."

"I missed you," he repeated, surprising even himself. For the first time ever, he'd felt the absence of a woman and he hadn't liked it for a single moment.

"I'm glad," she replied, a mischievous smile on her lips.

"And it's you that rocks." He looked into eyes that sparkled with joy and realized how accomplished the work made her feel. Her face glowed with excitement and she could barely sit still in her chair. "That byline is yours."

"Not necessarily," she said, sucking her lower lip into her mouth as two vertical lines of concern formed between her finely shaped brows. "Kat is a great writer. She's writing about Paris, the city of love. It simply fits for Valentine's Day."

"You have the scoop on romance and love for any day of the year. Not only that, but you're being exposed to that love." He interlaced their fingers and pulled her hand into his lap. "You don't need to stick with only traditional romance. Think outside the box. Write for a variety of readers. Reach more people."

"I like that," she said, her smile returning to her pink lips.

"I like it," Quinn added.

"I guess I do, too," Luis said. "*Querida*, I'd buy the magazine if it had different takes on relationships. I'm sick of people trying to fit everything into a neat little package. Not everything is for everyone."

The moment Charlie had asked for the kiss, the other men disappeared from Ford's radar. But they were back. Sitting with him and the woman that made his chest tight, her friends and confidants made for very unusual dinner company at the start of a relationship.

Quinn sat beside Luis, who sat on the other side of Charlie, and another man approached. Ford glanced at the maître d' and wondered if the man was pulling his leg. Setting up a *Charlie's Harem* joke or something.

"Good evening," the new arrival said. "I believe this is my table. May I?"

"Of course." Charlie piped up and indicated a free seat. "Welcome. I'm Charlie, and this is Ford, Luis, and Quinn."

"*Um*...you're all friends? All together?" The conservatively dressed, tall, and lanky man sank into the offered chair, tugging on the collar of his Polo shirt and looking around the table.

"We're all friends," Quinn offered. "We're not all together. For simplicity's sake, I'm with Luis. Ford here is with Charlie, and he barely leaves her side. I'm not sure if he bites, so be warned. He's a tad territorial."

Quinn may have been teasing, but Ford saw no problem with sticking to his woman. He'd be the one escorting her to all the events for the rest of the cruise. Not Quinn. Not Luis.

"My choice," Ford quipped. "Besides, some people know more about boundaries than others on this sailing."

"Agreed," said the newcomer. "I questioned the nature of the cruise and if it was what I was looking for. Initially, I had doubts. The staff assured—"

"My friend, tell us your name." Luis raised his hand, effectively calming the rambling.

"Grayson. Pleased to meet you all." Grayson rose from his seat, shook everyone's hands, and was lowering himself back to his seat when two women approached the table. He remained standing and greeted them.

Charlie welcomed the female company. The testosterone at the table was growing thick, so she also welcomed the sense of balance.

A willowy brunette, wearing a sleek designer dress that must have cost what Charlie paid for monthly rent, introduced herself as Emma. She then introduced her very sweet-looking best friend Grace. Unlike Emma, Grace was blond and wore a simple linen dress and a thin silver chain hanging between her breasts.

"Cute," Quinn said. "We have a Grace and a Grayson at this table."

A fifth man stepped up. "And a Tyler." He gave the table a casual wave and folded his large bulky frame into a seat. "Good evening. Nice to meet you."

"Good evening," they replied in a synchronized greeting.

Tyler didn't look like a Tyler to Charlie. He looked like a Jax or a Chief. She imagined him parking his Harley at the port and trudging up the gangway with a black leather backpack slung on his shoulder. Even though he wore a traditional white button-down shirt, it was rolled at his forearms and revealed non-traditional body art. His deep voice was proper and courteous, and more than anything, it demanded respect.

When the group settled into casual conversation, Charlie watched as Tyler's penetrating gaze traveled down Grace's body. Grace must have felt him looking, for she met his gaze and flushed. She curled her shoulders into her body, but Tyler gave a quick, almost impercep-tible, shake of his head and narrowed his gaze. Grace immediately straightened her back. He grinned his approval.

The man had keen and forceful dark eyes, and while she tried to keep her tablemates' names straight, Charlie couldn't help but be captivated by the silent dynamics between the stoic Tyler and some-how wounded Grace. How Charlie knew the other woman was wounded was a mystery, but she knew.

Two empty chairs remained, yet the conversation ensued and the itinerary dissection colored her mind with options. When it came to sharing their reasons for being there, following Quinn and Luis's lead, Charlie said she was there to enjoy the weekend with Ford. They were exploring the possibilities of their new relationship. It wasn't a com-plete lie, just a stretch of the truth.

"We don't need to be on this sailing for me to enjoy my time with you," Ford added. "I'd enjoy you no matter where."

Tyler studied them without bothering to voice his observation, but she could practically feel him scanning her mind for her true thoughts. Not that she had much experience with identifying the per-sonality, but Tyler had to be a Dominant who lived the lifestyle every moment of every day. And from the way he'd soothed Grace's ner-vousness, he was an effective Dominant. A good Dom.

She made a mental note to do some further research into the specifics of a Dom/sub daily relationship. She'd even ask Tyler for an interview, if she could summon the courage and he allowed it.

"We're here to celebrate Grace losing two hundred pounds of dead weight," Emma announced, flaring her hands to feature her friend. "Her drawn-out divorce was final on Monday."

"You opted for a single's cruise?" Grayson asked.

"Singles and kink," Emma corrected. "It's my present to her. She needs to have fun. My BFF hasn't had *fun* in over five years."

Charlie wasn't about to touch that one. The emphasis on *fun* was obvious. From the embarrassed drop of Grace's gaze and the pink spreading over her body, Charlie guessed the newly single woman was a born-again virgin.

"Fun she'll have," Tyler assured, and Grace's pink blush deepened to red. He stared at the woman until her gaze lifted and met his, which didn't take long. With a slight nod, he smiled. Reaching for the wine list, Tyler called for the sommelier and ordered two bottles of the Dom Perignon Jeff Koons Rose Vintage.

Charlie knew about the elite champagne selection from the days she'd subjected herself to family parties. She also knew that the two bottles were more expensive than the cost of her cabin. Wow. Just wow. She hadn't expected that sort of sophistication from a man with bulging muscles, an inch-long scar over his right brow, and tattoos that could have been featured on that tattoo artist reality show. The server wasted no time returning with the bottles and pouring the bubbly with practiced flair.

"To celebrate Grace's spirit and her rosy future," Tyler said, raising his glass in a toast and inviting the table to do the same.

"Thank you," Grace said in a soft voice, lifting the flute to her lips and sipping on the pink champagne. "It's delicious. Just beautiful."

"As you are," Tyler added. "Congratulations, sweet Grace. Wishing you all your heart and body desire."

The group echoed the congratulations and an easy camaraderie settled among them. Ford suggested his favorites from the aphro disiac menu. The broiled oysters sounded divine. Charlie went for them. For the entrée, he suggested either the Southern Oyster Casserole or the Lobster Risotto. Charlie loved lobster and wasn't about to miss the chance to taste the artful mix of her favorite dish with hot chilies, pomegranate, and vanilla bean. Just the description sounded orgasmic. But she exercised a little bit of control and decided she'd skip what sounded like the most mouth-watering dessert. Her hips wouldn't allow for champagne, risotto, *and* a dessert of cardamom-laced dark chocolate truffles with white chocolate ice cream. She'd order the fruit platter, which came with a dark chocolate dipping sauce. She'd skip the sauce. Save a few calories.

"Grayson, what brings you aboard?" Ford asked, doing the job Charlie had lost sight of while being too busy taking in all the sensuous details of the evening.

"It's a long story," Grayson dismissed.

"It always is," Emma added, a genuine smile on her face. "We have all of dinner to hear it."

Feeling unsettled for growing lax with her assignment, Charlie squeezed Ford's hand. He immediately turned and kissed her. Right there. In front of everyone. His tongue swept away the apprehension, and his undivided attention made butterflies dance in her belly—and lower.

"Thank you," she breathed against his mouth.

"My pleasure," he whispered for only her to hear, licking gently across her lips. "You'll have more than you need, sooner than you know."

"Well, it's not as exciting as Grace's motive for sailing away, and it's not as inspiring as the two couples so clearly in love in our presence, but I'll admit to wanting that connection with someone special," Grayson said, using air quotes around *special*.

Appearing traditional and reserved, Grayson did stick out in the crowd.

"First it was school that ruled my life. Now it's work." Grayson gulped down the remainder of his champagne and raised his shoulders. "I can't seem to find the right woman. I want someone real. Not someone looking for a sugar daddy or a free ride due to my career choice."

"I know exactly what you're talking about," Emma interjected. "It seems like potential partners are evaluating net worth rather than true compatibility. But you don't need to be worried about sugar daddy status. You're not old enough."

It turned out that Grayson was only in his twenties and five years younger than Emma. Upon hearing that detail, Emma quieted. She scooted closer to Grace, and Charlie could swear she saw disappointment flicker in Emma's eyes. Which probably meant Emma didn't consider it proper to date a younger man.

"Age is just a number," Charlie blurted. "It doesn't define a person."

"Maybe," Emma said, looking at her. "But there are certain stages in one's life that are more defined than others. Certain milestones that come naturally in our twenties or thirties or beyond."

Grayson shook his head, but didn't seem convinced. "I agree with Charlie. Age is just a number."

The young man's assertive tone was a surprise. Charlie's dinner companions were definitely an interesting bunch. They also seemed to have been purposefully grouped by the organizers to meet certain criteria. Maybe that was what the registration questionnaire had been all about? If so, Lovers Sail did a great job of matchmaking.

"Hello, kids," a silver haired gentleman said. "Sorry we're late. My bride and I got carried away celebrating our fifty-third wedding anniversary and lost track of time. Hope we didn't inconvenience you."

"Not at all," Ford said, indicating the empty chairs. "Welcome. Happy anniversary."

The remainder of the table congratulated the older couple, and quickly learned that Maggy and Sparky had married straight out of high school. "Well, after my Maggy graduated. It was an exercise in patience," he explained.

"Sparky waited three years," Maggy elaborated. Three years after they'd shared a dance at the local community center's Valentine's Ball to kiss her. Waited a total of four years to escort her to her senior prom and ask for her hand in marriage. Of course he'd spoken with her father prior to pinning her corsage. Their story seemed like a fairy tale.

Unfortunately for Charlie, she knew she was no Cinderella. With a sigh, she reluctantly accepted the temporary fairy tale relationship with Ford, settling her shoulder against his and relishing the feel of his fingers stroking her thigh. No question they were physically compatible. Probably more than physically. But he had been clear. He wasn't the relationship type. She was about to amend her original statement about exploring their relationship when their appetizers arrived and the scent of the wonderfully dressed broiled oysters had her mouth watering.

Before starting on his own, Ford offered her an oyster. "Just looking out for my own agenda," he said with a wink, sliding the treat past her lips. They exchanged tastes of their main courses and tangoed in a private dance of sensual promises while Charlie struggled to remain engaged in the conversation at the table.

"Is it the oysters or is it what you think I have coming for you?" He glanced at her nipples, clearly outlined against the black halter top, and let his gaze linger long enough for her to feel the tingles of his visual caress. But the physical touch of his fingers smoothing up her thigh to the juncture between her legs did more than make her nipples hard. The sweet spot between her legs throbbed with need and her heart pounded against her ribs.

"Here?" she breathed.

"Wherever I please," he said, caressing her bared heat, spreading her moisture and circling around the pulsing bundle of nerves at the top. He continued stroking her, occasionally sliding a finger, then two, into her, only to return his attention to the pulsing bundle of nerves.

The dessert arrived, and Ford set the fruit platter away, placing his chocolate truffles and ice cream between them. "This one first."

Eleven extra pounds, she mouthed.

The sting of a wet smack sounded in her ears, but no one else seemed to hear it. She bit her lip to stifle her surprise.

"Don't deny me," he warned, pinching her aching clit. "Show me how much you like the truffle between those pink lips and the ice cream melting in your mouth."

Charlie's breath hitched, and she looked around at the other guests wondering if they'd heard and understood his words. With a shaky hand, she picked up the spoon and cut into a dark truffle.

"I do like it," she replied, licking at the ice cream and sucking the truffle between her lips. "Really like it."

A trill of guitar chords sounded over the dining room's acoustic system and the servers broke into a festive performance, singing the classic "That's Amore." Emma and Grace picked up their napkins and gently twirled them over their heads, encouraging the others to do the same.

Charlie struggled but followed suit; Ford didn't. He kept his hand between her legs, stroking his fingers through her moisture and working a smooth and cool object snugly inside her. Suddenly, the toy vibrated to life, heightening her excitement and heating her whole body.

"The benefit of sailing on a kink cruise is that the promenade has a variety of merchants for our shopping pleasure," he said, gaining him a few confused glances from their dinner companions. The conversation had nothing to do with shopping. Certainly nothing to do with kink. They'd been discussing the variety of excursions in Cozumel.

"I guess that makes tax-free shopping less appealing?" Grace offered.

"Exactly," Ford agreed. "More time for swimming with dolphins and riding bareback on the beach. I hear that the latter is rather romantic." He glanced at Charlie, who managed to nod in agreement. Her booked horseback ride was the furthest thing from her mind as she rode the sensations of the tiny vibrator.

The tremors of ecstasy within her center intensified as Ford withdrew his hand from between her legs, adjusted the speed of the vibe, and let the sensations of the little contraption work. He picked up his napkin with one hand, dropped an arm around her shoulders and sang along with "The Way You Look Tonight" against her ear.

It was the first time Charlie listened to the words in the classic song, and with Ford's insistence that she breathe and enjoy, her climax crept closer and closer.

"It's not fair," she said softly. "My body is on overload."

"I know." Ford tilted her face to his.

"I can't control it," she argued.

"I know," he repeated. "Isn't it freeing to not have control?" His hand reappeared between her legs and his thumb circled in ecstasy. "Come for me, *chère*," he breathed, sealing his lips to hers. "Now."

She shattered in orgasmic bliss, moaning her release into his mouth. Pleasure raced through her body and exploded around her. The world faded, she wasn't sure how long the climax rolled over her, but then the sound of applause signaled the end of the finale and she sucked in a deep breath, forcing herself back to reality.

"Did you enjoy dessert?" Ford asked, trailing wet kisses slowly up her neck.

"It was decadent," Charlie said, worrying her lower lip and not fighting the trance her body had sunk into. "Pure decadence."

Chapter Fourteen

Ford's contentment faded as confusion clouded Charlie's eyes and her lips tightened in disappointment. It took him a moment to recognize the guilt and concern shadowing her face, but once he had, annoyance balled in his gut and he wasn't able to concentrate on the small talk happening at the table.

Charlie had angled her body away from him and refused to make eye contact. It didn't take much to see the effort she was exerting in order to renounce the physical euphoria she had relinquished control to only moments earlier. She immersed herself in casual conversation, refusing to play any longer. With the staff's performance over and dessert done, the guests' focus was the night's events.

She smiled and nodded, her back stiff and her knees clamped together, charming as heck with the other guests. The senator's wife image was back.

Why the swing?

Who had done this to her?

The majority of the table was heading to Always Kiss Me Good-Night, which Maggy assured the "youngsters" was the best advice she could offer on how to make a relationship work. "However, since that has always been a steadfast rule in our marriage, Sparky and I are going to pass on this particular event," she explained. "We've decided to attend the Nautical and More Knots seminar."

Ford squeezed Charlie's hand, and she turned to look at him, seemingly surprised that he'd ask for the kiss.

"It works both ways," he said, leaning in. "We'll catch up with you," he told the others. Waving over his shoulder, Ford looked only at Charlie. He waited until they were alone, no one else around for distractions.

"What happened?" Smoothing the lines edging the corners of her mouth, he skimmed his thumb over her lips and felt the tightening in his gut once again. This woman did things to him he'd rarely experienced before. It was all he could do not to demand she surrender to his desires to throw all other responsibilities away and just be together. Strangely enough, his desires weren't limited to the physical. "Why did you withdraw?"

"It wasn't a withdrawal," she said, closing her fingers over his, and pulling his hand into her lap. "The conversation reminded me that I did not come on the cruise to indulge myself—no matter how delightful and tempting the indulgence. You, my sexy Cajun, make my head spin, so I need to compartmentalize my thoughts and actions. I really should get back to the cabin and—"

"Don't go there," he warned. His chest burned and heat spread up his neck. "What the hell, Charlie? Why not indulge yourself?"

"I have work to do."

"I don't buy it," he said, dropping her hand and running his fingers through his hair. "You were handed, on a silver platter, more than a little material at dinner tonight. The guests sitting at our table come from all walks of life. Their experiences, motives, and wishes vary. And if I'm not mistaken, there are plenty of sparks already flying among them. Don't use your work as an excuse to pull away."

She folded her hands in her lap and stared at her thumbs, which she twirled with great intensity. "It's just that I lost track. I don't do that."

"What don't you do? Allow yourself a little decadence?" Ford pressed her to acknowledge what he'd seen in her eyes. She wanted it. Craved it. Even admitted to it. Yet, something held her back.

"Yes," she hissed. "I lost my head and let pleasure consume me. I made a mistake." Her thumbs picked up speed. "I pride myself on being practical and even keeled. I'm sorry if I gave you the wrong impression. I can't go around dismissing everything I've worked so hard for over the past few years for a few moments of stolen pleasure."

She hadn't given him the wrong impression. She'd allowed the real Charlie to surface. She'd let her guard down and guilt had crawled into the tiny space of truth she'd permitted.

Ford rubbed his hand over his chin and shook his head. He'd known Charlie less than twelve hours, and in that insanely short amount of time, he'd tossed his agenda into the air and let it fall at her feet in tiny pieces. Studying the confusion she attempted to mask on her pretty face, his annoyance grew. Annoyance that someone had instilled doubt and denial in such a beautiful woman. Annoyance that it mattered to him and she affected him on such a seismic scale. Annoyance that he felt at the mercy of the petite blonde. What the fuck was wrong with him?

He was getting nowhere with these kinds of thoughts. He was a doer, not a contemplator. Plus, she was blowing smoke up his ass and hers. No, no way.

"No senator's wife smile," he said in a low voice.

"What?"

He shook his head. "I was thinking aloud." He wiped his hand down his face and made his choice. "But I'm done with that."

A twinkle of hope glimmered in her eyes and he had no doubt what was needed. "Since we've decided to work together and help each other out, there is only one option for now. First, you will put the writing assignment to sleep for the night. You have more than enough material. We'll revisit your research in the morning. Second, we're attending Always Kiss Me Good-Night. We're going to immerse ourselves in the evening's activities, and you're going to enjoy it."

Relief sparked on her face. Tense shoulders relaxed and warm breath feathered over his lips. Yes, he'd made the right choice.

"Go into the ladies' room, retrieve the toy, and bring it to me." He wasn't giving her any time to argue and to insist on a change of plans. "You're being petulant about accepting what is given. We're not doing petulant."

Charlie dragged cool air into her lungs. She closed her eyes and nodded, secretly thanking the stars above for the man's high-handedness. "Yes," she breathed.

He stood and offered her his hand. She took it, followed him out of the dining room and to the nearest ladies' room. Leaving him in the corridor, she stepped inside and cleaned up.

She smiled at the remembrance of the concealed touches, the sweet sensations, and the explosive release. She'd practically passed out from it all. Or was that because she'd held her breath? How was it possible that no one else noticed?

116 · *Demi Alex*

Sinful. Just sinful. That wasn't the way for a proper lady to act. She truly didn't deserve orgasm after orgasm when she should be working. But she'd taken it like the wanton woman she was quickly learning she was. Not only that, but she was selfish. She hadn't once reciprocated the attention.

She frowned at her reflection. Douchebag-ex James had called her a sexual letch, with a deviant streak not appropriate for polite company. Her mouth instinctively formed a frown. Just because she wanted to get on top, try riding him for a change, she was a deviant. She was a letch because she'd touched herself when he wouldn't. Maybe she was selfish, or maybe he was a douche, but either way she finally knew what it was like to orgasm at someone else's touch ... someone else's sweet ministrations.

The door pushed open. *"Chère?"*

"I'll be out in a second," she called, reaching between her thighs and removing the tiny pink vibrator. She rinsed it off, wrapped it in a paper towel, then left the stall. Checking her reflection a final time, she fluffed her hair and went to meet Ford.

"Started to worry about you," he said, draping an arm over her shoulder and kissing the side of her head. "You okay?"

"Mmm," she mumbled and held out the neatly wrapped package. "As per your request, sir."

He laughed, then unwrapped the vibrator and dangled it from his index finger for all to see. She glanced around, grateful they were alone, and closed her hand around the vibe. "Ford. What if someone sees?"

He shrugged, pulled away from her, held out his finger, and the toy swung like a pendulum. "Stop hiding, *chère.* It is what it is."

Heat cruised up to her cheeks and her heart skipped. "What would people think?"

"Not that I care," he said, stopping the bullet from swinging and caressing it with his thumb. "But do you really believe a little pink vibrator would make much of an impression with this crowd?"

A tall woman, dressed in a fishnet cat suit that had two strategically placed black strips and thigh high boots, descended the staircase with a thick silver chain in her hand. The chunky chain was about two feet long, then it split into two shorter segments that were clasped to studded leather collars worn by two bare chested young men, each of them wearing black latex boxer shorts.

"I guess not," she replied, swallowing the lump of embarrassment in her throat. She watched him slip the toy into his coat pocket and sighed in relief. "I'm not used to this stuff."

"You're not used to a lot of things," he said, cupping her face. "And some things I don't mind, but others I do. I meant it when I said I wouldn't stand for you to hide your true desires from me. I won't."

He smoothed an open palm down the side of her neck to the center of her chest. Her skin tingled beneath his touch and her breasts grew heavy at the anticipation of more. Her nipples hardened and strained against the fabric of her dress, but he didn't soothe the ache with a stroke.

"Back at the table, you voiced your last 'no' to what you want." He leaned down, brushed his lips over her mouth, and looked her in the eyes. "The only 'no' these lips will let slide is one you feel in here." His hand splayed over her heart, his fingertips brushing her nipple, and her heart pounded twice as hard for the intimate gesture. It wasn't simply sexual in nature, rather it was a patient reinforcement.

Charlie didn't want to say no to this man. Not in any way. She needed to find a balance in her life and let herself live. As the energy from his hand seeped into her chest, she resolved to do exactly what he asked. Consciously and with complete awareness, she'd let herself fall for him.

"You're thinking a lot," he said. "Any questions?"

She shook her head.

"What was that?" Ford asked.

"None," she whispered, holding his gaze and feeling the joy settle over her heart. "Thank you."

His eyes brightened and he smiled. "With that pretty attitude, you're making me second guess taking back the toy." He playfully smacked her backside and straightened, pulling her into a tight embrace.

Smiling into his chest, she snuggled closer. It had been a long time since she'd felt that way. She slid her hands beneath his jacket and gathered his shirt in her fingers. "I don't need a toy to feel good. I have you. You make me feel wonderful."

"There's something about you, Charlie, something that makes me crazy." His hand closed on her nape and his fingers curled into her hair. He turned her face up to his and locked his gaze on hers. "We'll need to figure this out before we get back home or you're going to be my undoing, lady."

"That makes me feel powerful," she said, going up on her toes and pressing her lips to the underside of his jaw.

Maybe because of their locale or maybe because she was a romantic fool, Charlie couldn't help but reach for the fantasy. Freshly shaved, smooth, and welcoming, the chiseled lines were like a fine treasure map. Ford was the treasure. A treasure she'd never thought she deserved. A treasure she knew she'd search for, and then had to prepare to release when they returned to the United States. Bittersweet—but she wanted the sweetness, temporary or not. She didn't feel the "no" in her heart. The moment wasn't going to slip through her lips.

"It should. You hold all the power," he said, linking her hand through his arm. "Let's go learn about kissing good-night."

Dim lighting illuminated the lounge, but bright white lights bathed the stage and the four participants standing on it. Charlie watched as the MC blindfolded a woman with long red hair. He skipped over the lanky man, whispered something into a blonde's ear, and finally tied another blindfold over Grace's eyes. Their Grace!

"Holy cow," Charlie said, leaning into Ford as he guided them to the corner where their tablemates had gathered.

"I see." He scooted her in front of him and placed a hand on her waist for guidance as he continued to where Luis and Quinn stood. "Looks like Emma's plans for her friend's adventure are falling into place."

"Our recipients are ready. Two have chosen blindfolds to prevent them from seeing. The other two promise not to peek," the MC announced. "Close your eyes, my friends. It's time for three givers to line up before each of you. If one of the givers kisses you the way you desire, kiss back. You'll be his or hers for the remainder of the evening. What happens when the lights come on is up to you."

Givers formed lines before the four recipients, but when three men stood before Grace, Tyler shook his head. He glanced at Ford, took Charlie and Emma by the hand and paraded them up to Grace's line. Tapping the shoulders of the three men that had already taken their place before Grace, he glared at them with an intimidating scowl, and tossed his head to the side for them to scram. They did.

"Charlie has the right cheek," he said in a low voice. "Emma, the left. Give your friend a kiss good-night, ladies." Then he placed his large hand over his heart. "Thank you."

No way could Charlie argue with something so gallant. Tyler claimed Grace right before her eyes, and she found the caveman action very endearing, even sweet. Tyler didn't want another man kissing Grace, so he'd asked for platonic cheek kisses from them. She glanced at Emma, who smiled and nodded in agreement.

"You're very welcome," Charlie whispered.

The MC gestured for them to line up in order and continued explaining the kiss they were after was a lover's kiss. "A kiss that will send us into a fitful sleep, with sexy dreams, and hopefully a satisfying morning wake-up conclusion."

Emma stepped up first, hugged her friend tight, and cupped her right cheek. She kissed Grace's left cheek. "You deserve this. Enjoy."

When it was Charlie's turn, she reached for her hand and felt how Grace trembled at her touch. Intertwining their fingers, she squeezed and signaled her assurance. She brushed her lips on the other woman's cool cheek. "You're in good hands. Let loose, Grace."

The MC instructed them to move on, and Tyler stepped up. Standing close to the pair, Charlie witnessed Grace's reaction to Tyler entering her space. Her cheek flushed with heat, her chest rose and fell rapidly, and she wet her lips as his fingers trailed down the side of her face. He took his time, caressing her pretty skin and soothing her trembling chin as he used a finger to turn her face up to his.

"Mine."

Charlie heard Tyler's proclamation to Grace, and hope spread through her as he lowered his head and placed his mouth on Grace's. Her lips parted. She raised her hands and linked them behind his neck. "Okay."

Tyler snaked an arm around her waist and pulled her against him. Deepening the kiss until Grace had melted into his big frame, he pushed up the blindfold and smiled at her. "We continue in private."

Blushing, Grace agreed, and he scooped her into his arms and carried her off the stage. They didn't glance back. Didn't say good-bye to anyone. They were the only two that mattered.

Emma linked her arm through Charlie's and they strolled across the dance floor toward the others. "That was perfect. I loved the way he did that. He watched her all through dinner, bought champagne for her, and now he literally swept her off her feet."

"I think he's the kind of man that sees what he wants and doesn't hesitate to go after it. He wants Grace," Charlie said.

"I know," Emma agreed. "He's exactly what she needs. She lived with a floundering asshole for so long that she almost lost herself because of his wimp tendencies. She needs a strong man to remind her that she's a beautiful and sexy woman. Someone who won't allow her to back away."

"Tyler will only allow what he thinks is right. He's very dominant. Almost a little frightening," Charlie said.

"Not frightening. Reassuring," Emma insisted. "Grace needs that."

Reassuring . . . Charlie let the word and its meaning sink in as they reached the men and Ford draped an arm around her. He placed several soft kisses on her temple, but didn't speak.

"That was hot," Quinn said, fanning his face with his hand. He looked down at Luis. "You've never carried me off a stage like that."

"Skip dessert tomorrow and I may have a chance," Luis teased. Both men were big and powerful, but Quinn had at least four inches on Luis and a good fifty extra pounds of solid muscle on his frame. Luis bent and hooked an arm beneath Quinn's knees, sweeping him up into a romantic hold. "I'm up for it if you are, handsome."

"That's a sight to behold," Grayson said. "Hot, hot, and hot."

A surprised Quinn held onto Luis's neck for dear life, his long legs dangling, eyes large, and mouth gaping. "It's okay, lover. I'll walk where you lead."

They all laughed, and Luis lowered Quinn's feet to solid ground.

A server arrived with a tray full of drinks, distributed them, and placed two extras in the center of the table. "Did we lose someone?"

"Nope," Emma said. "We're drinking them all."

More laughter, and new sets of kissers got to work on the stage.

"Drink up, Emma. It's your turn to be kissed," Grayson said, as the MC's voice encouraged the couples in the background.

"No," she replied, shaking her head. "I'm just along for the ride. This trip is for my Grace."

"Everyone deserves to be kissed properly," Quinn said. "If you don't play, you can't win. Why are you benching yourself?"

"She's not," Grayson said. "She won't. She's disillusioned by freeloaders. Jerks who can't see the person behind her success." He gestured for her to finish her martini, and reached for the glass when she had. "Get on stage, Emma."

There was a longing in Emma's gaze as she looked at Grayson. They communicated silently until she relented and accepted his hand. She looked back over her shoulder at Charlie and extended her free arm. "Come with me."

"I'm not about to pass up the opportunity of getting kissed," Charlie announced, taking Emma's hand and winking at Ford. She turned to Grayson. "We'll find our way to the stage. No need to cut our odds in the room by having a good looking young man escort us."

With a nod, Grayson released Emma's hand. Ford swatted Charlie's backside. Quinn and Luis laughed.

"Blindfolds," Grayson instructed as they walked away. "Minimizes the nerves."

Emma knocked into Charlie's shoulder. "Too young. It's not right."

"What are you talking about?" Charlie asked.

"I just turned thirty-three. He's in his twenties."

"He's not your typical twenty something," Charlie pointed out. "That man has his shit together."

"I know," Emma said. "It still doesn't make it right."

"Do you like him?"

"What's not to like?" Emma answered with her own question. "If he were ten years older, he'd be perfect."

Charlie thought about it as they were ushered onto the stage. She looked at Emma and smiled. "You should look past the petty things." A staff member offered her a blindfold, and she nodded. While the woman tied it around her head, Charlie counted on her fingers. "Net worth. Level of professional success. A couple of years. Do those things make the person?"

Emma sighed, but didn't respond.

"Let the man kiss you," Charlie added. "You never know."

While her brain was in reporter mode and gathering information about Emma and Grayson's interaction, the blindfold settled her thoughts to what she was doing for herself. She had no doubt that Ford would be one of the kissers in her lineup, but she wondered if she'd be able to guess which one. Would her body react like Grace's had? What would be their end result? After all, he couldn't sweep her off her feet and carry her away to a private place.

"Are the receivers ready?" the MC asked.

Charlie exhaled, hoping she was right about Ford. Hoping she hadn't made a real mistake in letting him see past her façade.

Strong and confident hands cupped her cheeks, and the first giver sprinkled kisses on her whole face. A man with a sexy scent she recognized, a scent that lulled her to a comfortable and safe place, and a man who clearly enjoyed showing his appreciation. First, she felt his warmth on her forehead, then over her shielded eyes, on the tip of her nose, each of her cheeks, and her chin, and then he barely brushed his lips over hers and she felt, rather than saw, his smile. "So sweet, *querida*."

Luis's hands disappeared and she knew he'd stepped away. Sensing the next candidate, she immediately recognized Quinn's presence. Damn, why couldn't she have kept things simple and taken them up on their offer? Why did she need to complicate things and feel the way she did with Ford?

Feeling Quinn's broad chest brush over her breasts as he leaned down, she sucked in a breath. He kissed, warm and reassuring, from her collarbone, up the side of her neck, to her lips. She fell into the affection, reveling in the cherishment and relaxing her mouth against his. "You're an amazing kisser."

"You're amazing to kiss." Quinn pressed his muscled body against her softness, allowing his mouth to linger near hers. "He's a lucky bastard. You want him. And fuck me does he want you," he breathed between her lips. "He's burning holes into my back at this very moment."

Charlie giggled and stepped back.

"I'm here for you. Always." Quinn kissed her cheek and was gone.

Desire crawled over Charlie's skin in anticipation, but she didn't feel Ford's caress. She knew he was there. Felt his heat. Heard his breath. She waited, shifting her weight from one foot to the other, but he didn't touch her.

"You know what I want, *chère*." His deep voice and intent swaddled her in a passionate embrace. "I'm changing the terms on our deal. You need to accept. It's no longer anything. Not when it comes to you. No other man, I don't care who he is, will taste those lips once you kiss me. You'll be mine. Only mine."

Oh, Lord. Pressure built in her core with the understanding of a possessive Ford putting his foot down. She liked it. Liked him. *No other man ... Only mine.* His breath mingled with hers, yet he still didn't touch her.

She raised and wrapped her arms around his neck, sidling up against his body and going up on her toes. "Sounds good to me."

"Perfect." Then he touched her. Gently lifting the blindfold, he looked into her eyes and gave her that handsome and tempting smile that she'd come to adore.

Her insides melted just a little. And as soon as she smiled back, his mouth was on hers in a searing kiss. Ford claimed her breath as his, making her dizzy with desire, and bringing every nerve in her body to attention. Every nerve.

When his face lifted and his fingers smoothed over her jaw and down her neck, she saw something new in his gaze ... something she couldn't label. Intense, sincere, and consuming, he communicated silently.

This was no longer about research and work. Her body was his.

Chapter Fifteen

Charlie's phone chimed a new message. She turned from the computer screen and reached across the efficiently designed space for her cell.

You still awake?

Her gaze flitted to the bedside clock. Ten fifty-two.

Yes, she typed. My yacht isn't due to turn into a pumpkin until midnight, lol

She waited for his reply, but no little dots appeared in a text bubble to indicate he was typing. The screen eventually went dark. Her heart ached because, crazy as it seemed, she really missed him. She was also disappointed and confused by his decision to cut the evening short.

The moment they'd stepped off the stage, hand in hand, he'd said good-night to the group and taken her away from the party. Initially, she'd thought he'd show her a public-private space they could make that *only mine* statement come true. But, no. Her physical need to be *only his*, if only for the few days they'd have, went unanswered. Instead, he'd walked her to her cabin, announced he had work to see to, told her to get some writing done, and promised to be in touch.

Frustrated, she'd speechlessly watched him pull the cabin door closed and had immediately stripped and stepped into a cold shower. A damn cold shower.

The water had done its job at tempering her body's disappointment and the sting of rejection had faded. She'd concluded it was okay to combine work and play, and his calling it a night wasn't a personal refusal. She'd played. She'd work. And he was entitled to the same. After all, he was officially working on the cruise . . . as a manager on the crew. There shouldn't be a string attached.

Once she was comfortable in a pair of soft boxers and a favorite tie-dye t-shirt from her high school days, she'd settled before the computer and managed to write about how a romantic cruise setting was conducive to trying things one would never have the guts to do on land.

The quick knock at the door startled her from her thoughts. She unfolded her legs from beneath her, placed the laptop on the coffee table, and walked to the door. Looking through the peephole, she smiled at Ford. He was standing there, holding a gift bag, shifting his weight from foot to foot, and he appeared rather impatient for her to open the door. More smiles for her.

"You done?" Charlie asked, swinging the door ajar and stepping back for him to enter.

"I am," he replied, pushing his hands into his jeans pockets. He'd taken time to change, and wore faded jeans, tight in all the right places, with a simple black t-shirt outlining every muscle of his chest and every ridge on his abs. A shiny black bag dangled on his wrist, and he looked like a poster boy for a Naughty Gifts Galore campaign. "Did you get any writing done?"

She shrugged, but nodded with accomplishment. "Wrote about Grace and Tyler's inspiration. It's a good twist."

"Excellent. Join me for a nightcap," he said, holding out the gift bag. "Please."

"Okay," she replied, still waiting for him to come inside.

He shook his head. "I'll wait here. No cabin access, remember?"

She remembered. Her body remembered and resented.

He dropped the bag's silver handle into her hand and it dangled from her fingers. "Put this on, *chère*. There's a pajama party on deck eleven. Pajamas—of sorts."

Charlie pulled out a black silk spaghetti strap nightie with lace over the triangles meant to cover her breasts and a delicate black chiffon frill angled at thigh level.

"You may wear the panties. I'll wait right here," he added, pulling the door shut.

Without a moment's hesitation, Charlie rummaged through the tissue paper and pulled out the panties he'd referred to.

"Barely-there-panties," she said. She wasn't even sure if they qualified as underwear. Made of a pretty black lace, with a tiny rhinestone heart dangling strategically at the slit that cut down the crotch, they were a shadow of what she knew of as panties. She'd never worn crotchless panties. Never even owned a pair.

"What do you have in store for us now, Ford?" Charlie asked, whipping the t-shirt over her head and pushing her boxers to the floor. She tossed her comfort clothes on the couch and turned to her reflection in the mirror. "Sexy man is full of surprises. Nice."

Slipping the lace up her legs and settling it on her hips, she twirled and examined her reflection. Excitement settled low in her belly and her muscles contracted. The little heart hung just above the opening at the crotch and it teased the sensitive bundle of nerves with each movement. She slid the sexy nightie over her head, taking extra care to position her breasts inside the tiny triangles and keep from exposing anything she didn't want fellow passengers to see. And yes, it was a chore to get her nipples aligned and completely covered.

But the truth was that Ford had chosen well. She felt sexy, naughty, and on fire, but she wasn't flashy or raunchy. The nightie came to mid-thigh, and the barely-there panties did shadow the juncture at her thighs. The outfit required the use of one's imagination to see more.

She smoothed gloss on her lips and ran her fingers through her hair. Then, spraying perfume in the air, she walked through the mist and to the man who was waiting beyond her door. She stood behind it and cracked it open, leaning forward to look at him and check if anyone else was in the corridor.

"Am I supposed to walk out like this?"

"You are." He peeled her fingers off the cool metal, and while pulling her to the side, pushed open the door and smiled. "Beautiful, baby. Just beautiful."

Treasured. That's what he made her feel. She wasn't fat. Wasn't average. She was riding on clouds he'd summoned for her. Ford looked at her with true male appreciation. And she knew she wasn't imagining it. That sort of attention from a man like Ford empowered her. It gave her hope that what she wanted wasn't a fantasy.

"Let me get my shoes," she said, noting that his smile had turned into a cocky grin. He bent and positioned a pair of kitten-heeled slippers at the cabin's threshold. "You thought of everything."

"I hope," he replied. He leaned down and lightly kissed the sensitive flesh below her ear. Tingles danced through her in anticipation of the night ahead, and she instinctively nuzzled against him. "Grab your keycard and we're good to go."

"Okay," she breathed, and retrieving the card from the counter, she handed it to him. He slid it into his back pocket, then held her hand and helped her step into the slippers. Even with her in heels and him in flip-flops, she didn't reach his shoulder. But strolling beside him, she felt wonderfully strong and beautiful. Not small and meek. "It's like we're going to a lingerie ball, not a pajama party."

"It's definitely a pajama party. Sensual and casual, it's held in the lounge that we usually reserve for younger cruisers. There'll be bean-bags, popcorn, and a movie. But this time, alcoholic beverages will be served and some of the activities will be a little more risqué. It's a PDA party, rated VbC."

PDA stood for public displays of affection. She knew that much, and realizing they'd have an opportunity to be together in such a way set her sexual awareness to ultra-high. Heavy anticipation built between her legs as she wondered if, and how much, they'd actually participate.

Wanting to gauge how much he'd need to push her, Ford had chosen the specific event because of its nature. He already knew she got off on watching. Of course, he wasn't about to put his Charlie— Fuck! The sentiment felt more than temporary.

He shook his head, not only to shake the thoughts of her as his from his mind, but in realizing that no matter what, he wasn't going to put her on display. No. But a hint of public exhibition could be good if it primed her for his touch and made their coming together hotter than he knew it would be.

Seriously. Why was he thinking so hard on it? He'd never waited to have sex. Never anticipated being with a specific woman. He'd always seen what he wanted, went after it, and satisfied his need to get laid.

As he smoothed his thumb over the back of her hand, they stepped into the elevator. Ford settled her against his body, with her back to his chest. So damn beautiful. That's how she looked pressed against him. He'd had to force himself to leave her earlier, force himself to go away and let her work. If it had been up to him, he would have thrown all his plans out to sea and joined her in the cabin. He'd have stepped through that threshold, his job be damned, if only he hadn't believed that she needed to know *she* could have it all. A healthy balance of work and play. Something she craved, but didn't think she could have.

"Much more than beautiful," he whispered against her ear, meeting her gaze in the mirrored door. Dropping his shoulders and curling his body around her back, his fingers trailed down her arms, and he linked his hands beneath her breast and drew her closer. "How does the little heart feel, baby?"

"Sinful," she said. Pink colored her chest and she looked down to her feet. Perfect white teeth skimmed her lower lip and her body went stiff.

"No fucking way," he growled, immediately cupping her chin and lifting her face so she could see her reflection. "Don't look away. Look at us. Look at yourself." He waited for those big blue eyes to reappear in the mirror. "You don't have the option of looking away, Charlie. You need to see the gorgeous woman I see. You need to know she can have everything she's ever wanted, and you need to know she deserves it."

"Maybe." A slow curve shaped her lips and she gave a tiny nod. "Maybe while we're on this cruise it's doable. But in real life, what I want isn't compatible with what I can have." She turned in his hold and smiled up at him as the elevator came to a halt and the doors slid open. "Let's stay in the present and enjoy our night."

"Plan on it," he said, taking her small hand in his and leading her toward the lounge. Everything she'd ever wanted was compatible with what she needed. In the present moment and in *real life*. He'd show her.

An event staffer stopped them at the entrance. "Sorry, sir. Proper attire is required for entrance."

Of course it was. Ford kicked off his flip-flops, and flicked the button on his fly. Careful not to lose the contents of his pockets, he took off his jeans and folded them into a tight bundle at his left hand. Reaching for Charlie with his right, he strutted past the staffer in his boxer briefs and T-shirt.

Charlie's sweet chuckle pleased him. "You sleep in your underpants?"

"I sleep nude," he replied. "But seeing that my employees are tending bar, I figured a bit of coverage might be better for now."

"I think so," she agreed, still giggling. "It looks like Patrick, the bartender from our special place, has been assigned to this event."

Fuck, she was cute. The way she made him feel, he was glad he'd made sure Patrick was stationed here. It warmed his chest how she'd casually mentioned they had a special place, not to mention how other body parts reacted.

The woman's influence was morphing into so much more than a casual interest or temporary entertainment. Suddenly, what she meant was different from mind blowing sex and satiating his libido before his life went into high gear. Ford should have realized as much the moment he acknowledged he wasn't going to allow her to sail without him around to "look after" her.

He led them to a small table, draped with a floor-length black tablecloth, and invited her to scoot in across the crescent-shaped booth, which was also covered in a black fabric. If she noticed the additional outfitting of the lounge, she didn't comment on it. She simply slid in and made room for Ford to join her.

Patrick Swayze and Demi Moore worked the pottery wheel on the movie screen, as the server placed a bowl of popcorn on the table and took their drink order.

"This is one of the most romantic movies ever made," Charlie said, snuggling against his side. "A supernatural love story, proving the power of love does exist."

"This scene is sexy as hell," Ford replied, determined to keep it in the present and give her what she wanted. "I'd shape clay, or anything else, with you wearing that shirt any day."

With his fingers angling her face toward his, he brought his mouth to hers and licked along the line of her full lips until they parted and he tasted the addictive flavor of his Charlie. Tongues mingled, lips locked, and his mind filled with selfish images that he knew would make her wet and ready for him in the middle of the night.

Unfortunately, he wouldn't have her on their first night at sea. He could, however, make her realize how much he wanted her. He brushed the pad of his thumb across her lace-covered breast, then slipped under the soft material and circled the hard bud, taking his time as he kept his mouth sealed to hers. When he kissed her neck, and her breathing grew ragged, he moved her hand over his painful erection.

Small yet strong and determined fingers stroked him, sliding past the elastic of his boxers and wrapping around his cock. The other participants were too engrossed in their own activities to notice, and Ford liked the comfort of privacy in the public setting. Mostly because he knew what the thrill of exposure was doing to Charlie. "Take what you want, *chère*."

"I want you," she said, tangling her free hand into his hair and bringing her mouth to his. "I want to give you pleasure."

Only Patrick would possibly notice that the make out session with Charlie had gotten so heated, but Ford knew he could count on Patrick's discretion. The bartender was more than an employee. He was a friend.

The night before Patrick had married the love of his life, Rena, Ford had agreed to make her fantasy of having two men at once a reality. They'd fucked Rena every which way until thirty minutes before the ceremony. It was Ford who, while taking her mouth, had the sense to wash the sticky evidence of their night's activities from Rena's hair, while Patrick kneeled behind his then-fiancée's bent form and claimed her ass.

Hot as the memory was, he wasn't offering Charlie's mouth to anyone else.

"Want you so bad," he groaned against her neck and felt bumps form on her skin at his words. "I want that pretty little proper mouth of yours. I want to taste you, to bury myself inside you, and to hear you call my name as you shatter."

"Yes," she breathed, fisting him tight, and twisting her soft body against his in search of his lips with obvious excitement.

"Delicious," he said, reclaiming her mouth.

With an audible breath, Charlie broke the kiss and pulled away. She trailed a manicured fingertip up his chest and tapped his chin. Giving him a wicked grin, she quickly glanced at the other occupants in the room, licked her lips, and let her gaze skim to the shadow above his groin.

"It's my turn," she announced, folding her body beneath the coverage of the tablecloth and fitting herself between his legs. "Lift for me, honey." He heard the endearment and tangled his fingers in her soft as silk hair. When her hands were on either side of his hips, he lifted off the seat and she pulled his boxers down to his ankles.

They were breaking more than one rule, but he couldn't think past the fact that Charlie's breath swept over him and she was looking up at him with a pleading need in her beautiful eyes. He didn't get it.

Just a second earlier she'd seemed eager to take charge. Yet she was waiting for him.

Sipping on his vodka, he nodded and feathered a finger over her cheek encouraging her to take him in her mouth. "Yes, baby."

Soft lips went up his thighs. Her warm tongue licked over his balls, swirled, licked more, and she took first one, then the other, into her mouth. Pressure built on his spine, and she hadn't even reached his cock.

Tugging on her hair, he answered the question in those baby blues of whether her mouth was pleasing him, because yes, it was. He closed his eyes and dropped his head to the back of the seat, reveling in every sweep of her tongue as euphoric darkness swallowed his composure. Her lips closed around his left ball and suckled, then repeated the sweet torture on the right. She kept doing that, moaning soft noises of pleasure, like he was a treat to be cherished. She used both hands to stroke his shaft, and a grazing fingertip spread the moistness around the tip. She drove him mad with the need for her mouth. A battalion of red ants marched over his nerves, but in a very, very pleasurable manner. Sick. He was a grown man. It wasn't the first time he was in this position, so he shouldn't be about to lose it.

After a few minutes of being in Charlie's mouth, the sense to protect her head from bumping against the table disappeared because he concentrated on not coming too quickly. He felt her gentle strokes in every way and refused to have the sensations cease before he absolutely couldn't handle them any longer.

Charlie lapped up the side of his cock, her tongue warm and moist, as she continued to look up at him, silently urging him to watch, in the sexiest invitation of his life. He held the cloth away from her face, slid to the farthest edge of his seat, and watched as she took him fully into her mouth.

The gentle and tentative strokes disappeared. She fisted the base and sucked him deep until he hit the back of her throat. Holding his gaze as her cheeks hollowed and her tongue flicked, she worked him like she lived to give her man head at the dinner table.

"Want to take care of you," he said, as her head bobbed and she sucked harder. "Come up here."

She shook her head. He reached for her, pulled her slightly higher in his lap, and cupped her full breasts in his hands.

"Good thing you're such a tiny thing and can fit beneath this table. Between my thighs," he said, pinching the nipples he'd exposed. "Are you wet?"

She nodded, and he hit the back of her throat.

"Come up here for a bit. Let me take care of your sweetness. I want to feel that slippery heart against your heat, and when you're ready, we'll come together."

Her eyes went dark and her ear lowered toward her shoulder, but she shook her head no. "I take what I want," she rasped, between dipping her tongue into the slit at his tip, then swirling it around the edge of his head. "Now."

His balls drew up and he didn't dare, couldn't stop the pleasure from growing. She had him in her mouth, her throat working to accommodate his full length, and as he watched the beautiful and erotic intensity with which she gave to him, he lost himself.

Ford came with a force that made his thigh muscles clench, his breath hitch, and his heart pound so hard it could have broken a rib. Coming down from the explosive release, he reached for Charlie, as if needing to touch her and assure himself that she was real and not a figment of his imagination.

It took him several moments to steady his breath as Charlie swallowed and licked the last of his release, then scattered soft kisses on his thighs. She rested the side of her head on his leg and curled up against him with a content brightness illuminating her precious face.

"Come up here so I can kiss you," he managed at last. "Please, baby."

Chapter Sixteen

"I wasn't expecting that. My mind went dark and I can barely move my limbs. You give amazing head," Ford said. "Totally mind blowing."

"Thank you," she replied, her bravado wavering, but her ego stoked. He'd liked it. Considered it mind blowing. And Ford hadn't tried to control her head or move away from her. Receiving her mouth on him, he'd let her give and take as she'd pleased. And he'd liked it!

A sense of success fluttered in her chest and she took a deep breath. It had been a long time since she'd gone down on a man. She'd offered to do the same with James, but he'd insisted that no wife of his was going to perform like a ten-dollar hooker. At the thought, the pleasant fluttering balled into dead weight and settled in her gut. Would Ford think she was a wanton deviant because she enjoyed it?

No. Her hair fell against her face as she shook her head. She wasn't a deviant. James had been the problem. She wouldn't let him ruin her moment of bliss. Not again.

"You didn't come," Ford said, gently smoothing her hair behind her ear and caressing her cheek.

"Who's counting," she replied with a shrug.

"Not me," he replied. "But I'm dying to return the favor—first chance I get." Then he gently settled her against his side and dropped a kiss on her head. "I can't wait to be with you, no stupid rules, no limits. Just you and me."

She let out a long breath, relishing his words. Maybe it was his sexual acceptance that made him so appealing? Maybe it was the theme of the cruise? But at the moment, she wasn't going to think any further on it. She wasn't going to let negative thoughts from the past ruin her happiness.

"I'd like that, too," Charlie admitted, gaining another kiss on her head and a tight squeeze in his arms. Nestled against the man who allowed, even encouraged, her sexual explorations, Charlie relaxed and got into the movie and the pajama party theme.

"I can rectify that situation," Ford offered, sliding his palm up her thigh and tapping on the rhinestone heart between her legs. "Maybe I can't fit beneath the table, but I can be creative in other ways."

"Not now, Ford. Just hold me," she said. "I'd like to enjoy floating on cloud nine for a little longer. We're not keeping score."

A second drink later, with Demi Moore's character safe, and Patrick Swayze's character forever gone from her life, Charlie squeezed Ford's hand and turned her face up for another kiss.

"With pleasure," he responded. Sealing his mouth to hers and reinforcing how great it made her feel to be with a man that wasn't afraid of appearing vulnerable—even in public, even with the restrictions imposed on him because of his work position, he didn't hesitate to show her how he felt. He didn't hesitate to show her how she made him feel. His low groan reinforced her spirit. She barely knew the man, but she knew she wanted Ford in her life past the four nights at sea.

She smoothed her fingers over the five o'clock shadow that had settled there well after midnight, and rested her forehead to his. If only she could sleep in his arms, everything would be perfect. "Thanks for a great night, Ford. I never knew how exciting pajama parties could be."

"Pajama parties have a bad rep," he pointed out. "We'll have a movie night back home and I'll show you exactly how exciting they are."

It wasn't the first time Ford had mentioned them together—back home—but regardless, she didn't want to get her hopes up. She reminded herself that he'd also mentioned he wasn't a long-term-relationship kind of man. She *was* a LTR kind of woman, though. It would make any casual hookup in New York difficult to deal with. No matter how much she'd like to get to know him better, develop a relationship to take back home with her, she wasn't going to push her luck. She'd take their temporary arrangement for what it was. Temporary.

Charlie had to keep reciting temporary. Temporary. It had taken all of one day for Charlie to fall in love and lose her heart. Temporary. Yes, temporary.

"Do you have enough information to write the feature?" Ford asked, bringing up work and grounding her expectations.

"Not yet," she replied. "I'm surprised I have so much in such a short amount of time, but I'd like to see how things develop. I want to make this the strongest piece I can write, and I want it to open doors for future projects." She looked up into his face and found his jaw set tight.

"I'm willing to be booted off the ship in Cozumel, as long as you're with me. We could make our own way back home."

"I don't like airplanes," she said, pointing out the obvious.

"We'll drive," he offered. "I'll get you back on time to meet your deadline. You can write that kick-ass piece in the car while I drive. It'll give us a chance to discuss what I've observed on other cruises. There's plenty of romance on the high seas."

"What about your job? You'd burn your bridges."

"Georgiou will understand. I won't burn any bridges," Ford said. "And as for my duties, they're complete. Ramos has already stepped into his responsibilities and is doing great. The ship doesn't need my services, and I'll find a different way to supplement the money. I would much rather spend my last few days, before my world implodes, with a beautiful and sexy woman, driving to New York and getting to know every inch of her body while I do so."

The muscles low in her abdomen tightened. Heat rushed over her skin, but her mind shouted that she remain focused. She needed to shut it down before she gave in and was gallivanting across the US and Mexico just to spend more temporary time with a man.

"I don't mean to pry, and you definitely don't need to share if you don't want to, but you never elaborated on your future plans. So far, I gather it has something to do with your own café and that it's in New York." There. She'd turned the focus back on professional aspirations and managed to avoid dreaded personal relationship talk.

"You're on point," Ford confirmed, stretching his long legs and relaxing against the seat. "As Eugenia so eloquently puts it, and I must admit I like the way she puts it, I plan on building a java empire of my own, starting with a location that helped fund my graduate education."

"So you want to own and operate your own café?"

"More than one," he said, straightening in his seat and placing his hands on the table. "I worked at a place in the Village while I was at NYU. It was always busy, not only because the coffee and sweets were great, but because every single customer saw it as his place."

"That's nice. A place to belong," Charlie said, thinking of Mr. Wile's little shop a block from her apartment. If the old man had the energy to update the décor, add a few trendy pastries, and hire an extra barista or two so they could actually step out from behind the counter, he'd double his business. Not like he was doing bad or anything, but there were down times in the day. Down times that customers could use to make his little place their own. "We have a tiny spot like that in my neighborhood, but the owner is tired and doesn't want to do more than he already is doing. It's too much for him."

"I get that," Ford said, placing a big hand on hers and smoothing his thumb over her knuckles. The action immediately took her thoughts from Mr. Wile's café's potential, but she closed her eyes and forced herself to remain in the conversation.

"My old boss is ready to retire," Ford continued. "Almost. Thankfully, he's held out from selling. I approached him two and a half years ago and told him about my vision. We discussed what I'd like to make happen, and he really liked my ideas. I mean really. He's given me the opportunity to come into his business, grow and expand it, and he'll eventually phase out of the day-to-day operation and into full retirement."

"It's set? He's ready to retire and just hand you the café?"

"He's not handing it to me. I'm buying into it," Ford explained. "He's not stepping away from the business entirely, but he'll be taking on a passive role as things develop. He really wants to retire and visit with his children, who live in Colorado and California, as much as possible. Truth is, the man deserves it. He's worked hard and has built a solid foundation that I could take to a different level with more work and new energy."

Much like the energy Mr. Wile's place needed. She nodded and gave him a smile.

"The success of the current store gives us an advantage in the startup of multiple locations," he said, surprising her with the continuation of his explanation of his business plans, while taking her mouth in a kiss.

Tasting him on her lips, she wondered how he could go from one to the other. How he could kiss her and send tingles through her body while speaking about business was foreign to her. She'd never experienced it before.

It didn't take a long discussion to see that Ford wasn't buying a job. No. He was building an industry model with hundreds of jobs. His plans included two new locations in Manhattan by the end of the year, and five more the following, expanding to Boston, Washington, and Chicago quickly after that.

"Impressive," she admitted.

"Not yet," he replied. "All of it, even the first location, is still on paper. I have a lot to accomplish before it can be called impressive. Next week I'm meeting with landlords for location number two. When the third store opens, then you can tell me you think it's impressive."

Once again, he referred to them in the future. Once again, her chest ached from the impending loss.

"What about you, gorgeous career woman? Have you always wanted to be a reporter?"

"No." She shook her head, recalling how she'd ended up at Columbia University, which eventually allowed her the opportunity to land the job at *City Wings*. Her father had insisted that she needed to pull her eyes from reading fiction and use her time efficiently. He claimed her undergraduate degree in literature was the cause of her unattached love status.

A degree in English Literature had kept her from developing a relationship with the right man. At least a journalism degree, if used correctly, would have her interacting with proper subjects. According to her mother, she'd interview powerful and rising men.

"I've always had my head stuck in a book," she explained. A chill crawled on her skin and she rubbed her palms over her arms to chase it away. "I fell in love with reading when I was eight, probably before that, but I remember finishing the *Little House on the Prairie* series and moving on to 'mature' books." She made air quotes around the word *mature*. "Or so I thought. At first, I dreamed of escaping to Katherine Paterson's Terabithia. I learned that tragedy could happen anywhere, even in a magical kingdom, and I was hooked. I wanted to rewrite their fate. I did rewrite it."

"Didn't they make that into a movie?" Ford asked, shifting his body and cradling her against his warmth.

"They did. Just not with my ending," she said wistfully. "Plus, their situations were very different from my own. But for some reason, the book totally hooked me. Anyway, it was while we were on a family ski vacation that I found I could soothe my stressed emotions with fictional characters. I didn't know about the marital problems my parents were having, but I could hear the arguments and it hurt too much. Fiction was my escape."

"I'm glad your parents worked it out," Ford said, pulling her closer and brushing his lips over her forehead. "It's hard for a kid to be in the middle of her parents' drama."

"It was," she admitted. His words registered, and she looked up and studied his dark eyes. He knew of her parents. This wasn't a casual hookup. He knew. Their conversation sounded more like a real date than a sexual encounter.

"I'm sorry," he said in a low tone. "Sorry you had to go through that. Your brothers, too. Your family's firm has a strong reputation for family values, and meeting you, I can see it's not just a public image."

He knew about the family business. The knot in her throat tightened and her body went stiff. He couldn't have known when they'd met. She'd bumped into him by accident. He wasn't like her ex. Was he? Had he planned on being at the right place at the right time?

No. It wasn't possible. He'd had plans with Eugenia.

"They worked it out," she said, intertwining her fingers and twisting her hands in her lap. Swallowing her dread, she pushed air past the knot in her throat, and asked the question she wanted so badly to avoid, but needed him to provide a good answer to. "How do you know about the family firm?"

"Charlie, the Stanton name is all over financial publications," he said. No hesitation. No retreat to cover his knowledge. "A quick Internet search, and you appear beside your dad and brothers in numerous results. I'm well aware of your family's place in the investment world. Your mom isn't written about as much, but there are many family photos of her and your dad with captions at various charity events."

His thumb continued caressing her knuckles, his body remained comfortable, and he didn't show any regret in searching her name. He spoke about it like it was expected.

"I'm also sorry about the asshole you married," he added, a muscle in his cheek twitching and his features going hard. "I had the displeasure of meeting James Norrington a few years ago, and the man was a total ass. Don't know what you ever saw in him, but I do know you're better off without the dick. At least he won't be bothering you for the next two years."

He knew an awful lot. Knew James was in jail for embezzlement. Knew how he'd tried to throw Charlie under the bus and shift the blame on her, when she had known nothing about anything. Like she'd ever do something so terrible to her family.

Charlie wasn't sure what to think of Ford's knowledge, so she made a decision to shut it down. Shut it all down. The night had to end.

"I'm tired," she said. "Are you ready to go?"

"Sure," Ford replied, sliding out from behind their table and standing. He offered her his hand. "We have a full day tomorrow, and I don't want my Charlie skipping any events because she's too tired to participate."

His tone was easy, his body relaxed, and he didn't give any physical indication of feeling uncomfortable. It was as if he dismissed the possibility of the James nightmare holding any truth. If so, he was right. It didn't. Yet, she insisted on space between them as they walked. Ford clearly didn't approve. His fingers gripped hers something fierce. His hand didn't swing, but was stiff and held hers tight against his thigh.

She'd messed up. Let her guard down and ignored her place. A woman with her family's standing in the community had certain expectations to live up to, responsibilities, but instead, she'd just gone down on her knees, hadn't even bothered to hide her over-the-moon pleasure about it, and had sucked off a man who knew who she was. She'd even thanked him.

A Stanton woman didn't do things like that. Judgment was inevitable. Shivers, and not the good kind, caused her skin to prickle with the backlash. James hadn't bothered to disguise his displeasure with her sexual appetite, even in the privacy and dark of their bedroom, and he had gone as far as to discuss the unpleasant, unnecessary, and unsanitary, as he put it, hype of oral sex at a supposedly intimate business dinner. That dinner had been just after she'd tried to join him in the shower and been rejected.

It was all on James. First, he'd turned her down repeatedly. Second, he'd discussed—admittedly without specifics—but he *had* discussed their sex life with business associates. She'd never have guessed a man would act in such a manner at a business event. He was the messed-up one. Not her. Right?

"Baby." Ford's deep voice broke into her thoughts and she found her back pressed against the wall outside her cabin, his hands on either side of her head. "I'm sorry if the mention of the dick upset you. I won't talk about him. He's in the past. You're free of him. You're you."

Tears threatening to spill, she stared at his shoulder. Current need and desire battled with stern and disparaging expectations from her past. She wanted more than a sterile marriage. Needed more than limited interaction to procreate. Charlie craved the kind of passion that made her feel desirable, enough magnetism between her and her man that had them rushing back to each other every single moment available, and the undeniable attraction that set the butterflies dancing in her belly with a simple touch.

Shit. She craved those things. And for a single day, she'd experienced them with Ford, a complete stranger. A stranger who now knew her true identity. Any possibility she had with Ford, a self-proclaimed no long-term relationship man, was over.

"*Chère*, I'm not sure what is going on inside that beautiful head of yours, but I do know that I don't like your frown," he said. "I'm here. Nobody else. For as long as you're with me, it's on me to keep a smile on your face."

"On you? Why?"

"Because I choose to." Ford touched her chin and tilted her face to his. Looking into her eyes, eyes that lacked the brightness he'd seen from her all day, he was lost as to why she'd shut down and withdrawn. "You're with me. I have your back, Charlie." And he wanted all of her. Fuck the cruise line restrictions. If he made love to her, showed her how—made love? Where the fuck did that come from? They needed sex. Wild, animalistic fucks to satisfy their bodies and get on with scheduled life.

"Don't think, Charlie," he said, dropping his hand to her waist.

"Write the article. Do your work. And stay here, with me, in the present. I want you with me."

Yes. He wanted her. It was selfish, but he really wanted her. He needed to sate the need to have her, every which way, make it so damn good for her that the brightness in her eyes would light up the darkest of rooms.

She didn't reply, but hope sparked in the blue of her eyes. He'd said something right.

"I'll see to my work in the morning, and I'll let you write or do whatever it is you need to do for your work." He lowered his head and pressed his lips against the soft curve of her neck. "But after breakfast, you're mine. Good thoughts. Big smiles. Explosive orgasms. All mine."

The way her breath hitched at the mention of orgasms, and the manner in which she arched into him the moment his tongue tasted her delicious skin told him what he needed to know. His Charlie's physical desires had been knocked down by some asshole, probably the same asshole she'd married and who had tried to swindle her family out of tons of money. There was some warped sense of guilt that stole her light and weighed her down. Guilt that was unfounded. She held no responsibility in those actions. She wasn't wrong in wanting a good sex life.

"With me, you'll have what you need." Realizing he'd spoken aloud, he didn't explain when she turned a questioning gaze on him. He cupped her backside and lifted her onto her toes as he pulled her tight against him. The blush in her cheeks confirmed his instincts, so he pressed her further. He was going to make it okay for her to want.

"During this sailing, you're mine," he continued, bending down to accommodate her stature against his tall frame. His fingers roamed beneath the lingerie and skimmed the warmth between her legs. "This is mine." His left hand slid between her thighs, and sweetness coated his fingers. "These are mine." He moved his right hand to her breast and pushed back the lace triangle, uncovering a rose-tinged nipple and circling his thumb around the tip until it stood at attention. "You don't choose what is good for you and what is not. I do. You take what I give you, any way I choose to give it to you. Understand?"

She nodded, her hands linked behind his neck as she attempted to keep her feet on the floor. He didn't allow her to find her own balance. If she did, she could turn away and shut him out. Wrapping his arm tighter around her, he palmed her between her legs and lifted her off the ground, sliding his hand against her wet heat.

"You remain primed and sweet for me," he ground, nipping at her hard nipple and tearing away the material covering her other breast to pinch the tip.

She glanced at her exposed breast, having no idea that his body shielded her from the security camera's view, but she didn't object as heat colored her creamy skin. Charlie's breath came fast, and his body reacted to the brightness he saw in her eyes. Brightness glazed with desire. It was back. He'd brought it back. He had guessed correctly. She longed to be told, needed handling, and in turn gained security and relief when he stepped up with commands.

"You're going to lock the contents of your goodie basket into the safe. You will not indulge without me tonight. I will decide when and where you come next. Your orgasms are no longer up to you." There. He'd taken the control that weighed her down. Reluctantly, he lowered her feet to the floor. He kept a hand at her back, liking the fact that it took her some time to find her balance.

"I'm going to count to five," he said, pressing his fingers into her heated flesh. Wanting her to think of nothing but his words as she drifted to sleep, he issued an ultimatum. "If that sweet ass isn't locked inside your cabin by the time I'm done, I'm taking you right here."

She gasped, but didn't move.

"One," he began, sliding the keycard in the slot. "Bend you at the waist and satisfy my need. I'd appreciate it if you do stay."

Her hand nervously rubbed at her neck. She held her breath as she glanced down the hall and then back at him.

"Two." The lock clicked and he pushed on the door. "Make that little charm play against your clit."

"Ford," she gasped, settling her hand on his chest. "How am I supposed to sleep with your vivid storytelling fresh in my mind?"

"Three." He touched a fingertip to her mouth, and pushed past her lips, which suckled him in. "Make you drip pleasure down your thighs as I take you from behind."

Her lips parted, mouth gaped, and her pupils dilated.

"Four."

She turned and ducked past him and into the cabin. The lock clicked into place.

"Five," he breathed, dropping his forehead to the cold metal of the door. Fuck. Images of burying himself in her lush warmth burned in his brain. She'd been correct about vivid images causing insomnia. He would certainly never get any sleep.

He let out a long breath and turned away. Pulling his phone from his pocket as he walked to the stairs, he typed.

I'll pick you up at 9:45. Be done with your work. Be ready. You walk out to me and surrender yourself when I knock. Sweet dreams, baby.

Good night, Ford.

Chapter Seventeen

Charlie's gloriously pleased expression had disappeared with no explanation. He wasn't sure of the trigger, but it had happened at the point when he'd mentioned her ex. He could have kicked himself for doing that to her. He wanted to shake her and make her understand life wasn't about past hurts. And he would have, if he truly believed she was hung up on the asshole. Something else silenced her light and set worry lines on her forehead. More than James's sleazy money scam. More than the publicity of their divorce.

Rinsing the lather from his skin, he stepped from the shower stall and toweled off. He was in over his head. This obsession with Charlie had seeped into his pores and gnawed at him as only a woman's distress could. As only a woman who mattered could.

He grabbed a second towel and swiped it over his head. The unfamiliar pressure in his chest grew, so he resolved to get to sleep as soon as possible and to wake in the morning, thinking with his cock, not his heart. Thinking with his cock was easier than feeling. He'd get his fill of the woman, give her what she needed to break away from the chains that held her back, and through mutual sexual gratification—fucking awesome sex, he knew—they'd get on with the daily routines of their lives.

After tossing and turning in bed, and replaying his words in her mind for hours, Charlie managed to get ninety minutes of sleep. Not nearly what was required for the Sunrise Yoga class she was meeting Quinn for. It was just six thirty. They had half an hour of positions to accomplish and hold before the sun climbed into the sky. She should walk to his cabin and cancel, explain how the pajama party had kept her up too late. She absolutely would not admit that it was Ford's whispered promise of taking her in the hallway that had kept her awake into the wee hours of the morning.

She inched her way out of bed and into the bathroom, still trying to interpret his words. Would he? How? Where? Those questions had both thrilled and scared her in the dark.

A knock sounded on the door, and she realized she'd missed her chance to crawl back into bed. She wrapped a towel around her and stood behind the door as she motioned for Quinn to come in.

"You didn't need to dress for me, baby doll," he said, dropping an all-too-awake kiss on her head and swatting her ass. "Looks like someone needs some kitty stretches because she may have stayed in the very agreeable downward-dog position way too long last night." He looked down at her knees, one of which was a little red and scratched, and made a show of raising his brow.

"Ha ha ha, you're not funny," she said, pushing past him and opening the top drawer. She held up her favorite Lululemon pants, with pink and maroon splatters, that smoothed over her like a glove, and a solid maroon double strap bra. "Turn," she said, spinning her finger and asking for Quinn's back. "I need to dress."

"You walk out in those, I'll have a boner the whole class," he grumbled.

"Deal," she said, stepping into the pants and settling them just above her hips. She pulled on the top, bent over and fit her boobs into it properly, then gave him the okay to turn back around. "Hair up, then we can go."

"Damn, baby doll. You have a fine ass," he said, as she leaned over the nightstand for a hair tie. "A man could lose himself in that little piece of heaven all night."

From behind. Ford's voice sounded in her mind. She glanced back at Quinn, but didn't respond.

"Don't get me wrong, there's plenty of you to enjoy. You're the complete package, but we're not even going to speak about your incredible mind or beautiful heart. We're sticking to tits, ass, and pussy." He gave her a slow head-to-toe inspection and nodded. "Regardless of the definition or what we limit our conversation to, you're the total package, baby doll. Like I told you, that bastard is one lucky man. He gets inside that sweet ass and he's going to lose his mind."

"Stop," she said and sidestepped his big frame. Combing her fingers through her hair, she pulled it into a loose bun atop her head. "We're not going to spend the morning talking about dick and ass."

Damn, she'd spent the night thinking about those very things.

"What's up, Charlie? You don't like sex like that?"

She couldn't look at him, but he sounded sincere. Even concerned. So she just shrugged. "I don't know."

"You've never been—"

"No," she interrupted. "Stop."

"Okay, baby doll. I didn't know." Regret colored his good looks, creeping up his neck and settling in the pulsing at his temples. "Just wanted to tease you." He gathered her into his arms and pressed her cheek to his chest. "I was trying to wake you up and make you laugh. I didn't realize you were sensitive about it and it would bother you."

"I'm not sensitive." She was just totally inexperienced. "I *was* married." Married to a man who scheduled sex two times a week, in bed, with the lights off, and the routine lasted less than ten minutes for each session. "Maybe just a little sensitive," she admitted.

"Was he a bad lover?"

She shrugged, and then nodded.

"Your first?"

More nodding. James was practically her only . . . anything. Other than a few alcohol-encouraged heavy make-out sessions before him, and some attempts at foreplay since him, their scheduled missionary events made up the bulk of her experience. Until Ford, of course.

"Anyone better since?"

Shrug. She didn't think he was referring to Ford. Her vibrator didn't count. And while she'd dated, fooled around a little, there was nothing and no one who had rocked her world. But then again, there was Ford.

"I got my best kiss ever yesterday," she whispered into Quinn's shirt. "Best anything. Yesterday."

"It's about time. You deserve the best of everything. Just look at yourself in the mirror." He tickled the small of her back and kissed the top of her head. "I hate to say it, but Luis and I talked about the way you fit with him. You look real good together. As if you're made for each other. You should see the hungry way he devours the pretty sight of you."

"Ford says and does the right things. He meets every requirement on a hot guy checklist. And that's the problem," she said, pulling away and fixing her hair. She picked up the eye drops near the mirror and hoped they'd remove the red in her eyes. "I can get used to that."

"And why is that a problem?" Quinn asked, reaching into the bathroom and grabbing two folded towels from the shelf.

"Because," she said, leading them out of the room, "he's not a relationship kind of man." She glanced up at her friend and inhaled some courage to make her admission. Damn, they'd already shared so much. "I don't want to get hurt."

"No guy is a relationship guy until *that* person comes along." Quinn fell in step beside her and wrapped a reassuring arm around her waist. "I'm willing to bet you're that person for him. He's very into you. It doesn't look like a temporary fling to me." They reached the stairs and he gave her a questioning glance.

She shook her head. "Elevator."

"Baby girl, you have an opportunity to have the best sex of your life. Don't ruin that chance." Quinn hit the call button, and they watched the elevator ascend to their floor. "I think Ford knows how to do it right and make it good. Real good. Let him take the reins, and you enjoy the ride."

"Like I can do anything else," she breathed. "Anyway, we're kind of screwed. We can't be alone on the ship. Can't hook up in the traditional way. You know he can't come into the passenger cabins without losing his job."

"I know. He mentioned how he needs to invest this bonus he's receiving to make his plans a reality." This time Quinn shrugged. "But I'm surprised he's allowing his position to rule his actions. While you were working in your cabin, Luis and Ford talked about the benefits of self-employment and business startups for a long time yesterday. I get that he wants the money to make the transition smooth, but I thought he'd be able to come up with it some other way. So I'm not sure why a regular job matters to him so much."

"It doesn't," she said, stepping into the glass elevator and staring at the ornate promenade at her feet. "He's suggested we disembark in Cozumel. Says he's willing to drive us to New York so we could have privacy."

"You know Cozumel is an island, right?"

"Yes, I know. Ford said we could ferry to the mainland," she added.

"Then why not?" Quinn asked. "Take him up on it. Let loose and enjoy."

The corners of her lips immediately turned up in a smile. She'd heard that before. Said it herself. Funny how Quinn would use the same words. She went up on her toes and gave her new friend a quick peck as the doors opened.

"It's my job," she explained, grabbing a towel off his shoulder and turning toward the group that had gathered for the class. "It's too important to me. I want my byline. I want my name on the masthead, and in a very prominent way, one day. It's going to be hard, rewarding work. Plus, I want to prove that I have more in me than my family thinks. I can't leave the ship without all the material I need."

Quinn nodded and collected two mats off a pile. He handed one to Charlie, taking her elbow and holding her still. He leaned down, as if about to share a state secret, and kissed her cheek. "Some things are worth the risk, Charlie."

"I figured that out, my friend. I'm in."

Forty-five minutes of stretches and deep breathing did their job in relaxing and refreshing Charlie. Her disappointment had cleared and her doubts about a physical relationship with Ford had faded. He knew who she was, knew about her family, and yet he hadn't changed the way he'd treated her. Ford didn't handle her with kid gloves because she was a Stanton. He treated her like a woman he wanted beneath him in bed. And she was a woman who wanted to be beneath him, above him, anywhere near him.

"Thank you," she told Quinn as he handed her a skinny latte. "For the coffee and the advice. You're a good friend."

"Yeah," he grumbled with a grin on his face. "My pleasure."

Carrying a plate of mini pastries, they headed back up to sit on deck and enjoy the morning. "What was his name?" Quinn asked. "Your husband's."

"Ex-husband," she corrected. "James."

"How long were you together?"

"We were together for almost three years, married and living as husband and wife for seven months, then fighting in divorce court for twenty-two months." She sipped on her latte, grateful it was all behind her. "He thought the longer he could drag it out, the more money he'd get out of us—until all his doings came to light."

"Gold digger then?"

"Totally," she confirmed. "Good thing he's in the past. The lawyers made the prenup stick. Daddy terminated his contract. Then he got arrested for embezzling. He's serving time."

"So, James was a gold-digger crook who sucked in bed."

"No. He didn't suck or want to be sucked," she said, laughing at the predictable sex routine he'd insisted on. "Tuesdays and Fridays. No sucking."

"His loss. You're hot."

"Thank you." She was lucky to have found a confidant like Quinn.

Ford had a full day at sea to court, yes court, his woman. He intended to do so with everything he had. Charlie pulling away had raised red flags, not only for them, but also for him personally. A damn alarm had gone off in his mind, and he had no choice than to rethink his no-relationship policy. He'd thought. He'd decided.

Charlie was worth changing his policy. He wanted the chance at a relationship with Miss Charlene Stanton.

So after his morning meeting with Ramos, he shopped for more dresses. The choices had been limited, so he'd spent over an hour inspecting and touching each dress in the ship's boutique in order to find the perfect ones. They needed to be sweet but sexy, and totally classy while chic. They needed to be like Charlie.

He ordered flowers to be delivered with coffee and breakfast at a quarter to nine. He instructed the cabin porter to deliver the boxes of dresses he'd finally settled on, each with a pair of pretty panties; he included a handwritten note instructing her to wear the complete ensemble of her choosing. He planned to have a whole month's worth of Friday night dates in a single evening.

At one minute past nine, his phone vibrated. He looked down at the message on the screen and smiled.

How do I choose? Luv them! Thank you!

He would court the woman, just like his *grand-mère* used to tell him a woman dreamed of being wooed. *Grand-mère* always said it took time and effort to gain a woman's trust. Grand gestures were for show. It was the little things that captured a woman's affection.

"Remember," *Grand-mère* would say, "a lady wants to be cherished and feel secure. She wants to know she can depend on a man to know her heart and to deliver on his promises. You manage to give her mind and heart such gifts, she'll be your greatest *trésor, mon petit pirate*."

Ford had never cared to possess such a treasure before. But Charlie, well, she was worth having. He'd follow his grandmother's advice and slow things down.

Sex could wait if it meant building a relationship with Charlie. Sneaking around on the ship wasn't good enough for her. She'd almost slipped through his hands the night before. He wouldn't let that happen. He'd give her security and cherishment.

They'd be off the ship, alone, in Cozumel on Saturday.

At a quarter to ten, he texted. You ready, baby?

Yes. ☺ came her immediate reply.

He rounded the corner and walked to her door. Before he had a chance to knock, it opened and she greeted him with a beautiful smile.

"Thank you," Charlie said, holding her skirt in each hand and twirling for his approval. "They're all adorable; I had a hard time choosing which one to wear first."

"You chose well," he said, placing his hand on her waist and tugging her into the doorway and against his body as he lowered his head and brushed his mouth over her pink lips. "Good morning, *chère*."

"Good morning," she replied, tilted up her face, and cheerfully gave him her mouth. She let out a soft breath. "Good morning, honey."

A tightening in his gut had him craving to keep her close. He dropped his forehead to hers and closed his eyes, savoring the moment. She'd used the *honey* endearment. That was nice. Very nice.

"It is now," he said, smoothing her hair away from her face. "You're breathtaking in the morning, *chère*, absolutely beautiful."

"Thank you," she said in a soft voice. "That's sweet."

He kissed the pink on her cheek, lingering and inhaling her addictive scent. "While I'd like to stay like this for a long time, preferably alone and inside your cabin, I don't want to swim to Cozumel in order to see you tomorrow." He traced the pretty shape of her lips with his thumb and looked into her eyes. "You have your key?"

"Yes," she replied, fitting it into his hand.

"Good." He laced his fingers with hers and pulled her into the corridor. "Need anything from the room?"

"No. I'm ready." She let the door lock. "Did some morning yoga with Quinn, had two breakfasts, drank tons of coffee, and even managed to get some thoughts typed out for the feature. I'm good to go."

"Yoga?" He asked as they walked, surprised she'd been up on deck while he was working with Ramos. "You were up that early?"

"Quinn kind of forced me," she admitted. "But watching the sun rise on the horizon was well worth it. Not to mention the latte he bribed me with."

"The baristas are pretty kick-ass," he added, releasing her hand and draping his arm over her shoulders. "Glad you enjoyed the latte."

"I also enjoyed the coffee and pastries you sent." She smiled up at him and that gut clenching happened again. "It was very thoughtful of you. Made me feel looked after by a special guy. Also got me to sit down and type some thoughts as I sipped more coffee on the balcony. Thank you."

"You're very welcome, *chère*." Score one for him and his *grand-mère's* advice. It was the little things. Charlie thought he was a special guy because of coffee.

"So, with the coffee, exercise, and writing already tackled, do you need anything before the workshop?" Ford asked, checking his watch as he started down the staircase. The event was in the theatre. The blindfold required was in his back pocket.

She squeezed his hand, and he stopped on the landing. Glancing back at her, he grinned. "Forgot the e-cig?"

"Actually, no. I've thrown it out." She shrugged and pursed her lips. "Seems like I've been presented with a pretty good alternative and don't have a craving for it. However, I do have a craving for a long, slow, and proper toe-curling kiss."

He stepped up, wrapped his arm around her waist, and slanted his mouth over hers. Their first official date of the day began.

Chapter Eighteen

A VbC, vanilla but curious, workshop was an intimidating way to start their day. Charlie tightened her fingers in Ford's hand, and he immediately stopped at the entrance to the theater and kissed her—again.

"I'm not really into whips or chains," she breathed against his lips.

"No whips or chains, baby." He grinned, met her gaze, and skimmed his thumb down her cheek, stroking comfort through her antsy body with that simple touch. "Promise. No worries."

The nerves in her belly settled and warm tingles moved up her spine. Her uneasiness quieted, replaced by eager anticipation, and she decided she'd follow no matter where he led.

"Morning." The deep masculine voice had her glancing over her shoulder. Tyler lifted his chin in greeting, sidestepped around them, and guided a blushing Grace into the theatre. Charlie had expected to see them here when Ford had announced the nature of the event. After the way in which Tyler had gathered Grace off the stage and made an immediate exit, she could imagine Grace's night with the man.

"Good-morning," Emma and Grayson said in unison, surprising Charlie, especially with the hold Grayson had on Emma and the obvious way he'd made sure she'd follow. Grayson wasn't letting her go.

"Wow. That I wasn't expecting," Charlie said, as the obviously coupled professionals strolled past them.

"Things have a way of moving fast on the sea," Ford said against her hair, kissing the side of her temple and draping his arm around her shoulders. "A cruise, especially a singles cruise, encourages people to admit hidden desires. And there's a time limit to realize them. So people let their guards down and look for what they want. Relationships grow in fast-forward. I've seen it often, and you can quote me on that."

They walked down the aisle and took two seats in the row their new friends occupied. Despite being together, there were empty spots separating each couple, effectively allowing them the space to be alone. Charlie held Ford's hand, looked at the stage and waited for the group leader to begin.

"Good-morning, lovers." Surfer dude Bodhi waved at the audience.

Some participants waved. Others nodded. More returned the morning salutation.

"From the smiles on the beautiful faces looking back at me, I know you've all had an eventful and pleasurable night. Some with a sweet kiss on deck, others with a messy tangle between the sheets, but you're here, bright and early, as couples and a few moresomes. One way or another, you've hooked up and have decided to take the next step in your relationship." He pumped a hand above his head. "Give yourselves a hand for making the choice to attend Submission 101."

Were they taking the next step in their relationship? Ford may have sent her breakfast, may have even gone out of his way to buy her pretty dresses, but they, and their so-called relationship, had an expiration date.

She shook her head, negating the thoughts. She was going to let loose and have fun. Fun for at least two-and-a-half days. On Monday, when the ship was back in Miami, she'd deal with her aching heart.

"Contrary to common belief, submission is not about allowing a partner to use you and your body for his or her pleasure. It is about trusting the person you submit to. It is about earning the trust so that your partner or partners submit to you. Trust. It's a two-way street, my friends."

From the corner of her eye, Charlie saw Grace stretch and whisper into Tyler's ear. His large palm smoothed over her hair, and he kissed her temple. Emma and Grayson sat with their backs straight, hands linked in Grayson's lap and eyes trained on the stage.

Charlie wet her parched lips, wondering what she and Ford looked like to others. Was the expiration date looming over their heads visible to their friends?

"Stop thinking so hard," Ford said. "It's a simple workshop, baby." That's all it was. But she already wanted more. When she'd realized Ford knew who she was, knew about her family, doubt had entered her mind about the agreement they'd had regarding their sexual play. But when she'd also realized he had no further agenda, she'd relented to carnal desires and decided she was in the game. Her morning chat with Quinn had solidified her decision. She wanted great sex, needed great sex, and being with Ford guaranteed great sex. It was her heart she worried about.

Then Ford went thoughtful on her, giving her hope that her heart wouldn't shatter. She didn't know how to feel. She also wouldn't choose to walk away.

"We're going to make this enjoyable," Bodhi continued. "Trust isn't meant for only sex. It's continuous and necessary in building a relationship."

Shit. Relationship . . . again.

"Submissives, please stand."

Ford put pressure on her elbow and urged Charlie to her feet. "Please, *chère.*"

Standing, she joined Emma two seats over from her; then her mouth dropped when Tyler unfolded his long body and stood. She glanced down at Grace, who was tugging on his hand as if asking him to sit and for her to stand instead. He shook his head and remained standing.

Confused, Charlie looked back at Ford who spoke low. "Two-way street."

"Also contrary to popular myth, it's the submissive who holds the power. A submissive chooses where to place trust," Bodhi continued. "By standing, you're empowering your partner. It is your choice to do so. Trust is yours to share. Power is yours to share. No doubt, it's a huge responsibility you're handing to someone else, but it is the Dominant's place to know what you want, give it to you, and keep you safe in the interim."

With those words, everyone but Ford faded into the background for Charlie. He'd keep her safe. And he'd already delivered on her wants. She reached back and offered him her hand. He took it.

"Those of you in the back of the room need to come forward for the next step," Bodhi instructed. "There are small baskets beneath the seats in the first ten rows. Dominants, please take the supplied handcuffs and secure your submissive's hands at the small of his or her back."

Ford stood behind her and fit the lightweight toy around her wrists.

"Made of plastic, they serve only as a slight restraint—one that could easily be broken with a tug. They are a reminder. A symbol."

But Charlie didn't feel the need to tug. She settled into position, comfortable with the feel of Ford's fingers at her wrists.

"The handcuffs don't fit Tyler. He handed Grace the black scarf meant to be used as a blindfold so she could secure his wrists," Ford said into her ear.

Instantly, Charlie stopped from turning to look at Tyler and Grace and stared up at Ford. "Blindfold?"

"Could you imagine him in pink cuffs?" Ford continued.

"I can't imagine him as a submissive," Charlie said, intrigued as to why the big, tough-looking man would volunteer to be one. Tyler stood straight, loomed over Grace, yet his demeanor was accepting and soft. Yes, soft.

"Next, please use the black scarf to cover your sub's eyes," Bodhi said. "You accept full responsibility for them and their comfort."

Ford handed the blindfold in his basket to Grayson, who in turn handed it to Grace. Grayson motioned for Grace to tie it around Tyler's head quickly, as the large man, his hands tied at his back, had leaned down and was waiting on her.

A pink satin mask appeared in front of Charlie, so she closed her eyes and waited as Ford settled it over her eyes. "You knew?"

"I've worked this event before, *chère*. They change the details, but the concept is the same. I had a good idea we'd need a blindfold. This one matches the flowers on your dress. And besides, you please me in pink."

As warmth filled her chest at his statement, she made a mental note to wear more pink. She liked pleasing him.

"The last item in your basket is a list," Bodhi explained. "You're going on a treasure hunt. First four teams to return with all the items on the list win a tandem parasailing adventure over the crystal-clear waters of Cozumel."

"We got this one," she whispered conspiratorially. "You know the ship better than anyone else here."

She felt, more than heard, his chuckle, and leaned back against his chest. Strong hands closed around her body and his chin rested on her shoulder. He kissed the side of her neck, sending tingles through her. "I'll try my best."

Bodhi read off the rules of the hunt and instructed them to collect their loot in the baskets. "On your mark. Get set. Go!"

"Lucky we sat near the aisle," Ford said, turning her to the right and pasting his body against her back. "Take three steps and turn right. Two steps, then I'll squeeze gently when you need to step up. We'll repeat until we're out of the theatre."

The most difficult step was the first one, but Charlie managed. She turned right on the third, knowing they were in the aisle.

"Two small steps, then step up," he reminded.

She took them, and his fingers gently squeezed her hips. She felt for the stair, placed her thankfully non-heeled sandal on it, and continued. "Good girl. Two more." Squeeze. "That's it, baby."

Focusing on the sway of Ford's hips, which were pressed against her, and the instructions he whispered in her ear, Charlie almost missed the voice calling to them.

He squeezed. "Hold on a second. It's Grace."

She stopped, leaned against him, and discovered her hands hung where the denim of his jeans bulged in a hard promise. She moved her fingers and gently felt along his length.

"Don't," he warned, placing a handle in her hands and closing her fingers around the plastic. "We will not complete the hunt if you do that. And I'll be swimming to port behind the ship. Carry the basket."

She laughed and tapped the plastic container against the backs of her thighs.

"Ford, how do you feel about teaming up?" Grace asked in a quiet voice.

He squeezed Charlie's hip, and Charlie responded with a nod.

"We'd like that," he replied.

"Seems like I got the prettiest and smartest Dom on the ship," Tyler said. "I'm a rather lucky guy to have such a resourceful woman at my back."

"Looks that way from where I'm standing," Ford added.

Tyler groaned, and Charlie's hands itched to drop the basket, remove the mask, and see why. Ford tugged on her bound wrists and told her to settle down.

"I think we should collect these things out of order. Come back to the beginning of the list, especially numbers one and two," Grace said, her voice stronger and more authoritative than Charlie had heard before. "Let's start in the middle. I'm thinking most people will start at the beginning or the end and work their way through. There will be less of a rush for the middle items. It says 'protection and stripes on deck.'" She paused, and then giggled. "I got it. The pool towels are striped and the group's staff walks around with protection. Let's get to work."

"Sounds like a plan," Ford agreed.

"Told you she was smart," Tyler said, and Charlie felt a light nudge against her shoulder. "Sorry, darling. That was me. I meant to bump your man. Guess these two have us set beside each other."

"Makes it easier to maneuver your bulk," Grace explained. "Now walk. Baby steps, so I can keep up with you."

Ford angled her hips and tapped his fingers. "Go on, *chère*. We need to collect pool towels and condoms."

"Elevator to the starboard side of the pool?" Charlie asked, letting Ford guide her.

"You got it," he replied, the vibrations from his laughter rolling over her back.

"Doll," Tyler said, "we're heading to a wild part of the ship. You up to it?"

"The question is, are you up to it?" Grace shot back.

"Fuck me," Tyler grumbled. "I'm creating a monster and can't even enjoy the view." They all burst out laughing; Tyler pretended to cough with distress. "Seems like we, the innocent, blindfolded folk, need to look out for each other so they don't take advantage of us."

"Keep dreaming, big guy," Grace said, and Charlie felt Tyler being moved away.

Ford squeezed her hips, and Charlie stopped walking. "Good girl," he said into her ear as he wrapped his arm across her chest and kissed the side of her neck. The elevator sounded its arrival, and Charlie waited for Ford to steer her safely past the exiting passengers and inside. Just before the elevator started its ascent, he returned his lips to her neck. "You're doing beautifully, *chère*."

"Where are my words of encouragement?" Tyler asked.

Whack!

"Fuck," he growled, and the air around them pulsated with heat. "Can't wait for my turn, doll."

"*Mmmmm*," was all Charlie heard. She smiled, leaned her head to the side, and allowed a chuckling Ford more access to her neck. He trailed slow, wet kisses up to her jaw, then back down to her collarbone. His fingers caressed the aching undersides of her breasts, and she dropped her head back on his chest as the elevator climbed, happy in the arms of her man.

This submission thing wasn't so bad. And Grace and Tyler's bantering made it fun. "Kind of like a double date."

"What was that, *chère*?" Ford asked as the elevator doors opened and he motioned for her to walk. He turned her slightly to the right and returned his hands to her hips.

"I was thinking that this workshop is fun," she said. "Sort of like a double date. Grace and Tyler, glad you guys are here with us."

"Me, too," Grace said.

Automatic doors slid open and they walked out onto the crowded pool deck. He slowed their pace and halted when Grace gasped and yanked on Tyler's shirt.

While Ford was more than a little pleased with the confidence in which Charlie had accepted his guidance and seemed to be at ease, he looked at a very pale-faced Grace, whose eyes had gone big with all the activity she observed on the starboard side of the deck. Nude bodies were the smallest part of her shock. There was so much fucking going on around them. All sorts of fucking.

Once again, he dropped his forearm around Charlie's chest and held her tight. "Let's take this slow and give Gracie a moment to acclimate to the scene," he whispered only for his woman to hear.

Charlie nodded and leaned against him, accepting his decision with a very sweet smile. Trusting and comfortable, she lowered her face to kiss his forearm.

Keeping a hold on his beautiful angel, Ford wondered if he should reach out and steady the stunned woman leading her much-larger submissive. But Grace surprised him with a sudden, and very standoffish, glance. She met his gaze with a determined resolve to continue on their mission and shook her head to indicate that he should stop thinking of aborting. Her perfectly straight teeth released her lower lip, and she forced a smile that didn't quite reach her eyes.

"Thank you," Grace said, still shaking her head at Ford and communicating that she didn't need rescuing. "We're enjoying this, too. Right, big guy?"

"Right," Tyler said. He inched up his bound hands, clearly searching for Grace, but the little tease had released her hold on his arms and had moved to his side to get a better look around his massive body and take in the happenings on deck.

"Doll? Where'd you go? I like feeling you against me. Why'd you move away?" Tyler asked. Perhaps Tyler had accepted the blindfold, even insisted on it, but he clearly was the sort of man who liked to know where his woman was and what she was doing.

"I'm right here." Grace pressed her thin frame against his side and wrapped her arms around his waist. "Just taking a look around, Ty."

"Fuck. This is pure torture. I smell pussy. I hear skin slapping and dicks pounding," Tyler said, his pained restraint evident in the set of his jaw.

"Yeah," Grace confirmed, "it's a little wild out here."

"True. But the biggest reason I'm worked up is because you're with me," Tyler continued in a low voice, but not low enough to keep his remarks private, "and I want you again. Now. I want to touch and taste you. Take you right here and now. But I'm bound and blindfolded, so I only get what you allow." Even though he'd dipped his head and spoke against Grace's hair, he had no way of knowing they were standing too close for any privacy. "Your heart is beating so fast in that pretty chest. I can feel it against my side. But I can't wrap you in my arms. Can't see your face. Can't be sure you're okay with this."

Grace reached up and cupped his face. She pulled him down and brushed her mouth over his. "I'm okay, Ty. Just fine. Trust me."

She gave Ford a second glance. Silence. She was asking for his silence.

The timid woman from dinner was gone, and Grace was doing just fine. She'd see them through the jungle of bodies, deal with the scenes, and make her man proud.

"You wait for our towels," Grace said, her tone more authoritative with each word. "We'll get the condoms."

Surprised again, but in agreement, Ford told Charlie they were walking approximately ten feet straight ahead to stand in line for the towels. "There's about a dozen people ahead of us. Follow my lead."

"Yes, sir," she replied and started forward.

Avoiding the swinging basket between them, he wrapped an arm around her back and rested his hand on her left hip in an effort to protect his balls while keeping Charlie from coming into contact with anyone else.

"Is it as explicit as yesterday?" Charlie asked.

"More," he replied, remembering how her curiosity had spiked his libido. Then he remembered how she'd pulled away and how he'd decided he couldn't chance losing the opportunity to know her . . . honestly know her. "*Chère*, do you really feel like this is a double date?"

"It feels like a double date. Sort of different than everything we saw yesterday," she explained. "Being with Grace and Tyler makes it interesting, especially since they flipped the tables on the Dom/sub thing. I never would have guessed it would be that way for them."

Neither would he. But he knew where Tyler was going with this. Understood that Grace required special handling, and Tyler was apparently a master at giving the woman what she needed. Tyler was empowering Grace.

"Yes, it's interesting for sure," Ford agreed, not losing sight of his own plan. "Charlie, we need to try something different. A fast-forward button."

Soft lines marked her forehead in confusion, but she didn't speak.

"I want many dates with you," he said, watching the lines of confusion fade and her face relax. "A double date is a good beginning, and while this venue is far from traditional, I want to know you. More than typical vacation know-you. More than work know-you. As much as possible. I want as many dates as we can squeeze in today."

Confusion appeared again on her forehead, and her body went stiff. Puzzled by her reaction, he wanted to remove the blindfold and read the thoughts he knew he'd find in her eyes. But he wouldn't satisfy his own need to look into her eyes and break the rules of the event. They were on a fun double date. A date she'd said she liked.

He caressed the curve of her hip, working to smooth away the tension. "Dates? Numerous dates?"

"Okay," she said, her lips not smiling, but not showing any disappointment either.

"A round of miniature golf after lunch? Maybe a swim or a soak in the hot tub?"

"I'm not up to the lido—"

"No," he quickly agreed, "not on the anything-goes lido. The aft sun deck, which on most cruises is the adult-only area away from kid activity, is functioning in much the same manner on this cruise. It's serving as the place to take a break from scheduled events. It's quiet, and we can relax together and talk."

This time she smiled. "Okay."

Ford collected two towels from the young man staffing the booth and thanked the cruise-ship employee. He searched the deck for their friends and spotted Grace carefully choosing condoms off a tray held by a woman wearing only nipple rings and a butt plug. The plug secured a bright yellow paper umbrella above her head, shielding her from the sun. Pretty sight indeed.

The nude event staffer, while professional, appeared extremely friendly with Grace. They chatted animatedly and seemed rather engrossed in their conversation. Then condom girl reached out and pinched Grace's nipple, forming a large hoop with her thumb and index finger as she tugged. Grace nodded. Next, the nude woman turned and bent slightly, showing Grace exactly how the umbrella was being held in place.

Ford could only see Tyler's clenched fists and his tense shoulder muscles, but he could imagine what the other man was going through. Pure fucking torture. Poor Tyler. Having to listen to all of that but not being able to see or touch.

"I think Grace is into body jewelry and piercings," Ford said to Charlie. "Looks like Tyler is about to explode."

"What do you mean? What's happening?"

Ford explained about the condom girl and Grace's interaction with her, and there was no doubt in his mind that his angel liked the lust-filled images. Charlie's nipples strained against the floral dress and her décolletage heated. Ford bent his head and suckled her earlobe. "Do you like body jewelry?"

Nuzzling against his mouth, she shrugged. "I don't know."

"We'll need to find out," he said and straightened. He took the basket from her hands, placed her solidly before him, and pressed a painfully stiff erection against the lush softness of her ass. "Now keep calm. This is a double date, sweetheart. We have a mission to complete and win us some tandem parasailing."

And he had to stop thinking with his lower head. He wanted Charlie, really wanted her. Being with her made him feel good. When her beautiful blue eyes met his, happiness soaked his previously apathetic manner. And there was something about Charlie's spirit that made him want to hold her hand and leap off a cliff into cold waters with her at his side. Simply put, he wanted to spend time with her, learn what made her tick, and make her feel half as good with him as he did with her.

For some unknown reason, and maybe he was being selfish about it, he wasn't going to walk away from the sunshine she brought him.

"No more talk about nipple piercings or a dainty chain with a strategic charm, much like what you wore last night." Damn, he really had to stop thinking about sex. "Okay. Subject change. Now."

"Relax, honey," Charlie said, turning into his body and skimming her hand over his chest and to his cheek. "We're on a kink cruise. It's okay to have a hard-on. It's okay to be wound up about sex." She rose onto the tips of her toes and pressed her lips to the underside of his jaw. "I just hope I have something to do with your current condition."

"All the doing," he groaned.

"Good," she cooed on a slow and sexy sigh. "I like that." She angled her face up at him, smiled so damn brightly, and urged him to come down for a kiss. He did, and she pressed her mouth to his, a wondrous reward for indulging such a sweet request.

Running his fingers through her hair, he cupped the back of her head, and sealed his lips to hers, exploring the warm addiction of her mouth with his tongue. He closed his eyes and inhaled her essence, taking what she offered when it hit him. It wasn't the delicious kiss, it wasn't the tempting body, it was everything Charlie. And that had him wanting more.

From the little he knew about her, he knew she didn't wait for things to happen or accept the status quo. She went for it. Really went for it.

Fuck, he thought, sinking into the kiss.

Chapter Nineteen

Darkness behind the mask was a glorious thing when Charlie was in Ford's arms, his lips to hers, and she had nothing to worry about but following his directions on how to navigate through the ship. It was an escape from the toll of daily efforts to persevere and get ahead took on her psyche. It was a luxury.

"There are seven more items on the list," Grace announced, returning to where Charlie and Ford stood waiting. "I get most of them, but not all. It's like solving riddles for the treasures." She tucked a handful of condoms into Charlie's cuffed hands. "The first riddle is kind of weird. It says we need to grab a light from an English statesman."

"That's easy. We need a matchbook from the cigar bar," Ford said.

"Because the cigar bar is named Churchill's!" Tyler said.

"Yes," Ford said. "What else?"

Charlie leaned against his chest and smiled. "Told you my man rules."

"I'm familiar with the ship." Ford wasn't taking false credit. "You know I've sailed on it numerous times. It's not a huge deal to know the names of the bars."

"Someone is honest," Grace said, continuing in a businesslike manner, "but we have no qualms about using your knowledge to our advantage."

Ford dropped his chin atop Charlie's head and held her close. He shrugged.

"We also need the price list for Internet access from the lounge, a toy from one of the vendors in the promenade, something we've carried onboard from our stateroom, something borrowed, something blue, and then we're supposed to take a walk through the city of love and return with any sort of proof we've been there," Grace said, her voice trailing in thought. "I don't get the 'city of love' thing."

The illuminated Eiffel Tower at the entrance to the dance club and the French theme of the café flashed in Charlie's mind. "I know that one. It's the area the disco and café are in. We could grab one of their delicious lattes as proof."

"Paris, the city of love," Grace said. "Now I get it."

"Yeah," Charlie grumbled. "Everyone equates Paris with love. It's difficult to beat out Paris for ultimate romance." And that was the problem with her feature. There was definite romance on the cruise, but Paris was Paris was Paris, the city of love.

"Charlene? Charlene Stanton Norring—"

"No last names," Ford interrupted, reaching over Charlie's shoulder and shoving at the voice from the past. Standing taller than usual, Ford pulled her to his side and cradled her beneath his arm, offering her undeniable protection. His voice, low and controlled, rumbled from his chest. "What the fuck don't you understand about that?"

"Sorry about the slip, Charlene. I was caught off guard." Will's voice sounded sincere. Unlike his arrogant piece-of-shit stepbrother, William Norrington was not stupid.

Shit. Shit. Triple shit. She'd confided in him about their lackluster sex life. Hearing his suggestions, she'd also regretted it. They'd managed to stay friends once the divorce was official, but she'd quickly put the brakes on his suggestion of a relationship between them. Now he was on the ship she'd decided to let loose on. What would he think of her choices? Would he remain a confidant or turn on her?

"It's not the sort of event I thought I'd see you at," Will said.

"It's a fucking cruise ship." That was Tyler's growl adding to the mix. "What's it to you?"

"It's a kink cruise," William said. "Charlene isn't meant for such activities." She heard him shift. Perhaps attempt to touch her? She also heard a thud of sorts stop him from reaching her. "You okay with all of this, Charlene?"

Worrying her lower lip, she wondered how fast news of the kink cruise would get back to the family. Wondered what the family would say.

"Please remove the blindfold," Charlie said, trying to keep the trembling out of her voice by speaking low.

A soft touch brushed the sides of her head and the mask disappeared. Bright sunshine flooded her sight. She blinked, leaned closer to Ford if that was possible, and allowed her eyes to adjust. Ford had one arm wrapped around her, the other pressing on Will's chest and effectively barring the man from coming any closer. Tyler stood next to Ford, blindfold off and hands free. Gracie was at Charlie's other side, the pink satin mask in her hands.

"Charlene?" Will asked, his tone showing more concern than he had a right to.

"She's with *me*," Ford said, his jaw squared. "Her well-being is *my* concern, not yours."

"It's okay." Charlie shifted and offered her bound hands to Grace, waiting for her friend to release them while Ford pressed her even closer to his side. For some reason, the dread she'd initially felt seemed frivolous. Her being on a kink cruise was no concern of Will's. She was with Ford. She was his concern. She was safe in his embrace. It didn't matter what Will or anyone else saw or thought.

The moment her hands were freed, she curled her fingers around Ford's bicep, and then realized a second tidbit about their situation: She wasn't the only one on a kink cruise. So was Will. And just like she didn't care why the wild boy of the family was there, it was none of his business why she was there.

"Charlene?"

"It's Charlie," she replied, straightening her back and tilting her chin up. "These are my friends. Friends, this is Will. An acquaintance from back home."

With that introduction, Will's brow lifted. Fine, she deserved that challenging look. He was much more than an acquaintance. She met his gaze and held it, unwilling to share details of their past and communicating that she didn't want his interference.

Ford continued to hold her tight at his side and made it obvious that Will wasn't getting close to her. No way. A sense of security and belonging washed over her.

"It's not a big deal," Charlie said. "Will forgot where we are and made the mistake in using last names." In all fairness, Will didn't know her circumstances. He didn't know she was with Ford. And snug in the crook of his arm, it dawned on her that she was completely his for the duration of the cruise.

"Baby?" Ford asked, his gaze softening as he looked down at her and she smiled.

"Really. It's fine," she offered. "He's okay."

Ford dropped the hand he had plastered against Will's chest, but didn't release her. Instead, he angled his body, making it impossible for the other man to reach her without going through him. He glared at Will. "What part of anonymity don't you get?"

"Guilty," Will said, holding his hands up in a sign of surrender. "I didn't mean to put Charlene—Charlie," he corrected, "in a difficult spot. Just checking on an old friend."

"You checked. She's fine. Now go enjoy your cruise," Ford said.

In an attempt to end the standoff, Charlie nodded her agreement and smiled as big as she could manage. "Enjoy yourself, Will. This is exactly the type of *activities*"—she threw his previous description of the events back at him—"you're into."

"Touché," Will replied, grinning as he bowed at the waist. "I'll be around if you're so inclined."

"You're not so inclined," Ford said in her ear as Will backed away.

Tension diffused, Tyler extended his arm to Grace, and she stepped closer to him. Ford still held Charlie, but his body relaxed and the veins marking his neck became less pronounced.

"Who was that?" Grace asked.

"My ex-husband's stepbrother," Charlie replied.

The stiffness in Ford's body returned. Breath hissed through his teeth.

"Honestly, he's okay," Charlie said. "He's not like James. Nothing like James. Will even tried to warn me away from him."

Regardless of how much Charlie insisted Will was "okay," Ford hadn't missed his introduction as an acquaintance. An acquaintance was not a friend. An acquaintance was not concerned. There was more to the story, but it would need to wait for when they were alone. That was third-date material. He kissed her temple and squeezed her shoulder.

"Okay, baby. I'll let it go." *For now*. But he wasn't dismissing the guy being there and especially not disregarding the fact that he'd approached Charlie. Nor was he going to let him within any proximity in the future. He was simply going to keep her to himself and court his lady as he'd intended to do. He'd woo her, get her, and figure out the rest later. He went for a lighter approach. "After all, this is our first date. Shit happens on first dates."

"I'm sorry the scavenger hunt is ruined for you," Charlie said, reaching for Grace's hand. "Heard things were getting interesting."

"Interesting is putting it mildly," Tyler grumbled. "More like blistering. I need to get my girl some accessories since she's expressed a specific liking or two."

"It was fun while it lasted," Grace said. "Lugging this big guy around got us some amused looks from the other participants." She snuggled close to Tyler and turned her face up for a kiss. He obliged, and she turned to wink at Charlie. "And he thinks I'm responsive."

That comment earned her a swat on her backside, and they all laughed. Charlie's mood had significantly improved, and Ford knew his *grand-mère* had it right. A woman enjoyed being courted. The double date had also been a good way to go. It was nice being with another couple. Easy, fun, and just plain nice. Then it hit him. She wasn't just his; he was also hers. They were a couple. Fuck.

"How about a stroll through the city of love for a delicious latte?" Charlie asked.

"More coffee?" Ford looked down at her and shook his head. "You're going to be wired. I won't be able to keep you under control."

"You complaining, Mr. Control?" Charlie retorted.

"No, ma'am. No way."

As they walked off the pool deck and to the elevator banks, Grace cleared her throat. "Speaking of control, has anyone seen Emma?"

"Grayson led her toward the aft of the promenade when we left the auditorium," Ford said. "They didn't even wave good-bye."

"Aren't the vendors with the toys on the promenade?" Tyler asked, and Ford confirmed they were.

"That's good," Grace breathed, and wrapped her hand around Tyler's arm. "Maybe Grayson could remind her of how good it is to play?"

"It's kind of convenient how things have developed since dinner," Charlie said. "You think Lovers Sail played matchmaker by seating us all at the same table?"

"For sure," Ford said, looking away before she had time for another question.

* * *

Over coffee, they learned that Tyler had a seven-year-old son named Chase who was being looked after by Tyler's sister. He also owned a motorcycle repair shop that specialized in Harley-Davidsons, and was an avid fan of country music. Recently divorced, but officially separated for almost three years, Grace had no children, loved reading the classics, and was currently in between jobs. She was considering going back to school to get her teaching degree. Tyler pointed out the plethora of universities in Wake County, North Carolina, and she blushed with appreciation.

Tyler and Grace looked good together. They complemented each other.

"What about the two of you? You're a perfect couple," Grace said, throwing that adjective around.

Strangely, with Charlie tucked against him, Ford didn't mind the reference. Even if he had seen enough to know that couples didn't last, he'd take it while he could have it with Charlie. Having her against him felt too good not to. Fuck, he was a damaged selfish bastard. And fuck him when she figured it out and turned tail and ran.

"Well, *um* . . ." Charlie shifted in his arms.

"The way we met was perfect," Ford said, rubbing his palm down the gooseflesh on her arm. His Charlie didn't like deceiving anyone. He wasn't about to let her down. So he chimed in, answering the question and giving her some breathing room. "When a gorgeous angel flies into a man's arms, he has no choice but to catch her. I caught her."

He relayed details of their meeting the previous day, even how Charlie had mistaken Eugenia for his wife, but didn't bother to include a timeline. He didn't lie, but he didn't elaborate. Every word, every feeling was true. He'd caught an angel. He was holding onto her.

"There's no denying this cruise is temptation personified, but we still have work to do. Charlie uses some of the downtime to work on an article she's writing for *City Wings* magazine, and I'm storing up energy reserves for a new business venture that awaits me in New York." The conversation between Ford and Tyler turned to business and the pace of expansion, effectively removing the focus from the state of "couplehood."

Charlie's body relaxed and her skin warmed again. She gave him a relieved smile and kissed his cheek. He grinned when he heard her mumble a promise to Grace that they'd get their girl talk in at a future time.

Once they returned their baskets to Bodhi and his staff, they made plans to attend the comedy show after dinner.

In the meantime, Ford had a second date to plan.

"Miniature golf or rock climbing?" he asked.

Chapter Twenty

Charlie chose rock climbing, which meant a wardrobe change. Ford made a few pointed comments about her picking that activity because she wanted out of a dress that showed off her pretty curves just right, but his reaction to her cuffed khaki shorts, which she'd paired with the neon-pink shirt that read *Ask Me* across the front, wasn't lost on her. He gave her a head-to-toe inspection, then his gaze returned to the scrolled lettering and the braless boobs behind it.

"You trying to give me a heart attack, woman?"

"What?" She gave him her most innocent and wide-eyed look, handed him her room card, and strolled past him on four-inch platform sandals that put his mouth within reach. With a touch of her hand on his arm, she led him toward the elevator. "You think the shoes are too high?"

"No, ma'am. We supply climbing shoes on deck." Placing a hand on each of her hips, his fingers splayed over the rounded flesh of her butt, he walked her back against the wall near the elevator. "Those heels are just fine. They make it easy to reach everything I want. But the total package on such pretty display, and being unavailable, well, that's reason for bodily pain."

He dropped his mouth to the curve of her neck and brushed his lips over it before his tongue licked down to her collarbone. His erection pressed into her belly, and his thigh fit between her legs. "I'm trying to be a gentleman. Trying not to think of all that delicious beauty covered by your clothes, but those breasts jutting out are driving me insane. No matter how slow my mind says to take it, I'm aching to take you fast. Fast and hard. You're making it very difficult for me to stay on track with my original plan for the day."

"Which is?" Charlie looked up at the fire burning in his eyes, and heat spread over her body.

"To date you. To win you over with charm and witty chitchat." One hand moved from her ass to the side of her right breast. His thumb stroked over her nipple, and she arched against his touch for more. "There's so much more to you than a sexy, mouthwatering, hot little body, and I want to get to know as much about you as I possibly can. This sailing and you being so oblivious to your physical appeal are testing my control."

She shook her head and pushed at his chest, smiling sweetly as she put a few inches between them.

He placed the pink bikini bottoms in her hand. "Go back in and put these on for later."

"Give me a minute." Reaching into his back pocket, she retrieved her room card.

And a minute was all it took for her to return to her cabin, peel off her shirt, put on her bikini top, and then pull her shirt back over it. She stepped out of her shorts and panties, pulled on the pink bottoms, and her shorts again, then walked back out, took his hand, and suggested they take the stairs. No need for more elevator make-out sessions.

"Baby, you could wear a potato sack and I'd still find that sweet ass sexy as heaven," Ford said from behind her, laughter in his voice. "Not to mention the way those tits bounce with each step, making me want to suck them until you come just from my mouth on them. And you will come like that, because from what I've tasted of them, and the way you squirmed when I had my mouth on you, those nipples are prime routes to a climax. So, for your information, *chère*, wearing your suit beneath that shirt does little to relieve my pain, but thanks for trying."

She kept climbing the stairs, grinning at his exaggerated frustration, but glad he groaned as she turned on the landing and touched her lips to his.

"Honey, we have many dates—your words, not mine—to go on and an article to write. No time for daydreaming and such sweet talk." Even if the mere thought of having him made her sex pulse like mad. "Maybe you'll surprise me with another romantic movie in the dark as one of our dates today."

"Maybe," he replied.

And she really wished he would.

They hadn't even had lunch yet, but Charlie had stepped outside her comfort zone and climbed a thirty-foot rock wall, beat Ford at a round of miniature golf while he stood behind her and showed her how to move her hips for the perfect swing, and had even spent time in the arcade playing air hockey and pretending to ski a double black diamond on a simulator.

"That was some play date," she said, walking into the restaurant, her fingers interlaced with Ford's. "It was the most fun I've had in a long time. Thank you."

"You're very welcome," he replied. "Thank you for the date, *chère*."

They chose a table for two in the back of the dining room with a view of the sea. He ordered a burger and fries; she decided on the Mediterranean antipasto plate. She was biting on a green olive when he put down his burger and leaned back in his seat.

"Your shirt says to ask you, so I'm asking: What's the story with William Norrington?"

She dropped the remaining half of the olive on her plate and shrugged. "He's not like James. Not in many ways."

Ford didn't speak but waited for her to continue.

"Will is the bad boy in the family," she said. "He is wild, reckless, and takes no shit from his father and grandfather. Doesn't care which fork he uses for the salad, and doesn't care if he drinks beer out of the bottle rather than a fine wine in a crystal goblet at dinner."

"And what does that have to do with warning you away from James?"

Shit, now he was asking the more difficult questions. Part of the answer, he'd undoubtedly discovered with his Internet search. The other was something she'd never discussed with anyone other than Will.

"*Chère?*" Ford prompted. "No matter your answer, I'll understand. I simply want to know what we're up against with him."

"Okay," she said, shaking her head. "You already know who I am and the kind of responsibility that comes with my family name. You didn't freak over it, so I'm guessing you understand why I'm hesitant in laying it all out."

"I also identify with it," he said. "My father cut me off when I told him I wasn't joining his firm and I decided against a law degree. I wanted nothing to do with his business and wanted him nowhere near mine." He covered her hand with his. "I think we have that in common. Not that your family cut you off, but that we each want to be our own person and not a puppet of our family name."

They did have that in common, but Ford not following in his dad's footsteps wasn't exactly as public as her being torn to shreds over making the wrong choice when it came to fortifying her family's fiscal position. She'd fucked up and chosen wrong. Both for her family and for herself.

"James is a con artist," she continued. "Proof is that he's doing time for embezzling and trying to take the whole family for a ride. He's also a con artist when it comes to personal relationships. He's incapable of a personal relationship. He never wanted me; he only wanted access to my family's money." She bit her lower lip with the admission, and her vision went blurry from the tears in her eyes.

"I'm sorry, *chère.* You were young and inexperienced, and the fucker took advantage of your nature."

She shook her head. She'd known all along that it was a financial arrangement on James's behalf. She had. She wasn't stupid. But she'd believed James had loved her in his own way and would eventually come to love her the way she wanted to be loved. She had accepted the lack of affection until that time would come. James had the exact ambition and business savvy her parents thought appropriate. He was charming in public, phenomenal at networking, and always closed his deals.

"I figured out what he was about rather quickly. I knew." She didn't meet Ford's gaze because she didn't want to see the pity in his eyes, so she stared at her lap. "Will knew, too. We became friends, and he tried to warn me before I married the asshole. I didn't listen, and eventually Will had to back off."

"So Will stopped being your friend?" Now Ford looked pissed. "He left you alone, without any support to face that fucker?"

No, Will wasn't the reason for the defeated mess she'd crumbled into when the shit hit the fan and she couldn't look away any longer. That had been all her doing. She carried all the responsibility, because she should have walked away from the messed up situation, but she hadn't. She should have seen James's true colors and not rationalized them away.

No sane man would let his woman, not one the likes of you, sleep alone, Will had insisted. *The jerk is fucked in the head. You need more than he is capable of giving. Call it off, sweetheart. Call it off.*

"No. He didn't actually back away during the marriage. Just stopped insisting I see the light. We became even better friends," she said, and Ford's gaze narrowed on her. This conversation was proving harder than she'd originally thought. "Like I said earlier, he was the wild one in the family. He made it his personal mission to make family vacations fun and bearable for me." She attempted a smile that she knew wasn't real.

"James never did that for you?" Ford asked.

"We really didn't interact much when we weren't expected to," she said, hearing how nuts it sounded and rubbing her forehead to ward off a headache. It only got worse after she had accepted his ring. He'd acted like she was an inconvenient appendage, not a lover. "As for Will, I got to know him during the family vacations. He would burst into the sedate gatherings with a sexy woman on his arm and a ready joke on his lips."

In typical Will fashion, he didn't care that his brother complained about being kept awake into the wee hours of the night because he banged "the latest slut"—James's words not Charlie's—into submission without any consideration for the family. The truth was Will made certain she'd hear . . . on purpose. He'd admitted as much to her. *You deserve to scream and moan in pleasure. Can't you see what you're missing?*

"So Will is easygoing, likes sex, and doesn't bother to hide it," Ford added. "Guess that explains his presence on the ship."

She nodded, but once again lowered her gaze to her lap. "James was not into sex, didn't like it, and didn't bother to hide it."

"He wasn't a good lover," Ford said, pulling her back into the moment and out of the sadness that had consumed her. "That's all him, baby. Nothing to do with you. You're so sexy and sweet, a man would have to be crazy not to do everything in his power to learn how to please you."

"I don't think James noticed or cared that our relationship lacked intimacy," she said. If he did, he didn't do a thing about it. "He didn't try to please me. It was more his husbandly duty."

"That's nuts. Did anyone else notice his attitude and say anything?"

Will had noticed, and he had told her as much. In fact, he'd repeatedly told her she deserved better. She deserved laughter with her man, wild sex that led to multiple orgasms, and everything his stepbrother wasn't giving her.

"I already said that Will warned me. But I didn't listen." Not until it was much too late. Not until she'd lost herself and had felt like something to be scraped off the bottom of a shoe. "And in the end, it didn't matter. James stole from my family. He used me to do it."

Will had stood by her side and kept her sane throughout the horrific ordeal. Once the divorce was final, he had also suggested they give it a try. Not his typical hookups, but an earnest try at a true relationship. Unable to see past the family connection, she'd refused, and that was when they'd drifted apart. How was she supposed to share these details with Ford?

"It's over," Ford said, reaching for her hand. "You're rid of James, and you're doing great without him. You're making your way as a journalist. Working to make your mark and do what makes you happy." He felt her hand relax as he stroked his thumb over her knuckles. "Plus, look at where you are. You're on a damn kink cruise. You're surrounded by glorious sex and romance. No more boring sex for my girl. None. You do deserve better. You're going to have better."

She gave him a smile, and she knew this one made it all the way to her eyes. She deserved better, wanted better, and was going to have better.

"I'm up to the task," he said, squeezing her hand and insisting she hold his gaze.

"What?" Charlie asked.

"*Chère,* I don't care what it takes, and I don't care what kind of barriers I need to deal with, you'll take your pleasure."

Take her pleasure? What did he mean?

"I rarely make a promise, but this is a promise," Ford said. "A priority to keep." His brown eyes reinforced the sincerity of his words, and her body tingled with that promise. "We'll deal with today. Find a way to deal with being forced to interact only in public. But clear your schedule for tomorrow."

"Tomorrow is Cozumel," Charlie said, her forehead wrinkling in confusion. She tried to rub it away, but the pressure continued to grow. "That's what's on our schedule."

"Wrong. *You* are the only thing on *my* schedule," Ford corrected. "Forget tandem parasailing, horseback riding on the beach, swimming with the dolphins, and snorkeling expeditions. Tomorrow, we're going to make up for lost time. Tomorrow is nothing but us. And it's us off the damn ship."

Chapter Twenty-one

"Due to recent revelations, I'd like to press the fast-forward button on our dates," Ford said, dropping an arm over her shoulder as they walked off the elevator.

"I'm good with that," Charlie replied, snuggling against him. "What do you want to do next?"

"Body Bingo."

"What?"

He stopped walking and turned her to look at him. Cupping her cheek, he swept his thumb over the perfect line of her jaw. "Body Bingo," Ford repeated. "With your body as the card, the marker in my hand, it's a sure win."

Her eyes went dark with desire, and he knew he'd struck a chord. She wanted, no needed, the physical and sensual connection. While *Grand-mère* may have been correct about feeling treasured and the little things, when it came to relationships with women, she was wrong about giving it plenty of time where Charlie was concerned. She deserved to be cherished and treasured in every way, and she needed it sooner rather than later.

"The game starts in ten minutes." He looked over her beautiful curves, his gaze settling on the outline of the bikini beneath her neon shirt. "Are you wearing the bikini bottoms?"

She nodded in confirmation.

"If you're attached to that bathing suit, we have two choices," he said in a low voice, angling his body against hers and running his finger beneath the pink string straining with the weight of her breasts at her neck. "You can go nude, lay that gorgeous body on my table and take my marker—I wouldn't mind in the least bit—or you can change into a different suit before we head to the lounge."

A pretty line of white teeth scraped over her lower lip, as her nipples peaked at the thought. Yes, she needed sexual play. She craved it.

"Actually," he added, waiting for her to take a breath and then continuing, "it may look cute if we use pink and purple daubers. Tie-dyed, with strategically placed marks."

"Okay," Charlie breathed, the heave of her chest reclaiming his attention.

"Fuck, *chère*. You're so beautiful. Forget the feature and spend every minute with me." No joke. He'd make every second count. He'd find a way around the rules and regulations to please her.

"I'm working, Ford. You know how important a byline is for me, no matter how tempting your offer," Charlie said.

He agreed, but his agreement didn't stop him from asking her again once she was stretched out on the table, in a corner booth of the lounge, in a tiny pink bikini that barely covered the creamy flesh of her gorgeous breasts.

"Ford," Charlie warned, raising her arms and linking her hands at her wrists above her head as the moderator instructed.

He shifted in his seat, making sure his body concealed the majority of her body from the camera. The truth was he didn't like her on display like this. On the other hand, having her on display like this validated their covers. Still, it didn't mean he liked it.

He marked the inside of her left elbow, the top of her right foot, her belly button, which happened to be an adorable little innie, but hesitated when the moderator called for the right nipple. "It'll ruin your suit."

"Well, I'm not taking it off," she said, turning her head and giving a big smile. "What's under there is reserved for your eyes only."

"Thank you, Lord," he whispered, tossing the dauber over his shoulder and cradling her face in his hands. He took her lips. Gratitude mingled with relief as they yielded and her tongue met his in a delicious kiss.

When he raised his head and looked down at her, she smiled and got up on her elbow. "We're never going to win one of these events," Charlie said.

"No? Why?"

She smoothed his furrowed brow and touched her lips to his. "We can't seem to finish them."

Sitting up, she brought her legs next to him and slid off the table and into the booth beside him. She reached for her shirt and pulled it over her head. Then she took his hand and held it in her lap.

"What's up, *chère*?"

"I'm thinking I'd like some quiet time alone with you." She held his hand in both of hers, tracing over his knuckles in a bashful manner. "But since we can't be alone, I like the idea of the pool at the back of the ship. The one that's being used to give us a break from all the events."

More than willing to keep her to himself, he nodded in agreement and kissed her again. Ford collected her shorts, bent and picked up her sandals, then stood and held out his hand to her. "Let's go."

As Ford wrapped an arm around Charlie's waist and pulled her wet back to his wet chest, he swept her golden hair over her shoulder and brought his lips to her neck. "So damn perfect, baby. I can stay like this all day."

He rested his cheek on her head and closed his eyes. He inhaled the floral scent of her shampoo and kissed her temple. Having Charlie in his arms was a greater reward for remaining on the ship for the extra voyages than the financial benefits it afforded. Being in the company of a beautiful woman was in no way work, but he didn't want to leave her for a minute longer than he had to. And he had to be apart from her only for her to sleep.

"Thank you," he said.

"For what?" A slippery Charlie turned in his embrace; her bright, blue eyes that sparked with sincerity awed him. He blinked and swallowed the lump of gratitude that had gathered in his throat.

"Sitting in the hot tub with my woman beats playing bingo any day." He traced down her nose and tipped up her chin, trying to keep it light and fun for her while keeping his own feelings in check. "So thank you for suggesting it. You made me very happy. You *make* me happy," he corrected himself, and lowered his head, rubbing the tip of his nose against hers as he brushed his lips over her mouth. Then, waving his hand between them, he grinned. "Mostly, thank you for this. For letting me get to know you."

She smiled, unaware of the glorious effect of that smile, and his chest constricted. No one had ever affected him the way she did. When the time came for them to go their separate ways, he'd miss that smile. He'd miss her sweet curious gaze and determined exuberance. He'd miss everything he knew about her, and with every layer she revealed, he knew he'd miss her more.

"Ford, I feel like you know me much more than I know you," Charlie said, gently stroking his jaw.

"Ask anything you want to know. I'll answer."

Adorable as hell, she tapped a finger to her lips and let out a long breath. "Start at the beginning. Tell me about your parents."

He stiffened and turned her to look forward, gathering her back to his chest again. His parents weren't his favorite topic. "That's a long story."

"We have time," she said, settling softly against him.

He groaned, but nodded. "Okay. My parents are probably the shortest part of the story. My father knocked up my mother the night of his law school graduation. Duty had them married three months later. It wasn't a love affair or even close. My father knew she'd planned it. Accused her of wanting into the pants of a future success because she wanted into his wallet."

"That's horrible," Charlie gasped, attempting to turn and look at him, but he held her still. It would be easier to finish without those brilliant blue eyes studying him, so he kept his chin on her head and kept her looking forward.

"It was true. I don't remember my mother." He took a breath and worked to release the pressure in his jaw. "In exchange for giving up her parental rights and signing divorce papers, my father wrote her a check ten days after she gave birth to me. She cashed it and hit the road. She hasn't been heard from since."

Charlie gripped his forearm, and without saying a word, she kissed a slow line to his bicep, offering silent support. She nuzzled against his arm and rested her cheek on it. She let him continue.

"Before we'd even come home from the hospital, my father had hired a great nanny, Marianne, who stayed with us until I went to school. Between my grandmother and Marianne, I had more nurturing love than other little boys ever know. I was lucky she'd left." He moved his shoulders, wanting to throw off the dread that crawled through him at the thought of constant interaction with such a mother.

"Lucky I had the women in my life who stayed. My grandmother and Marianne are wonderful."

"And your dad?" Charlie prompted.

"He tried," Ford said grudgingly, because his father *had*, in his own warped way, tried. "But he wouldn't win Father of the Year. He was never home for dinner. Always working. He lived like he was a carefree bachelor, which he wasn't because he brought home three stepmothers, two of whom were stepmonsters. The third was Eugenia, who you met. The funny thing is that Eugenia, even though she's only a year older than I am, was the best wife and stepmother. She gave him a wonderful daughter, my sister Emily. But in true Keaton fashion, he fucked that up, too. He's a womanizer who can't keep it in his pants, and women are always willing to accommodate him because of the size of his wallet. That's what he knows. That's what he does."

"So he made good as an attorney?"

"Oh, yeah." Ford shook his head, his palm sliding across her middle and absorbing the warmth of her skin. He wasn't angry, wasn't upset. He'd accepted his father for what he was and had moved on. "He was born to be an attorney. Like my uncle's, Father's life was plotted like a detailed novel from the moment he was born. They're partners in the firm my grandfather and his brothers established. All the males in the family were expected to follow in their shoes. Bruce, my cousin, is next in line to assume control. His brother, Remy, is also practicing there. I was supposed to do the same. You know: *and sons*."

They sat in silence, letting the water swirl around them as he held her. Ford's hold was tight, as if he was assuring himself she'd stay regardless of what she'd heard.

But Charlie knew a thing or two about expectations, and a heaviness settled over her heart as she thought of Ford clashing with his dad. She turned, smoothed her hand around his shoulders in a gentle acceptance, and then swung her legs over his thigh. She placed her cheek on his chest and a soft palm over his heart.

"Sometimes, regardless of their intentions, parents mess up their kids with wrong expectations. It's not that they're malicious, it's just that they're misguided," she said, remembering how he'd said they had so much in common when it came to choosing their own paths.

She also understood why he'd made the effort to explain he wasn't a relationship kind of man. With all he'd seen in his dad, he didn't believe relationships could last.

"Father lost it when I decided against law school," Ford confirmed. "Our already rocky relationship crashed and burned. Now, he sends Eugenia as an ambassador to keep the connection alive. But no matter what he says or what he offers, I'm not going to change my mind. I'm not a lawyer. I'm going to launch the cafés on my own."

Sighing, Charlie touched her lips to his chest. "I get it. After the James debacle, my parents backed off on making me a proper wife. We were all duped, so they had no choice but to acknowledge my hesitation to get involved again. Unfortunately, they didn't forget about finding me the proper husband. Numerous dinner party ambushes followed. Eventually, I moved out of the house and into a small apartment my grandmother had from her college days. I make my own way. Pay a fair amount in rent. Refuse to agree with my parents' suggestions on the social scene. And my brothers think their little sister is crazy for not accepting the family's financial help." She pressed her mouth to his heart and closed her eyes.

"I get it. I do. I want to do it on my own, too." His fingers curled at the nape of her neck and he massaged away the tension. "But, *chère*, you're different. Bright, efficient, gorgeous, you don't hide your curiosity or sweetness. A man loses himself in all that's you."

Not the man she wanted, though. Not the man in the hot tub with her. With a sharp intake of breath, she gathered her strength and decided not to hide behind an acceptable façade. Something he claimed a man would lose himself over.

"But not you?" Charlie surprised herself by actually delivering her question.

"Fuck. Yes, me," Ford instantly replied. With a finger under her chin, he angled her face up. "Baby, you don't get it. You're addictive. No matter the cost, I'd lose myself in you as long as you allow." He touched his lips to hers and spoke against her mouth. "I'm already lost when it comes to you."

His voice trailed off, but his gaze held hers as he dropped his forehead to hers.

He's already lost? How? And why as long as I allow? Charlie thought, letting his words float in her mind and push any hesitance aside.

"Kiss me, Ford," Charlie said, running her tongue over his lips and tasting a hint of the pleasure he'd promised over lunch. Decision made. She'd take it.

His kiss was gentle and soft, and she committed the feel of every sensuous stroke to memory as her body heated. In the short time she'd known him, Ford gave without reservation, only asking for her to let him give. She was open to receiving.

"Does this mean we're done with the family history?" Ford asked between kisses.

"We're done," she said.

"Good," he replied, lifting her from between his legs and turning her to straddle his lap while he kissed her. His hands cupped her bottom and he fit her against his erection, rubbing her throbbing center through the pink suit.

She linked her hands behind his neck, and took her own advice. She'd let loose and just live in the moment. Charlie played with his dark hair and made out with the sexiest man she'd ever met like no one was watching.

The pressure of fingers on her hips and the sound of a low growl at her mouth pulled her from the haze of ecstasy. Ford held her up and off his body.

"Jesus, baby, you're incredible." He shook his head and grinned. "My mind keeps telling me we're working, therefore we're being watched. That means we've given them enough material to make us real. Now, either you peel that gorgeous body away or we agree to swim for it."

"No swimming," she said, tucking her swollen boobs into the pink triangles. "I'll wait until we're on land."

"Don't forget you said that. The minute the ship is tendered, we're off."

"Agreed," she said, touching her lips to his. "You up to helping me with more research today so I can take tomorrow off from the writing?"

"Absolutely," he agreed, but raised his brows indicating a condition to the quick agreement. He reached for his discarded shorts. "Keep your legs wrapped around me."

Her heart skipped a beat as he reached into the pocket and retrieved the small pink bullet. Pulling her bottoms to the side, he slid a finger in and out of her as her thigh muscles tensed with need. His thumb found her clit and circled in sweet strokes.

"No sign of petulant Charlie today. Today's Charlie owes me some orgasms. And since I can't have you the way I truly want, I'm going to let the vibrations of the toy put that pretty pink in your cheeks for everyone to see. You're going to come for me on demand, baby. Over and over." He slipped the bullet inside her and returned her bathing suit into place.

"Now breathe," he said, standing and pulling her to her feet. He helped her out of the water and wrapped a towel over her shoulders. "I heard that part of the group is going to the Dating Game, and Maggy and Sparky are going to It's All About the Sting. Want to hit both of those before dinner?"

"Perfect." She reached for his hand and gave it a squeeze.

"My pleasure," Ford said, lowering his head and kissing her.

"Thank you. Best way to keep these lips occupied." And it was. She didn't miss that vanilla vapor at all. "When do I get my next orgasm?"

"Looking forward to it?" Ford asked, sidling up against her and pulling her against his hips.

"Yes, but I can wait. You said you're willing to lose yourself with me as long as I want." She smoothed her fingertips over the chiseled contours of his face, watching the questions form in his eyes. "Since you're willing to leave our time to me, I've decided that I can have it all. I'll earn my byline, and then a permanent spot on the masthead of *City Wings*. I don't need to choose one over the other, because I have time on my side. And since I so enjoy your lips and hands, with you . . . well, with you, I want more than four nights at sea. I want private dinners in my little apartment at home. I want breakfasts in bed. And I want all of that with you. You promised."

"So I did." His hands tightened on her hips and he pulled her lower body against his as his lips turned up in a sexy grin. "Stretch out and use the whole mattress while you can, *chère*. When you're in my bed, you'll realize how little room you'll truly have. And that's a second promise."

Then he crushed his lips to hers, and Charlie lost herself in Ford. Lost for how long she didn't know.

She surfaced when, keeping the towel wrapped around her, Ford instructed Charlie to lift her arms and fit the neon T-shirt over her head. He untied the bikini and pulled the wet suit from her body as he slid the shirt down. Next, he kneeled and held her shorts open for her to step into. Right before he raised them over her hips, he removed the suit bottoms.

She stared at him, her mouth gaping in shock, as he dropped the bikini to the deck. "I thought my nipples showed."

"They do," he said, stripping off his wet suit and giving her an unobstructed view of his naked and beautiful body, before stepping into his shorts—commando.

"I thought you didn't like that."

"Wrong. I do," he replied, snapping his shorts in place and entering her space. "And knowing that no one else gets a shot at that sweet little body of yours, I want you as excited and wet as can be. You need to come often and hard. If that means letting everyone else drool over the gorgeous view, so be it. It's mine. So is that mark next to your nipple."

She glanced down at her shirt, seeing the hard outlines of her nipples poking through, and remembered the love bite he spoke about.

"You like watching, baby. You were breathing so hard at the scene, clutching the railing with those talented hands and steaming up my belt buckle."

Charlie was about to deny the buckle again, but he raised his hand and curled his fingers around her neck.

"The risk of being caught excites you. While you're shy, you like the camera. You clenched on my hand so tight when you learned there were eyes on your back. You dropped to your knees and sucked me off so pretty, knowing that anyone could have walked up to our table."

Ford was right. Totally right. It was like she was tempting her luck, pushing things that had never been an option for her in the past.

"And you know what?"

She raised her shoulders, but didn't speak.

"You give great head, *chère*. Makes me lose my mind just remembering that wonderful mouth and talented tongue." He pulled her close and spoke against her mouth. "And while I won't let another man touch what is mine, I'll do anything to get that mouth wrapped around my cock again. So keeping you on edge with those nipples hard and that pussy wet works for me." He trapped a taut peak between his thumb and finger, squeezing just hard enough so pain pulsed to her sweet spot between her legs.

"Ford," she breathed.

"Yeah, baby. You'll give me your next orgasm when you least expect it. But I can tell you it won't come close to what you'll give me when we come together."

Chapter Twenty-two

Charlie squeezed the drops into her eyes and closed them tight. She couldn't believe all that had happened in two days. The fast-forward button had definitely been pressed at boarding. She opened her eyes and stared at her reflection. A new woman, confident, happy, and eager to face the day, stared back at her.

Ford had seen to her multiple climaxes. She'd shattered with pleasure during the Dating Game—on stage while answering questions. Clearly, she'd been too distracted to give witty answers and win. She shattered again in It's All About the Sting, in which the demonstrations kept her on the edge of her seat the whole time. He'd served up a repeat performance of the previous night at dinner, which proved very fruitful for her writing, and she'd more than enjoyed herself on the Dungeon's dance floor after the comedy show. So much so that Luis and Quinn had stormed out of there, proclaiming they needed to find a woman . . . pronto.

She laughed at the remembrance, and reread the notes Ford had insisted she take the time to enter into her computer after dinner.

- *Tyler's strong hand empowers a once-defeated Grace.*
- *Grayson proves that age is only a number, and Emma gazes at him with longing.*
- *Maggy and Sparky, well they're Maggy and Sparky. Made it mucho years by keeping things spicy. Today, Sparky wears collar & Maggy holds leash.*
- *Quinn and Luis are the best. Best couple. Best friends. Best. I love them.*

But the butterflies dancing in Charlie's belly confirmed that nothing would compare to what was to come. She dressed in one of her pretty new dresses, applied mascara and lip gloss, and looked forward to Ford knocking on her door for morning coffee. Coffee with a man who had penetrated her shield and had changed her life.

A message popped up on her screen.

Good morning, chère. Pack day bag with wallet, passport, laptop, and panties.

Panties? She typed back.

Panties. Then dots as he wrote. **Be there in five.**

Like she could wait five minutes to see him.

Charlie leaned against the doorjamb, smiling at an approaching Ford. Her fingers tangled in the soft material of her dress, which did nothing to keep the goose bumps at bay once she spotted Ford. Broad shoulders and a sexy-as-shit saunter filled her mind with naughty thoughts and her heart with hope. His long legs ate up the distance and she smiled.

Shit, shit, triple shit. She'd never wanted to run up to a man, jump into his arms, and kiss him like he provided sustenance. She'd never seen a more attractive man in her life. She summoned her composure and retained a tiny bit of control, shifting her weight from one foot to the other, but aware that she worried her lower lip with anticipation.

"Don't just stand there, *chère*. Get your sweet ass moving." He reached her, snaked an arm around her waist, and lowered his lips to her neck. With a wicked grin, he stole her practiced composure.

She tangled her fingers in his hair and lifted his head to seal her mouth to his. "Kiss me first."

He did, and with each stroke of his tongue and sweep of his hands her angst subsided and a strange sense of belonging replaced it.

"Good-morning, baby." He looked at her like a starved man holding a plate of hot stew. "No more kisses for now, or I'll snap and devour that sweet little body of yours right here. So, food. You need food and coffee for energy before they let us off the ship. Then, when we are off the ship, I'm going to deplete every last drop of that energy. It'll be my turn to feast."

Less than an hour later, they were on the pier and Ford was holding open the door to the taxi he'd waved down. Four minutes after that, the taxi pulled in to the circular drive of a portside hotel. Ten minutes after that, Ford tossed her day bag, which also held his passport, onto the couch in their room, leaned his butt against the granite counter of their rented studio, and crossed his arms over his chest. His gaze moved up and down Charlie's body, zeroing in on the way she struggled to catch her breath.

"Strip," he ordered.

Moisture pooled between her thighs at his command and her lungs worked twice as hard. But determined to let loose and truly let herself go, Charlie shed her inhibitions and kicked off her sandals. She didn't have a chance to remove anything else before Ford was on her, his hands at her waist, lifting her off her feet and tossing her onto the bed.

"Fuck waiting." He urged her knees to the sides, and then he fit himself over her like a second skin. Burying his fingers in her hair, he tugged her head back and looked into her eyes for long steamy seconds, offering her a glimpse of the day in store, and pressing his obvious excitement against her aching core.

"Ford?" She turned her head to the side, unable to accept the promise she read because of the consequences it carried.

"Look at me," he said, using a finger to guide her chin and make her turn back to him. He captured her gaze and she couldn't miss the fire in his dark eyes. "I'm going to make you want to keep me around for a long time, *chère*," he said, working her skirt up over her hips and hooking his thumbs in the lace of her panties. "But first I'll have my mouth on you, your taste on my tongue, and your release."

Charlie shivered as he pulled her panties down her legs, and she silently admitted that she already wanted to keep him around. She closed her eyes and gave into the pleasure of knowing Ford was going down on her, seeing to her like no one had ever before . . . and wanting it.

She reveled in the ecstasy of Ford's mouth trailing up her thigh to the ache at her core and shut out everything other than the fiery sensation of his mouth. He licked through her heat, up to the pulsing sweet spot, then back to her opening and feasted. Her body bowed when he closed his lips on her. Then he slid his masterful tongue deep inside her and took her somewhere she imagined was much like heaven.

Pressing and circling his thumb against her clit, he worked her with his tongue, devouring her excitement until her breath grew ragged and her legs trembled with need. He didn't speak until her hips jerked high and his strong hands cupped her ass, holding her off the mattress and high off the bed. He blew softly, soothing the heat and dropping tiny kisses on the throbbing skin.

"Open your eyes and watch yourself come for me, baby."

She did as she was told, and seeing her man's face between her legs, his dark eyes showing how she pleased him, she reached for it. Tingles started in her toes and moved through her like wildfire. Ford gave and took, in patient and generous indulgence, then a decadent burst of pleasure consumed her and she couldn't think at all.

Charlie came undone, her control splintering into a prism of bliss and consuming her reality as she called his name and gave herself over to her man.

She hadn't caught her breath or managed to come down from the sweet rapture of the greatest orgasm she'd ever experienced when Ford lowered his zipper and pushed his jeans off. She didn't question the foil package in his hands or where he'd found it, but she attempted, rather poorly, to focus on his progress as he tore at the wrapped condom, rolled it on, and held her pleasure-hazed vision the whole time.

With one hand fisting the base of his beautiful cock, he reached between her legs with the other and ran a finger through her soaked folds. "So lovely. Wet and sweet and totally ready for me."

"Yes," Charlie managed. *So damn ready*, she thought.

He positioned the large, smooth head at her entrance, and anticipation quivered deep in her core as he teased her with a taste of what he'd deliver. She wanted to reach for him, to pull him in, but her leaden arms wouldn't move. Angling her hips, she moaned her agreement as he nestled closer, and a feeling of pure and fulfilling bliss spread through her chest and wrapped around her heart.

"Damn, Charlie," he said with a guttural groan. "So perfect. So damn perfect." His hand skimmed over her hips and swept the skirt of her dress higher around her waist. "Wrap your legs around me and hold on. Together. We're going to come together. I need this to be a hard and quick ride, baby. Slow later."

Ford semi-lied. Hard? Yes, his "hard" slid through her swollen folds, nudged her clit, and kept her floating like a beach ball on a summer breeze. Quick? "Quick" to return to her entrance, drive inside her, and stretch her aching core as he pushed in to the root with an intensity she'd only dreamed of.

"Okay?" Ford asked, buried deep, his weight on a muscled arm, as his eyes searched hers. She nodded, and he gave her body time to adjust to the wondrous invasion as he lowered his lips to the curve of her neck. Tender fingers stroked down her cheek, over her shoulders, to the space between her breasts. He slowly, slow as hell, single-handedly worked each of the tiny buttons of her dress, all the way down the skirt, then pushed the material away and exposed her completely to his view.

"Beautiful. Gorgeous," he groaned, lowering his head to the crook of her neck and touching his grinning lips to sensitive skin. "I'm not going to last." She felt him grow inside her. "The total package is better than I'd imagined."

Charlie found the strength to raise her hand and tangle her fingers into his hair, inhaling his scent into her soul. The lingering effects of her first orgasm mingled with new sensations from Ford's ministrations, causing her to hold on to the feeling and not let go. But Ford didn't allow her to settle, rather he stroked deeper, faster, closing his hands on her hips and lifting her off the bed and into his deep thrusts.

"Ford," she breathed against his neck.

"That's it, baby. Feel me. It's me and you," he said, bringing her back up to the edge. "Give it to me, Charlie. Take it."

There it was again. He'd insisted on it. Wanted it. Demanded it. Take and give.

He slid out. A moan of protest escaped her mouth to be met with his encouraging growl as he pushed back in to the hilt. He lifted his head and captured her gaze. She fought the urge to close her eyes and guard her heart. In a split second of lucidity, she recognized the erratic beat of her heart for what it was. Hope. Love.

"Ford," she breathed against his neck, lowering her mouth and closing her lips on his shoulder. She surrendered any remaining strength to his capable hands.

"Breathe," Ford said. His fingers moved between them and he touched her sweet spot, coaxing her body further and her face back to his. He slipped his tongue past her lips and with a kiss, charmed her lungs into restarting.

Charlie's hands roamed his back, her body writhed against his front, and her eyes remained open and focused on Ford. With his intense gaze piercing any barrier, he rolled his hips, stroked her every desire, and took her high above the protection she'd feebly attempted to keep her heart safe.

"Reach for it, baby," he said. "Now. With me."

Defenses shot, she let go. Her climax flared where Ford urged and spread through her body. Her muscles clenched. Charlie held him tight. And he drove into her sex, claiming more than just her body as she accepted a man she'd known for only days.

"Ford," she rasped.

"That's it, baby. This is me and you," he said. "Together. We're coming together. You and me."

A final thrust, and he brought her to the edge of reason, taking her over, safe in the embrace of his arms.

Knowing he wouldn't be able to sate his desire for Charlie in the foreseeable future, Ford looked into her sparkling blue eyes and exhaled his relief in the knowledge. He wanted her again. Wanted her like mad. Grinning, he brushed his mouth over her lips, and shared oxygen with the woman he knew he'd bring into his life in New York. And he'd stay in her life . . . as long as she'd keep him around. He dropped his damp forehead to hers and tasted her sweet lips.

She responded, as she had to his every touch, and she kissed him back. The feel of her arms tightening on his back gave him reason to believe she'd give him the chance to grow used to the way she made him feel. She kept one leg hooked around his waist, offering more of an opportunity for him to adjust to this new feeling. What the fuck was the foreign emotion swelling inside his chest? What the fuck?

"*Chère*, I could get very used to this. Could stay like this for a very long time," he admitted, reaching behind him and trailing his hand over the softness of the calf wrapped around his leg. "So push me off so I can get rid of the condom, and we can start from the beginning. This time around, it'll last longer."

"That sounds like a plan, Ford." She moved her leg and released her hands. She tapped her finger in the center of his chest as if to push him off. He pulled away and started for the bathroom.

Ford looked over his shoulder and saw that Charlie had turned on her side, gathered a pillow into her chest, and was watching him. She gave him a smile and his chest squeezed. Damn, she gave with her whole self, and when she lowered her shields, she received with her whole self. Pure heaven. Pure Charlie.

He wanted to give her more to experience. He wanted her to have all she'd ever dreamed of.

When he returned, he had her again, nice and slow as he'd promised. Then he carried her into the shower and took her hard up against the tile until the water ran cold. Back on the bed, she fell asleep in his arms, and when he couldn't allow the opportunity to give her another orgasm slide away, he woke her with her clit in his mouth and his fingers buried deep inside her heat.

Now, he reclined on the pillows at his back, his hands folded behind his head, and watched her walk across the room with the last bottle of water from the mini fridge at her lips. Her creamy skin wore his mark and the mere remembrance of her tugging on his hair as he sucked those full breasts made him hard. He took himself in hand and stroked. Fuck she was addictive.

"Baby," he began, "I'm not near ready to return to the ship."

Shaking her head, she lowered the bottle and gave him an easy smile when her eyes discovered his hand working his cock. She licked her lips and took a deep breath. "Are you telling me we need more time to get this right?"

"I didn't say anything of the sort." He sat up, and while fisting himself with one hand, reached for her wrist with the other and closed his fingers around it. With a searing look, he moved her hand to his eager erection and communicated his intent of keeping her in no uncertain way. "I'm saying that you have a man to see to. And I'm saying that now that I've had you, I can't think of spending one more night without you in my bed. I can't wait a whole day to have you again."

She kept smiling, placed the bottle on the nightstand, and then kneeled on the bed at his side. Lowering her face to his, her breasts pressed into his chest as she brought her mouth to his and smoothed dainty fingers over his hand. Her thumb rounded his crown and shivers raced down his spine.

"Who said anything about having to wait?" Charlie asked. Her free hand stretched to the box of condoms on the stand.

Damn. The woman gave. Hot and responsive, she didn't hide her appetite for sex. Now she didn't only respond to him, she instigated more physical activity.

He leaned back on the pillows and motioned for her to proceed, his erection growing painfully hard as she grinned and tore the foil package with her teeth. This playful Charlie who was willing to captain their next encounter held his complete attention and made his heart pound hard against his ribs. She amazed him in so many ways, and he would explore each one of them.

With Charlie straddling him, grinding herself over his sheathed cock, she rode him in total abandon that lit up her gorgeous face with her beautiful warmth. Wanting to bathe in her bright light, he raised his hips and pushed into her as she lowered on him, wanting more and more of her with each thrust. Her hard nipples peeked from between long strands of blond hair, on display for his pleasure. He wrapped his arms around her back, sat up, and sucked her between his lips until her moans filled the room and she convulsed around him. No shyness. No reservation.

"You and me," he repeated, and Charlie threw her head back, called his name as she came.

She trembled over him, her body coloring with pleasure as he stroked down her back and watched her chest heave for air. He coaxed her higher, rubbed his fingers on her pleasure point, but he didn't let her come. He wanted to see the heat in her eyes as she climaxed, and he was a greedy bastard that hadn't had his fill. Cradling her body in his arms, he rolled her beneath him and took her mouth.

"You explode like a fucking rocket, baby. It's the sexiest thing I've ever seen. So damn hot. But this time, you're going to hold it. I'm going to watch that fuse simmer and burn," he said, sinking deeper into her sleek heat and rooting against the ecstasy offered him. "You're not going to come until I say you can come. And that will be after I've fucked you good. Fucked you hard. And I'm coming deep inside you."

She moaned in agreement, biting her lower lip and closing her eyes.

He moved his mouth lower, suckling a nipple and rolling the other between his thumb and finger. He pinched hard enough for her eyes to open and her hips to buck up against him.

"Not yet," he warned, taking her roughly, knowing he was pushing her limits. Knowing her delayed release would be stronger than any before.

With his mind blank, he pounded into her pulsing heat, his body demanding every piece of her. Every piece. And when she gave it, his name on her lips, he took it. Then he gave, calling her name, truly lost in everything that was Charlie.

"Together, love. Now."

He wrapped her in his arms and held her as the world shattered.

Eventually, an exhausted Charlie shifted beneath his weight. He rose onto his elbow and pushed her hair off her face. Her lashes fluttered against her cheeks. Her beautiful and swollen lips turned up in a smile. She opened her eyes and looked at him.

"Baby, we need to talk," he said.

"We need to eat," she replied, turning away and swinging her legs off the edge of the mattress. "I'm starved."

Chapter Twenty-three

"I don't know if I should be flattered or annoyed," Charlie said, giggling at Ford's grumbling that they were wasting time they could have had alone rather than in a restaurant—in public—again.

Ford shrugged, checked his watch for the umpteenth time, and signaled for the waiter to bring them their check.

"I think we should have dessert," Charlie added, just because she wanted to see him cringe. Surprised at how much she enjoyed getting a rise out of him, she laughed aloud when he did cringe, then laughed even harder when he tossed a hundred-dollar bill on the table, grabbed the day bag, and pulled her from her seat because the waiter was taking too long to bring their bill.

"Ford, all you think about is sex."

"Not so, *chère*. Even though no one would blame me when it comes to you." Ford stopped walking and she bumped into his solid side.

"When it comes to me?" Charlie asked as his hand dropped to her waist and his fingers curled into her soft flesh.

"Yeah, you. Other than the obvious—meaning how fucking gorgeous you are and the way every man in that restaurant cannot keep his eyes off you—you have a beautiful mind and a soul that attracts people. That's the problem. I want alone time with you." He held her still, the bag touching the side of her thigh, and stepped into her space. Pressing his hips to hers, he moved his hand into the small of her back, and pulled her even tighter against him. "I don't care if they look, just not at too much, as long as I get to have this. I get you."

Shit. Shit. Triple shit. She was so screwed. She wanted him again. Her body hummed at his touch.

"Damn Paul and his suggestion of bodies humming," she mumbled, dropping her face against his shoulder and closing her eyes.

"What's that?" Ford asked, squeezing her hips and making her look at him.

"Nothing," Charlie replied, but shifted uncomfortably under his scrutiny. "Something my boss said. He was being silly when he gave us the assignment and said silly things. It's silly."

"Silly?" Ford grinned, shaking his head and smoothing her hair from her face. She felt his phone vibrate in his pocket, but he ignored it. "You're so adorable. So damn cute. Who says *silly* like that anymore?"

"I do," she said, vying for some space and not getting any. She changed tactics. "Get your phone, Ford."

"Forget the phone," he said, lowering his head and touching his mouth to hers. "Do you really need to get back to New York? Stay with me for the next voyage."

She shook her head, but raised her arms and wrapped them around his neck. "Wish I could, really wish I could, but the feature is due in a few days. I have to get back and present," Charlie said, going up on her toes and kissing the man who made her body hum.

His phone vibrated again. He broke the kiss and answered. "Yes."

Holding her hand, he walked toward the hotel and listened to the caller. After a few minutes of listening without responding, he nodded and veered them in a different direction. "When?"

His face had gone stoic, but he wasn't angry. More like disappointed.

"No. I understand," he said. "We're on our way." He pointed toward the pier. "Yes. Tell him I have his back. No worries." Giving her an apologetic look, he lingered at a kiosk while he continued listening.

She released his hand and walked around the stall, surveying all the colorful ceramic goods she believed were made locally. She liked them. They reminded her of their time in the hotel, and she considered buying something to take home. She was about to call the clerk over when someone pulled on her wrist. She turned to find Will.

"Hey, Charlene," he said, looking through the open kiosk at Ford, who was watching them. "Are you okay?"

"I'm fine, Will. Are you enjoying the cruise?"

"You know I am, babe. Like you said, it's my kind of activity." He angled closer to her and lifted his chin at the monitoring Ford. "Is he treating you good?"

"He is. He really is." Charlie smiled and gave her once-friend a quick hug, leaning up to his ear. "Isn't he hot?"

Will chuckled, staying close and lowering his voice. "He's hot. I'll give you that much." Will glanced back at Ford. "But I don't trust him. One of my buddies told me he looks familiar, he's not sure from where, but he doesn't think that his name is Ford."

"Technically, your friend is right," Charlie agreed, not elaborating. She stepped back from Will as Ford rounded the kiosk. *I don't care if they look, just not at too much, as long as I get to have this. I get you.* Ford wouldn't appreciate Will being so close and having a clean look down her dress. She didn't want any issues, so she held her hand out and gave her man a big smile. It was time for a decent introduction. "Honey, you remember my friend Will. Will, this is Ford."

The men each tipped a chin up to the other.

"Ford." Will's face held no expression.

"William," Ford said, moving both bags to the same hand and draping his other arm over her shoulders. "Sorry to cut this reunion short, but we need to get going, *chère.* I need to be back on the ship as soon as possible."

Will's gaze flitted to hers and inquired. She sighed, glanced up at Ford, informed him that Will could be trusted, and asked him if he minded if she "shared." He shrugged, so she turned to Will.

"Ford actually works for the cruise line. He's undercover as a passenger to make sure policies are being properly observed," she explained. "So work calls. See you on board?"

"See you on board," Will said, looking slightly appeased.

"Later." Charlie waved, and then linked her thumb in Ford's belt loop. "I'm ready when you are."

"Ready," Ford replied, leading her through the shops and restaurants to the pier. He didn't speak until they'd swiped their cards and passed security. "Ramos, my replacement, needs to catch a flight to Miami immediately. His little girl has been admitted into the hospital with a very high fever. His ex isn't very good at keeping it together when it comes to their daughter."

"Is she okay?" Charlie asked, concern lacing her voice.

"Ramos thinks it's just a regular kid thing. Like a virus," Ford said, his manner calm and collected. "She's five. Little girls get fevers. But the little beauty is the love of his life, and since I'm still on staff and available, he asked if I could finish off the sailing for him."

"Of course you could," Charlie insisted. "He should be with his daughter."

Ford stopped walking and turned her to him. "I'll be in uniform. I won't be able to be with you in the workshops, and—"

"It's okay," Charlie said, cupping his face and feathering a thumb over his chiseled jaw. "I've got this. I know which ones to attend and which ones to steer clear of. I'll be okay as long as I get to see you a little."

"Dinner. I'll join you then." He touched his mouth to hers and her lips parted.

When his tongue found hers, she melted into him, wrapped her arms around him and hooked her hands on his shoulders. She could stay like that for hours. Kissing him. Tasting him. But he lifted his head and she saw the hesitation in his eyes.

"What is it?" Charlie asked.

"We need to talk, Charlie. Really need to talk."

She didn't want to hear it, so she kissed him again. "Later."

Chapter Twenty-four

Charlie felt Ford's absence the moment he left her and went to report to the captain. She knew it was irrational because he was working and still near, but she missed him. She'd grown accustomed to his presence and wanted to be with him.

Reminding herself she wasn't on vacation, she turned her energy to work. That sufficed for a while, then Quinn insisted she join him for dinner, but explaining what had transpired to her new friends dampened the mood again. Feeling betrayed, they questioned Ford's intentions toward her. Quinn and Luis tried to explain, but the tension was thick, and dinner was difficult to get through.

Her mood instantly brightened when Ford walked in during dessert. While she'd managed to get a lot of work done, had managed to laugh, and had been tickled to within an inch of her sanity during the sensual massage workshop that Quinn had asked her to join him at, she'd missed Ford. Not a good sign with only a day left on the cruise.

"Good evening," Ford said to the group, placing a hand on Charlie's shoulder. "I hope you're enjoying dessert."

"Are you speaking in an official capacity or on a personal level?" Grayson asked. He had been seriously offended when Charlie told the group of Ford's employment.

"Both," Ford replied, pulling out his chair and folding his long body into it. "Correction. Personal. On an official level, I've heard of no complaints." He caressed Charlie's shoulder, squeezing out an apologetic message for placing her in an awkward situation with her new friends. "Allow me to apologize for not being forthcoming when we first met. Our initial contact may have been in an official capacity, but I, we, consider you all friends. And as a friend, I thank you for keeping an eye on my wild girl while I'm forced to be away from her and see to work."

It didn't take much more for their friends to accept the cruise-staff Ford at their table and resume chatting over dessert. Charlie passed on invites for the remainder of the evening, and she asked Ford if he had time for a stroll on deck before escorting her to the cabin. He took her hand in his and walked her out of the dining room.

"Technically, I can't drink in the bar now, but I'd like for us to visit our spot and talk." Ford swept a finger across her forehead and pushed her hair back. "Even knowing this arrangement is temporary, I'm not liking it. I'm going to inform Georgiou that I'll honor the rule of no staff in passenger cabins, but I'm bringing you back to my cabin. I want you with me."

"No." Shaking her head, Charlie stepped back. "Please don't."

Ford looked confused when embarrassment warmed her cheeks, but determination settled in his eyes, and his thumb tilted her chin up so his gaze seared through her. "You're not shutting me out, *chère*. If this is about your work, fine. I'll accept that you need time to work. I'll give you time the way you give me time. But you're not pushing me back out after I've managed to get through your defenses. We're in this together."

Shivers raced up her spine. He was too close. She needed space.

"And don't give me some bullshit about it being proper, or caring what Georgiou or the rest of the staff will think." He lowered his head and kissed her. His tongue stroked hers, and she abandoned the bricklaying and melted into him, moaning her agreement.

"It's you and me," he said softly, smoothing his thumb over her lower lip. "Care to share what's bothering you?"

She wasn't sure what he was looking for or what to say, so she shook her head and licked her lower lip.

"You keep using that tongue in any way, don't expect me to put off speaking to Georgiou about moving you into my cabin for a single minute."

"Don't," she breathed, trailing her palm down his abs and hooking her fingers in his belt. "If you do, it'll be admitting defeat."

His brows furrowed, and he tilted his head. "Baby?"

Earlier in the day, specifically the time she'd spent naked with Ford, she'd grasped on to the hope she could have it all. She wasn't ready to let go. Love, great sex, and even a successful career danced within reach. If one crushed the other, it spelled defeat.

"Ford, please understand where I'm coming from." She changed her tone and went for serious logic, rather than emotional upheaval. "You said you'd help me earn the byline. You'd help keep me focused. I won't focus if I'm in your cabin. I won't do my job, and you'll set a bad precedent for your staff. Can you imagine the rest of the crew doing something like that?"

Ford wrapped his fingers around her forearms and gave them a squeeze. "I don't see your point. But I'll support you. Any way you want." He relaxed his hold on her arms and took her hand. He walked through the corridors and to her cabin door, not saying another word until he took her keycard and inserted it into the lock. "Do what you think you need to do. Once we're in Miami, all supportive promises are done. Over. No more bull. No more keeping me at a safe distance."

Holding her gaze, he touched his lips to hers, sending shivers through her body and stoking the hope for having it all. Then he pushed on her door and motioned for her to step inside. She did. He turned and strode down the hall and back to work.

Quinn cancelled yoga, but Charlie was determined to stick with it. She promised herself a latte as a reward, and was waiting in line for her prize when Will came up behind her and cupped her elbow. His gaze scanned the patrons, probably for Ford.

Not that the tall Cajun could be missed, but she could have saved him the effort of looking. Ford was working. She was on her own.

Will planted a friendly kiss on her cheek. "Good-morning, gorgeous. Nice to see you're alone."

"Good-morning to you," she replied, glad her friend was back to himself. "You're cheery today."

He nodded, but then shook his head. "We need to talk," he said, adding an espresso to her latte order. Will handed his keycard to the barista and signed for their coffees, then led her to a bistro-style seating area. He didn't continue smiling though. He didn't attempt any more small talk. He just sat across from her and leaned his elbow on his knees.

"What's wrong?" Charlie asked, wrapping cold fingers around the hot coffee cup for support. "Why the look?"

"His name isn't Ford. It's Keaton."

"I already know. It's not a big deal."

"Okay. You know his name, but why are you standing for being treated like that?" Will asked, clearly annoyed. "After what you've been through with dickhead James, you know you deserve more."

She searched his eyes, but couldn't piece together his problem. "Will, I'm not following you."

"He left a woman like you to sleep alone on a damn kink cruise," Will spat. "I saw the two of you last night. Saw him leave you at your cabin. You deserve more." He pinched the bridge of his nose as if to maintain control. "I know you said that nothing more than friendship can ever happen between us. I accepted it—after a lot of thought and kicks in the ass for not being more obvious with my feelings from the start—I understand why you said that. But I'll always care for you and look out for you." He rubbed his palm down her arm and squeezed her elbow. He wasn't being obnoxious or rude, simply protective like he'd always been. "Ford, Keaton, whatever-the-fuck his name is, isn't doing right by you."

"That's for me to decide."

"We've talked about this, Charlene. A proper man looks after his woman. He would never leave her alone on a romantic cruise; rather he'd make her climb the walls with pleasure. He'd make her his number-one priority. Not his fucking job. Don't repeat the same mistake—"

She held up her hand, palm forward, and pushed up from the seat. "Conversation is done. I'm not discussing Ford with you. Later, Will." She turned on her heels and left him sitting alone at the small table. Will had managed to ruin the calm she'd worked an hour for on deck.

Ford was nothing like James. Nothing. Will was so off-base it wasn't funny.

Determined to stay on track, she hurried to her cabin, retrieved her laptop from the safe, and set up on the balcony. An hour later, room service delivered a tray of pastries and coffee. She snagged a mini-croissant, devoured it in four bites, then grabbed a second before she reached into the drawer and checked her phone. She had multiple text messages from Ford going back to last night.

Sleep well and dream of me, chère. I'll be dreaming of you.

That had been five minutes after she'd watched him walk away.

She scrolled to the next message, which had come in during yoga class. Warmth spread through her chest as she read.

Spotted you in those tight little pants. Looking good. Text me when you're done.

She tapped the reply function. Done.

☺ Lunch? was his response.

When?

Soon.

So she tossed the phone onto the bed and headed for a shower.

Ford made a fist, but kept looking at Charlie as she mentioned her run in with Norrington and his wrong interpretation of their relationship. Problem was, he agreed with the fucker. Charlie did deserve more than he was giving her. She deserved his full attention, not someone who checked his watch for the next staff meeting. "I'm sorry, *chère*."

"For what?" She wrinkled her nose and leaned her head to the side. "Why?"

"Norrington is right. You shouldn't be left alone. Any man lucky enough to be with you should see to your every pleasure . . . especially on a kink cruise. You shouldn't be denied physical desires. Neither one of us should."

Not only was he barred from her cabin, but his being in uniform limited their public interaction. While able to enjoy lunch or a casual stroll on deck, they couldn't participate in Lovers Sail events. He could barely touch her. Couldn't even kiss her the way he wanted. And it was torture for him, but mostly he didn't want to think of what Charlie was settling for. She wanted to explore. Craved the experience. Fuck, she needed the sexual pleasure to complete what she'd started. And he wasn't giving her what she needed.

He wiped his palm down his face. "There's a masquerade party tonight. It's a full-kink event, but something I'd like to share with you."

A twinkle played in her eye and a huge smile brightened her face. "Full kink?"

"Yes," he said, carefully choosing his next words. "While there will be an abundance of scenes, and even though you've grown comfortable with the public activities, you must place yourself completely in my hands. You cannot think to question my choices. Once you decide we will attend, all remaining decisions are mine."

Excitement bloomed on her chest and the soft pink of her skin confirmed she needed this. He'd do anything to give her what she needed.

"I considered suggesting you stay in tonight," he said, looking into her eyes. Anticipation. Thrill. Hesitance. "What you've seen over the past few days is tame compared to the things that will happen on the ship tonight. It's the last night, last opportunity. People have connected and have established their limits. They're going to push those limits and have them pushed."

Her hand rubbed at the base of her neck, then her finger twirled a strand of hair.

"I know it isn't very progressive of me, but I don't want you wandering alone. If you decide we attend the party, I'll ask Luis and Quinn to escort you to dinner." He didn't like placing her in the care of other men, but he'd grown to respect both of them. They wouldn't allow any harm to touch her. "If we attend the party, I cannot make dinner."

She worried her lower lip, but she shook her head. "I'd like to go."

"Then we'll go," he said, offering her his hand and closing his fingers around hers once she'd settled her small hand inside it. "I'll come by your cabin at eleven with a mask. Feathers or rhinestones?"

"Both," she replied.

Chapter Twenty-five

"Charlene, may I have a word with you?"

"No," Tyler growled, placing his hands on the table and standing to face Will.

"It's okay," Charlie insisted, looking up at Will, before turning back to Tyler. "Really. We've been friends a long time." Will leaned over her back, so she met his eyes and pushed at his shoulder, silently asking him to step back for her to stand. She laced her hand through Will's arm. "We'll only be a minute."

Will led them through the dining room to the atrium.

"Are you crazy sneaking up on me like that? What were you thinking? Tyler is a big guy, and he was pissed. He could have gotten physical," Charlie said.

"Where's your guy?" Will asked, his green eyes narrowing and his fingers squeezing her elbow.

"He's working," she said. "And why are you acting like this?"

"Working, my ass," he said, dropping her elbow, looking away, and pacing as if contemplating his next words. After a long silence, he threw his hands up and shook his fists in the air. "He's working you, Charlene."

"What are you talking about?"

Will turned to her. Sadness crossed his face. He stepped up to her and cupped her cheek. "Please tell me this isn't because of James. He's so not worth it. Not worth anything you do."

"James?" Charlie studied his face, but couldn't understand. "What does James have to do with any of this?"

"Everything. You're fucking Keaton Fitzgerald Rutherford III."

"Rutherford?" Charlie breathed, and all the oxygen seeped from her brain as the lobby swayed in her vision. Her fingers closed around

Will's forearm and she held on to remain standing. Tears pooled in her eyes. "Like in Bruce Rutherford?"

"Fuck," he growled. His eyes filled with regret, and he let out a long breath as he gathered her in his arms. "You didn't know. I'm sorry I told you like that."

"I don't care if he's a Rutherford. He doesn't have anything to do with the firm. He told me about the family."

"Did he tell you he's fifty thousand short on cash?" Will asked, his fingers gripping her upper arms. "The bastard is looking at your bank account. He needs money to make his business venture happen. He needs your money."

No. It couldn't be. Ford didn't see her as a bank account.

She couldn't hold back the tears, so against her better judgment she walked into his arms. "He lied to me?" Charlie asked, burying her face in his shoulder. "Led me to believe he was a decent guy. Told me I could have it all." She tried to quell the sobs, but couldn't stop them. "I've been dreaming of a fairy tale with a Rutherford. A Rutherford who has shaky ties with his family and needs cash. I'm so stupid. So stupid."

"You're not stupid. You're too trusting. He doesn't look like James's attorney." Will pointed out the obvious. "Bruce is short and stocky. No resemblance."

"Did he play me?" Her heart ached. "Is it all for the cash or is it revenge for his cousin who lost the case?"

"I don't think it's because of the legal stuff. They aren't exactly James supporters. Bruce runs the New York office of the firm. James hired him because of the firm's heavy-duty business connection. He was his divorce attorney, but their firm didn't represent him when the criminal charges were made," Will said, cupping the back of her head. "Darling, I want to protect you, so I'm going to be honest with you. I'm sorry if I hurt you with the way I said it. Do you think there's a chance I'm wrong about him making the connection about who you are?"

"He knows who I am," she said, stepping back and wiping away the tears with a shaky finger. "He knows of my family. He knows."

"Did he tell you about his?" Will asked in a soft voice. "Did he tell you about his father's firm?"

Replaying his words in her mind, she remembered him mentioning the family business and Bruce's first name.

"He told me he had a falling out with his father when he decided he wasn't going to follow in his footsteps and be a lawyer." She inhaled and nodded. "He told me that his cousins, Remy and Bruce, had chosen to practice law and were at the family firm."

"There you go. Maybe, just maybe, he's okay. Has he asked for any money?"

Charlie glanced up at her friend, wondering if he really believed what he was saying or if he was just trying to soothe her broken heart. She shook her head. "It won't work. He knew about James. Knew what he did to me. To my family."

A calm and logical persona had replaced the angered friend. Will bent and looked into her eyes. "Was he good with you? Make love to you and take care of your needs?"

"That doesn't prove anything," Charlie said.

"Only it might." His expression softened. "A man who cares about a woman makes love to her, Charlene. He doesn't just have sex," he said in a gentle voice. "You know the difference." He rested a finger on her heart. "You know it in here."

All she felt was pain. Confused and upset, she just wanted to curl up on her bed and sleep until it went away. "Will you walk me back to my cabin?"

"Of course. Whatever you want," Will said without hesitation. "Charlene, think about it. Think carefully. It's about you, not your family, and not James. He hasn't asked for money, and maybe he won't. If he does, cut him off immediately. If he doesn't, give him a chance. You deserve to be happy, regardless of how others see your life. Don't let the family's social expectations decide your happiness."

She thanked him and asked if he'd wait for her to clean up and say good-bye to her friends. She returned to the table, exchanged phone numbers and emails, then said her farewells. When Quinn and Luis stood to escort her, she insisted on leaving with Will, saying they had family business to discuss.

Ford being the cousin of the lawyer who'd represented James was difficult to digest. Keaton Rutherford . . . of *the* Rutherfords. Ford needed money . . . well, he'd admitted that was the reason he'd stayed on for the extra cruises, but was he manipulating her feelings to gain access to her money? She rubbed the heel of her hand in the center of her chest, but the ache wouldn't fade. "How bad is it when

I want the cause of my pain to hold me and tell me it would be okay?"

"Bad," Will said, his voice troubled. "You are a beautiful, smart, and great woman. While you may not realize it, you can have any man you want. Do you want Rutherford?"

She looked down at her feet and walked, not answering, but considering his words. Her heart wanted him. Her mind told her she was crazy.

When they reached her door, Will took her keycard from her hand. "I don't think you should be alone tonight. Stay with me or with one of your friends. Better yet, do something totally out of character and throw caution to the wind and continue your sexual liberation. It looks good on you. Beautiful. Crook your little finger at any man you choose, and let him make you feel good until Rutherford is a mere bleep on your radar."

It was impossible not to smile and release some of the sadness. Charlie went up on her toes and touched her lips to Will's cheek. "Thank you. Right now, I need time alone. I'll decide while I pack."

"I'll turn my phone on. Call me with anything." He unlocked the door, handed her the key, then stood back for her to enter. "Anything, Charlene."

She took off her dress, washed her face, and brushed her teeth. With a heavy heart, she hung the *Do Not Disturb* sign on the door and set the carry-on bag on the bed. Charlie folded and refolded, quickly determining that sticking with original plans kept things easy.

She fit the pretty new dresses and lovely nightie in a plastic bag, placing it on the shelf in the closet. Not only did they add bulk to her suitcase, they reminded her that she could only have it all for a weekend.

The weekend was over. The fairy tale was complete. She took the phone off the hook, turned off the lights, and crawled into bed.

Allowing five minutes for tears, she resolved not to regret her time with Ford. She'd cherish it. Unfortunately, like in packing, sticking with original plans kept things easy. A fling was a fling, which meant there was no longevity in the plan. Ford had never promised her more. Her fairy tale was over.

She hugged her pillow to her chest and closed her eyes. There was a knock on her door. She glanced at the time. Ten thirty. Charlie turned over and buried her head in the covers. A message chimed on her phone.

Open the door, baby.

Sorry. I'm tired and not up to the masquerade party.

Open the door!

She let out a long breath and threw back the covers. The moment she turned the handle and the lock released, the door's movement forced her back, and Ford stepped in. He cupped her cheek and touched his lips to her forehead.

"Are you well, *chère*?"

She nodded, trying hard not to meet his concerned gaze.

"Luis and Quinn said you didn't look good at all, and that you left the dining room sick." He looked over her T-shirt, her boxers, to her toes and back up to her eyes. "You don't look sick. You look beautiful."

That earned him a smile. Beautiful, even with red eyes. Well, maybe they could never work. Maybe the tabloids would have a field day with a Stanton-Rutherford affair, but Charlie deserved a good-bye kiss from the man who had stolen her heart. She deserved a good-bye hug. She stepped into his arms and placed her cheek on his chest.

"What's wrong? Were you ill? Why did you run out of the dining room like that?"

"It's nothing like that. I'm not ill, but it's true I didn't feel great. I'm a bit overwhelmed with everything that's happened these last few days, and I need to sleep." Sleep and transition back to real life.

"Okay," he said, dropping a kiss on her head. "Get back in bed."

She looked up at him. "What about no staff in passenger cabins?"

His arms wrapped around her and lifted her off the floor. He walked her to the bed, and once he'd gently lowered her to the soft surface, he caressed the side of her face. "You're so tired. You didn't feel well. We're going to bed, and we're going to sleep. Now."

"What about the captain?"

He returned the phone to its base, then lifted it and dialed. "It's Rutherford. She's okay. Just tired." He nodded as the other person spoke.

She silently rejoiced in his words. He hadn't hidden his name but had identified himself as a Rutherford. It wasn't a devious plan. It was a huge negative factor fate had thrown their way, but Ford wasn't hiding his identity.

"Thank you. We'll be fine." He placed the phone on its cradle and looked at her. "The doctor said to ring him at any time if we need him. And in order to put your mind at ease and help you sleep better, Georgiou has been informed that my girl will not be alone. He sends wishes for a quick recovery."

He leaned over her, touched his lips to her forehead again, and then turned off the light. She heard the water running. Charlie stayed in bed and didn't question him anymore. He returned, showered and with wet hair, and climbed into bed beside her.

"Sleep well, baby," he said, fitting her against his chest. He kissed her again, and then tucked the covers around her shoulders. "Good-night."

"Good-night, Ford." Charlie had one more night of her fairy tale.

Chapter Twenty-six

Ford inhaled her sweet scent and kissed the back of her neck. "I don't want to let you go yet. Sail with me, Charlie. Stay for the next cruise, finalize the feature, and submit it via email."

"I can't," she replied, curling her back and bringing her knees against her body. "It's okay, Ford. We had a great weekend. Let's not push our luck."

A chill crept into his bones. She was blowing him off, cutting ties, and he hadn't had his fill of her. He wasn't about to let her get away that easy. "*Chère*, I'm going to report to work and tie up loose ends with the ship. I'll call you as soon as I'm free. We'll figure this out after all the guests have disembarked."

She nodded, but didn't turn to look at him. He didn't like it. Didn't like it one bit. But Ford was determined to find a way to be with her and convince her to keep him around. They were not done.

He touched his lips to her shoulder, and then he reluctantly released her. He was scheduled to report to duty. But more importantly, he needed time to think. There had to be a logical solution.

Charlie checked her phone as the train pulled into Penn Station. Ford hadn't texted or called since she'd turned it on. She didn't blame him. She hadn't returned his texts before she'd disembarked, and she'd turned off the phone completely after the third time she'd sent him to voicemail.

After a futile attempt to have her fly back with him, Will had taken her to the train station and seen her off. He'd offered to ride the train with her, but she'd claimed that she needed the time to work on her piece. Well, at least it wasn't a lie. She'd drowned herself in her work and the time had passed without too much notice.

She'd only turned the phone back on to call Kat and Paul the previous night and let them know she was on her way home, continuing to send all others to voicemail. Her parents had called twice, Will five times, and even her grandmother had phoned once. Not answering her grandmother felt bad, but she didn't want to hear dinner-date plans from her parents or warnings to stay away from money-grubbing men from Will. She'd just wanted to finish the feature and get home.

Now she was home, with a feature and a proposal for a three-part series. She had no idea why Kat had insisted on meeting her train, but neither did she mind. Charlie could use a hug to keep her together. She raced up the concrete stairs and wrapped her arms around Kat. "Oh. My. God. What an amazing trip."

Kat hugged her tight, as she'd expected, and then looked over Charlie's skimpy attire. "You'd better get some clothes on before you freeze that gorgeous tan off. Are you even wearing socks?"

"Yes, I'm wearing socks. They're no-shows." Charlie dropped the suitcase on its side and unzipped the main compartment. She needed a moment to compose herself and remember to stay positive. No way was she going to pop Kat's romance bubble.

"Please tell me you're wonderfully in love," Kat said, squatting and helping search for her coat.

"Got them," Charlie said, pulling out her jacket and a scarf. "I had amazing, earth-shattering, bone-rattling sex. The best sex of my life."

"Obviously," Kat replied, rolling her eyes. "What's his name?"

"I'm not saying." Charlie didn't want to dampen the mood. She'd revel on the great sex part and get her dose of romance via Kat. She wasn't willing to share how easily he'd let her go. She wasn't willing to share Will's theory that, once Ford had figured out Charlie wouldn't be taken for a fool, he'd moved on to finding a more susceptible rich woman on the final cruise. Actually, that was something she didn't even want to think about.

The proof in his giving up was that once the ship had sailed again, he'd stopped calling. It hurt.

"What?" Kat's gaze narrowed in disbelief. "Why won't you tell me?"

"Because my personal activities don't relate to the article. I'm not writing about what I did, but the opportunity to find love on a cruise." Taking hold of Kat's arm, she started walking. She danced around the subject, managing to remain vague and not lie. Even if it was the logical conclusion, losing Ford was painful. And while she'd decided to remember the good parts, the fact that he hadn't tried to contact her again hurt.

"Is it possible to find love on a cruise ship or not?" Kat asked.

"It definitely is," Charlie confirmed, thinking of how beautifully her friends had paired off. Grace was relocating to be with Tyler and his son; Grayson and Emma were in negotiations on the path their relationship would take; and Quinn and Luis were more in love and lust than when they'd set sail. "Did you find love in Paris, my friend?"

"I did," Kat breathed, searching for a cab. "It's obvious why Paris is always listed as one of the most romantic cities in the world. The history, the flavor, and the zest for romance are everywhere."

They hailed a taxi and settled into the back seat. Kat told Charlie about the architecture of the buildings, the beautiful streets, the unique life of the river, the delicious food, and especially the allure of the café life.

"And where did you find love?" Charlie asked.

"At the airport." Kat smiled as she spoke. "Marko was waiting for me when I landed."

"Marko? School Marko?" Charlie smacked the seat. "Did Paul have anything to do with that?"

"Of course," Kat said, laughing like a woman in love. "But it's okay. I still love him. They had the whole thing planned before you or I knew about the assignment. Everything. When Marko learned about what had happened with the jackass and the company's expense account, he and Paul brainstormed the premise of the feature. Marko paid for everything. Both of our trips. You were right, such expensive research wasn't in *City Wings*' budget."

"I knew it. There was no way Paul would have paid for my cabin. No fucking way." So many details to absorb. So many to share. Absorb first. "Why didn't you tell me Marko was loaded?"

"It's not about the money. Marko is more than a damn bank account."

"You're preaching to the choir, Kat. I get it," Charlie said, pointing a finger to her chest. "I really do." Charlie knew that money didn't make people, but she also knew that money often controlled their fate. But in this case, her friend's unease had nothing to do with socioeconomic standards. Kat had found love in Paris. She also worried she'd lost it there.

"Tell me everything," Charlie said. "Start from the beginning. The good and the bad. Don't leave anything out."

They were in their apartment when Kat shared details of her rendezvous with sexy Marko Renard. He'd met her at the airport and romanced her like mad in Paris, all hot and steamy, very intense, and extremely determined, then he'd put her on a plane and sent her back to New York.

"I think he 'sent' me away on purpose. He's a bit of a lovable tyrant, but he's also arrogant enough to think he always knows best. I'm afraid that something bad has happened. He thinks he can protect me if I'm away from it."

"Like all that talk about going to Provence and eating his mom's Sunday dinner meant nothing," Charlie added. "Not."

"Exactly." Kat placed her glass on the coffee table and stood. "I have to get back to Paris. He needs me."

"What time is the flight?" Charlie hopped up and carried their glasses to the sink.

Kat checked her phone. "I'm waiting for Paul to call. I need to ask if he'll purchase the ticket with his credit card for me. I maxed out my card and I have twenty bucks until payday."

"You're shitting me," Charlie said, reaching for her bag and pulling out her computer. "Why didn't you ask the minute I got off the train?"

Outraged that her friend would think that not accessing her money was more important to her than Kat's happiness, she told her as much while she booked Kat's ticket back to Paris . . . back to Marko.

Charlie watched Paul and Kat pull away from the curb, wishing her friend would find all she wanted in Paris. She entered the building lobby as her phone vibrated. Pulling it from her back pocket, she read Ford's text.

Hold the door, chère.

She turned and walked out to the sidewalk, searching to her left and then her right. She didn't see him until he'd crossed the street and approached her straight on. Dark and brooding in a navy wool blazer, he didn't smile or call out a greeting. Instead he reached her in a few long steps, closed his hands on her arms, and pulled her up on her toes.

"You were supposed to wait for me."

"What are you doing here? You're supposed to be on the ship," she breathed.

"If you would have waited as we'd agreed, you'd know that I left the cabin and went to turn in my resignation."

"You said you needed the bonus for your coffee empire," she said, trying but failing to keep her feet flat on the ground. She wrapped her arms around his neck for support.

"I did, but I need you more."

Before she could formulate her next question, Ford lowered his head and sealed his mouth to hers in a branding kiss. Her arms tingled beneath the sure hold of his fingers, her chest heated as he pressed her into him, and her heart danced with joy when he didn't allow her to pull away. Charlie stayed and melted into him as his kiss seared through her, stealing her breath and releasing her apprehension.

With his forehead against hers, she closed her eyes and let the knowledge of Ford not giving up on them soothe her soul. He'd come to her. He stood with her.

"You missed a few items while packing," he said, holding out a package with her dresses.

"How did you know where to find me?" Charlie asked in a whisper.

Ford looked at her, a simmering twinkle in his eyes. "Once I realized you'd pulled a disappearing act, I called Bruce to see if he had any forwarding information on you after the divorce. He didn't, but he had insight on your relationship with William Norrington. He'd interviewed him and had placed him in the not-to-be-called, or hostile witness, group as far as the divorce went. Apparently, William's loyalty lies with you."

It did. And she knew it. But Will's strong views on his stepbrother's behavior could have also skewed the judge. Will was never called to give his opinion on her marriage.

"You scanned off the ship at the same time, so I assumed you left together," Ford continued. "I contacted him and met him in Little Havana. After much conversation, he admitted to taking you to the train station and that you were on your way to New York City. Then, after he'd interrogated me on my intentions, he relented and gave me your address."

This wasn't a conversation for the sidewalk. The night chill permeated her thin sweater. She took his hand and led him into the building's foyer in silence. She didn't speak until they were in the privacy of her apartment.

"Will was satisfied with a great-sex-for-now answer?" she asked, but hoped he'd correct her. "A no-commitment, short-term-relationship man for me?"

Ford shrugged off his jacket and threw it on a chair. He walked to her and cupped her face in his hands, forcing her to meet his gaze and hear his words. "*Chère*, that was before you. You're a game changer. These last few days were a game changer."

Her belly tightened with hope. He'd come. He'd followed her.

"I'm not going to lie. The sex is great, and it may have been the catalyst for us to connect, but we are not a temporary arrangement. I want you. I need you. In an insanely small amount of time, I've realized that I don't want anything without you. Sleeping without you was torture. The only night I slept well was Sunday, when I was able to hold you close. And truth be told, I knew you were troubled, knew you had doubts. But I was too selfish to risk being told to leave. I figured you'd understand how I felt and want to keep me around if I held you."

"I do want you," she said, trying to step away. He held her still. Didn't let her turn her face down or step back. "I'm a Stanton. You're a Rutherford."

"That didn't bother you on the ship," he replied, his tone short and annoyed.

"I didn't know," she admitted. "I was so wrapped up in getting the information for my article, that what you shared didn't register. Will told me at dinner on Sunday. Didn't know why I'd stand for being played by a Rutherford."

"Fuck everyone else," Ford growled, his right hand lowering to her nape while he held her face up to his. "This is you and me. Only you and me. I won't let anyone or what they may think keep us apart. We've both fought to be free of family expectations. And while I love my family, and believe you feel the same about yours, this is you and me."

Hope consumed her and she wrapped her hands around his neck, going up to touch her mouth to his. "You and me?"

"You and me, *chère*. Give us a chance."

Always quick to decide, Ford had known he'd wanted her from their very first kiss in the taxi. He hadn't known to what extent until he'd let her sleep alone after Cozumel, but that sleepless night had proved she was his. Without her, he had been empty and lonely. Holding her on Sunday had only served to solidify how he felt. She completed him. Gave him purpose and faith for a future with love.

Not once did her being a Stanton influence his feelings. It was all about Charlie and who she was on her own. Gorgeous, smart, capable, and full of energy, she filled him with desire. He wanted to stand by her, support her, and fucking benefit from her light.

"It may sound crazy because you've known me less than a week, but I won't sleep without you one more night. You belong in my bed, at my side, with me." He tangled his hand in her hair and angled his mouth over hers. "Collect your things and come home with me."

Her throat worked as she swallowed, and a tiny groan escaped her lips.

"Not Louisiana," he clarified. "I've already been there."

"I don't understand," she admitted.

"With the monetary benefits of the last cruise no longer an option, I swallowed my pride, tucked my tail between my legs, and asked my father for a loan equal to what the investment would have earned."

"You asked your father?" Charlie rubbed the heel of her palm over her forehead. "Why would you do that?"

"Because being here with you is worth anything to me," Ford replied. "I can eat a piece of humble pie to make that happen. But I can't be at sea without you for a week."

Charlie took a deep breath and ran her fingers down his strong bicep. "You're really here. You have the money for the coffee empire. You're here. With me."

"Of course I am. Now come home with me, *chère,*" Ford repeated. "Home. Here. In New York. You said you have a roommate, and we need privacy to talk this out."

She smiled, her blue eyes alight with yearning, and she leaned into him. "My roommate is heading to Paris."

That was all he needed. He brought his mouth to hers, determined to show her how right they were together. Her lips parted, and he swept his tongue into her welcoming warmth, tasting sweetness and love in the woman who held his heart in the palm of her hand. "Damn, I love Paris." Ford bent and hooked his arm beneath her knees. He lifted her into his arms and carried her to the bedroom. "Tell me you want this. Tell me you'll keep me around, baby."

"Okay," she breathed, as he stood her by the bed. Her warm hands fit beneath his shirt and pushed it up. "It's you and me."

Pulling a condom from his pocket, he placed it on the nightstand and had her naked and beneath him in minutes. There was no delay, no time to waste; he needed her. And from the lovely moisture glistening between her thighs, she needed him, too.

"You're always ready for me, baby. Always beautifully ready." He handed her the condom, freeing his hand to slip a finger deep inside her and feel the woman he couldn't imagine being without. She moaned and rolled her hips, grinding against him as she tore at the foil.

"I'm dying to get inside you," he said, adding a second finger and stretching her tight heat. "Dying to show you that when I said you were mine, I meant you were mine. No outs. No turning back."

Her small hands worked to roll the condom over his erection, while his mouth found her neck and his fingers coaxed her to move faster.

"And tomorrow, we see the doctor. We're getting checkups and you're going on the pill," he said, his mind working out the details his body demanded. "I want nothing between us when I make love to you. Just you and me."

Her gaze went soft, unspoken love filling the space between them. She wrapped her arms around him and pulled him down to her mouth. "Just you and me."

She kissed him, hard, long, and strong, showing him that she was in as much as he was. Charlie took control and gave herself.

"Take," he encouraged. And his beautiful angel rolled onto his body and straddled him. Her body rose above him, and then lowered to take him. "You and me."

Chapter Twenty-seven

L ost in his thoughts, Ford sent up silent gratitude for the woman he loved. Charlie completed him and made every day a wonderful adventure. She'd kept him around, and he was determined to assure she always would.

"I can't believe I'm totally done and free for a whole week," she said, folding a new dress into her case and handing him a pair of jeans for his.

"That's three stories in three months. *City Wings* is lucky to have you, *chère*." Paul had offered her a position as a staff writer, with a cruise series as her first official assignment. She'd turned in the third piece last night.

Ford stopped packing and gathered Charlie in his embrace. "I went through hell waiting on you to decide to move in here. It took you another month to get you to agree to sublet the apartment and accept that you're stuck with me."

She shrugged and touched her lips to his jaw. Mr. Wiles sold to Ford, and with some creative financing, Luis had bought in to the location. With Kat in France, Charlie had packed up her personal belongings, and Luis and Quinn had moved into the old apartment. "How could I refuse when the operating-owner of your second location, which just happened to be down the block from the apartment, needed a place to stay? I sacrificed the apartment for your success."

"Right, *chère*. Finish packing so we can talk," he said, tapping her butt. "We have a four-month anniversary to get underway and a wedding to attend."

"You're proving to be very sentimental for such a successful businessman."

"Four months ago, you fell into my arms and turned my world up-side down."

"You mean right side up," she corrected.

"It's never been righter," Ford teased. He lifted her off her feet and fit her legs around his waist, tapping her naked bottom. "Why are you torturing me by not wearing panties?"

"I'm not wearing panties because we have a flight to catch, and you've agreed to distract me with repeated orgasms en route." She smiled wickedly and moved her hips, shamelessly rubbing herself on his jeans. "Plus, we have an opportunity to scratch number seven off your places-to-make-love list."

Mile high. On a plane. En route. The little nymph had come out to play. And while his body reacted to her arrival, he couldn't wait any longer. He placed her on her feet and studied the naughty invitation on her angelic face. He wanted to have that every day of his life.

"Strip, baby. It's only you and me," Ford said, waiting for her to pull the dress over her head.

Once she stood naked before him, he unbuttoned his shirt and tossed it to the floor. Then kicking off his shoes and socks, he dropped his pants and stepped out of them. The two of them, alone with each other, meant everything in the world to him. Not money, not work, not surnames. Nothing they'd been given by their families entered their private sanctuary. It was only what they had of themselves that mattered.

He ran his hands down the side of her body, bringing them to rest on her hips. Kneeling before her, he touched his mouth to the valley between her breasts, which housed her generous and beautiful heart.

"Charlie, I love you. I treasure every moment you give me, and I want many, many more."

"I love you, too. I want more, too," she said, tracing his face with gentle fingers.

"I didn't know what was missing from my life until the day you ran me over in South Beach. That's when I learned I was missing my other half. You, *chère*."

"Stop, Ford. You're going to make me cry." She wrapped her arms around him. "Stop speaking and make love to me."

"While I will never pass up the chance to make love to you, not now on our bed, nor on the plane in three hours, I want to do so with my ring on your finger." He reached into the pocket of the pooled pants and pulled out a little blue box.

Charlie gasped and her mouth dropped open. Her blue eyes went as dark as the deep sea, a sight that thrilled him each time he saw it, and she stared at him bewildered.

"Marry me, *chère*."

She caressed his jaw and leaned into him. "Yes." She brought her lips to his. "With pleasure." She wrapped her arms around his neck and kissed him again. "Just you and me."

"You and me," he said, sealing the proposal with another kiss.

"I hate airplanes," Charlie groaned, burying her face into his shoulder and tightening her thighs around his waist. "Why does Kat's wedding need to be in France?"

"Because you get to come, repeatedly, over the Atlantic Ocean. You're doing beautifully, baby." In the first-class lavatory, Ford cupped her behind and angled her hips so he stroked her swollen clit as he thrust into her. Much like the woman who had taken a bus from New York to board a kink cruise in Miami searching for romance, his Charlie's curiosity spurred her spirit. "This distraction works well for me."

He held her higher, suckling on her pink tips and loving the way she rolled her hips to take him deeper. His climax built and his legs quivered with need for release, so he leaned against the cold metal of the sink and let his woman take control and ride him hard.

Ford loved the way she let herself go, took her pleasure, and soared in the freedom she'd once envied. Freedom she now found with him. He gave that to her. His woman. His angel.

Throwing back her head, Charlie moaned loud. "Hold me, Ford. Hold me."

He tangled his fingers in her hair and guided her head up, sealing her mouth with his and swallowing her moans as she tightened around him and lost herself in orgasm. He followed, holding her tight in his arms, as they both became official members of the mile-high club.

"Perfect, Charlie," he said, moving his mouth over hers and feeling the throb between her legs as her eyes cleared and she slowly resurfaced.

He lowered her sandaled feet to the floor and straightened her skirt. Reluctantly, he fit her full breasts into her top and did up each button to the middle of her chest. He turned her to look at the mirror, and admired the snug fit of the white cotton shirt across her chest.

"You're smoking hot, baby. All flushed and pink and beautifully mine." Ford intertwined their fingers and lifted her hand in the air. The diamond sparkled in the light. "You joined the club with my ring on your finger."

"With you, I would do anything," she said, as she watched him in the mirror.

"You can, *chère*. Anything." He skimmed over the swell of her breasts. "You go first. I'll follow."

"Together," she said, bringing their joined hands to her lips and kissing his knuckles. "It's you and me. Together."

Charlie slid the lock and opened the door. "Good thing the passengers in first class are offered sleep masks," she whispered, stepping out and walking down the aisle, holding his hand at the small of her back. She reached the fifth row, and moved to the window seat.

Ford reclined in his seat, held his arm up for her to scoot over, and pulled her against his chest. "I love you, *chère*."

"I love you, Ford."

His woman rested in his arms, her airplane nerves a thing of the past. She smiled up at him. "I truly have it all."

"Me, too," Charlie breathed, snuggling close against him and placing a soft kiss on his bicep. "Me, too."

About the Author

Demi Alex writes steamy romances, blending emotional fulfillments of the heart and carnal desires in her work. Born in Athens, Greece, and raised in her own version of a big fat Greek life in New York, Demi was infected with book and travel bugs early, and currently admits the only therapy for this condition is to combine the two in fictional stories that allow her characters to let loose and experience all they crave. She attended SUNY at Stony Brook, and after changing her major numerous times, graduated with a degree in Public Policy and International Studies. Her characters are loosely based on people she encounters while she travels or during the time she spends matching homes to owners as a Realtor. She simply has a passion for matchmaking that can't be put to rest. Readers can visit her online at www.demialex.com, on Facebook, and on Twitter @DemiAlex2U.

Look for Demi Alex's next International Affairs romance in June 2017, and don't miss *26 Hours in Paris*, now available!

Magazine writer Kathryn Taylor is traveling from New York to Paris for work. But the flirtatious Frenchman she left long ago is waiting at the airport—and he wants to play . . .

No one can guide Kat through the sensual city's delights like Marko Renard. He let her get away once, and now he's determined to make her stay—even if he has to tie her down. He will wrap her in cashmere, tease her tongue with chocolate, and take her to the peak of the Eiffel Tower. . . . But can he convince the bohemian beauty she belongs with him, in his luxuriously decadent world? In business, he's the master—but it's Kat's body and soul he truly longs to rule.

He has just enough time to show her the pleasures of the boulevards, the boulangeries—and the bedroom. To finally get her to just say *oui*, he'll have to seize the day—and the night. . . .

26 Hours in Paris

DEMI ALEX

www.ingramcontent.com/pod-product-compliance
Lightning Source LLC
Chambersburg PA
CBHW021243260626
47155CB00004BA/1291